JOURNEY INTO THE JAWS OF DEATH

There were ten of them—nine British soldiers and a lovely young woman—trapped behind French lines and doomed to capture and execution unless they could somehow rejoin the British army.

To Keith Graham, the young ensign who was no longer a boy but not yet a man, fell the task of leading the little band through the jaws of death to safety. He had help from Gwyneth, the widowed camp follower who was as cunning as she was beautiful—and who taught him a few lessons in manhood along the way.

The excitement of battle, the heroism of desperate men, the tragedy of death, the tenderness of young love all come stunningly to life in this suspenseful, moving novel by the author of *God Is an Englishman* and *Give Us This Day*.

TOO FEW FOR DRUMS
was originally published by Simon and Schuster.

Too Few for Drums

R.F. DELDERFIELD

PUBLISHED BY POCKET BOOKS NEW YORK

The characters of this book are entirely imaginary and bear no relation to any living person.

TOO FEW FOR DRUMS

Simon and Schuster edition published 1973

POCKET BOOK edition published May, 1974

L

Standard Book Number: 671-78360-2.
Library of Congress Catalog Card Number: 78-162712.
This POCKET BOOK edition is published by arrangement with Simon & Schuster, Inc. Copyright, ©, 1964, by R. F. Delderfield. All rights reserved. This book, or portions thereof, may not be reproduced by any means without permission of the publisher: Simon and Schuster, 630 Fifth Avenue, New York, N.Y. 10020.
Cover illustration by Lou Marchetti.
Printed in the U.S.A.

For my son Paul,
the first to encourage
the file,
affectionately,
R. F. DELDERFIELD

Contents

〜∾〜

Shall they return to beatings of great bells
　　In wild train-loads?
A few, a few, too few for drums and yells,
May creep back, silent, to village wells,
　　Up half-known roads.

WILFRED OWEN
The Send-Off

Too Few
for Drums

CHAPTER ONE

The Bridge

✦

THE DRAGOON must have been the best marksman in the French army or his shot one of the luckiest of the war.

At that range, all of two hundred meters, Graham would not have expected a carbine ball to do more than dent the tough leather of Captain Sowden's shako. He had seen the dragoon appear on the rocky platform above the town but had paid little attention to him. The main body of the French was known to be several leagues to the north, and the dragoons, as skirmishers, had been following them all the way from Busaco, observing the withdrawal but making no attempt to bring the British rearguard into action. As far as Ensign Graham was aware, this was the first shot of the retreat. It was a fatal one for Captain Sowden, penetrating his forehead as he stooped to examine the explosive charges under the bridge and laying him stone dead on the cobbles of the approach.

Graham heard the report and the harsh rattle of Captain Sowden's accouterments on the stones. He turned and looked over his shoulders, to see the captain lying face downward, his brains oozing from a hole in the back of his head where the dragoon's ball had emerged. For a few seconds he was too surprised to do more than stare at the dead man and then across the roofs of the town to the rocky platform on which the dragoon was standing, his carbine resting on the crupper of his saddle, the wind from the pass catching the tail of his big horse and trailing it like a pennant. Then the instinct of self-preservation asserted itself and Graham threw himself across the open

13

space to the shelter of the last house in the town and at once began to take stock of his position as the only British officer this side of the river.

The moment of panic passed, for he could not be fired upon so long as he remained under the lee of the wall. Moreover, as he took a swift look around the angle of the jutting stones, he saw the dragoon thrust his carbine into the saddle bucket, mount and ride slowly into the narrow cleft between the overhanging rocks. In place of purely physical panic, however, came a nagging sense of responsibility, followed almost at once by a feeling of acute isolation now that Sowden was dead and the river ran between the squad and the rearguard. He glanced across the narrow bridge and could see the two squadrons of Brunswickers moving off at a trot along the road leading to Condeixa, and in advance of them a long thin line of red representing the last company of the Fifty-first Foot, to which he and the squad had been attached during the retreat. The bridge, he knew, was mined and engineers were posted on the far side awaiting Sowden's orders to light the fuse and cut off immediate pursuit. Remembering this, he sat thinking a moment, pondering Captain Sowden's last words addressed to him a moment before the dragoon's ball had stretched him dead upon the ground.

Sowden had said, "Tell Sergeant Fox to break down the jail gate. Some Portuguese are inside and we have orders to leave no one behind, *no one,* you understand? But look sharp about it, boy, we have less than five minutes!"

Graham fancied that Sowden had resented giving these instructions, as though he considered it presumptuous on the part of General Crauford, commanding the rearguard, to risk British lives in order to prevent the French from making prisoners of Portuguese jailbirds, but it was clear he had no intention of disobeying the general's order. The jail must be emptied, and the jail was situated in the square three hundred meters north of the bridge.

Graham found himself sweating despite the chill wind that swept down from the Sierra behind the town. He had almost no military experience and the dragoon's shot was the first he had ever heard fired in anger. He had not been in Portugal more than a few weeks, and his duties up to that moment had been limited to escorting an ammunition train up the dirt road from the coast. He had never been called upon to make a single decision. Every order had been passed down to him from experienced officers like Sowden. The company's attachment to the rearguard dated from the previous evening, when the ammunition train had been halted and turned back and Wellington's triumphant army, fresh from the victory at Busaco, had come pouring down from the mountains, where its ebullience had turned to gloom the moment word filtered down to the ranks that they were withdrawing to the coast.

Graham, fresh from the Hythe training battalion, had not had leisure to consider the strategy of the campaign, and now he was completely preoccupied with his own situation. At any moment the bridge would be blown and anyone this side of the river would be at the mercy of the oncoming dragoons. Perhaps the brown-faced cavalry would take prisoners, more likely stragglers would be sabered on the spot.

The thought made him spring up and run down the littered street toward the square, bawling for Sergeant Fox at the top of his voice and noting the movement of red tunics through gaps between piled-up furniture, dragged into the street and abandoned earlier in the day, when the rearguard had marched down to the bridge driving panic-stricken civilians before them.

He called, "Sergeant Fox! Sergeant Fox!" in a voice shrill with urgency, and suddenly Fox was there with a bunch of the most grotesque men and women Graham had ever seen, men wearing sacklike smocks and women whose nakedness showed through their filthy rags, a prancing, gibbering group of about two score, the sergeant and

Private Lockhart urging them down the streets with curses and occasional jabs of the bayonet. As they swept past Graham, Fox checked his stride, half saluted, and said crisply, "They weren't jailbirds, sir, they're looneys! We only took those who could climb over. The lock on the gate was too heavy for musketry!"

Graham looked past Fox and saw other bedraggled creatures swarming down a ladder set against the huge wooden gate of the town jail. Under the ladder were two more men of the Fifty-first: Privates Watson, the grimy little ex-sweep, and Strawbridge, the huge countryman with the bovine eyes and straw-colored hair. Strawbridge was standing erect as though on sentry-go, but Watson was obviously enjoying the novel sensation of emptying a jail, for he wriggled, grimaced and shouted ribald advice to the capering fugitives, sometimes threatening them, but without conviction.

Across the square from the jail Graham saw two or three other redcoats—Lickspittle and Croyde, the two licensed felons, and Morgan, the Welsh Methodist. Close by, emerging from a house, was young Curle, the company drummer-boy, his black gaiters seeming to reach almost to his waist, and his tunic, several sizes too large for him, reaching halfway down his calves. Lickspittle and Croyde had obviously been looting, and this fact registered in Graham's brain as Sergeant Fox said, "We'd best hurry, sir, they'll be blowing the bridge!" so that suddenly Graham felt hopelessly inadequate, for this was the warning he had meant to give the NCO.

"Captain Sowden is dead," he told Fox, remembering to speak arrogantly. "Collect the men and move off at once, Sergeant!" And he made a very great effort to calm himself and walk rather than run across the square to where Lickspittle and Croyde were shoveling odds and ends into a haversack under the melancholy eye of Private Morgan.

"To the bridge, at the double!" he shouted. But the men did not immediately respond, so that he struck

Croyde on the shoulders and added, "The engineers are lighting the fuse now."

That got home to them and they exchanged a swift look of consternation before Lickspittle, the smaller of the pair, swung the haversack, grabbed his musket and set off at a run, followed by the cumbersome Croyde and then, but with less haste, by Morgan, the company Bible-quoter. The drummer-boy remained, looking up at Graham like a lean, trustful mongrel. There was no fear in his eyes but a look of anticipation as though Graham, who wore gold epaulettes and was therefore half a god, could transport him across the river by a lift of the hand. Graham looked down at the little starveling and felt a swift rush of compassion which he at once stifled under a snarl.

"The bridge, you little fool! Quickly!"

The boy opened his mouth to say something but thought better of it, picked up his drum in one hand and cartridge belt in the other and broke into a shambling run as Graham walked back across the square to the foot of the ladder.

The two men here, Watson and Strawbridge, were awaiting him, and Graham saw that the last of the lunatics had now disappeared up the street. From behind the gate came a hideous cacophony of screams and cries, and Watson, interpreting the officer's look, said in his harsh London accent, "They're all cripples, sir! None of 'em can't get up an' over! We'd better leave 'em, 'adn't we, sir?"

Graham nodded and waved his hand toward the bridge, and at that moment the blast of the explosion struck each of them in the face and the far end of the street dissolved into a vast gray cloud, debris sailing in a wide arc and pitching almost at their feet.

The roar of the exploding mine was still ringing in Graham's ears when Strawbridge, the countryman, said involuntarily, "Christ! 'Er's gone, zur!" Terror showed in the Cockney's narrow face, his tongue shooting out and curling around his lips.

Then, as the dust began to settle, Sergeant Fox appeared at a run, butting his way through the cloud of dust and followed at staggered intervals by Lockhart, the ex-gamekeeper, then Croyde waving his hands in despair, and finally, in a little bunch, Lickspittle, Morgan and the boy Curle. They assembled under the jail wall and even in the extremity of his alarm Graham realized that the lunatics inside the building had ceased to scream.

"Most of the looneys got across, sir," Fox said breathlessly, "but I reckon the engineers mistook us for the French!"

Graham made another tremendous effort, feeling his lip quiver and his heart thump and pound like the irregular beat of a steam-driven pump. His mouth was parched and he felt sick and unreasonably cold.

"How many are left on this side? How many of *us?*"

The sergeant looked around and made a rapid count. "Nine, sir, including yourself."

A little of the sergeant's calmness communicated itself to Graham. Fox was a big-boned, gangling man in his early thirties, tough, spare and weatherbeaten, with the faded tunic and worn equipment of a soldier with several campaigns behind him. As he addressed the officer his eye was cocked at the mountains immediately behind the town, but Graham realized that he would never mention the nearness of the enemy or, indeed, offer any advice that was not specifically demanded. Yet he knew now that he needed advice most desperately and he jerked his head, indicating that he wished to consult the sergeant out of earshot of the men now herding together in a muttering group under the gate. Fox understood at once and they moved into the center of the square.

"Have you been along this road before, Sergeant?" Graham asked.

"Yes, sir, several times, but I don't know of another bridge. There might be a ford higher up, sir, I did hear on the way up that cavalry of the German Legion swam their horses over."

A ghost of a smile puckered Graham's lips. It was the last flicker of a carefree boyhood spent in the woods and fields of the Kent-Surrey border, where his tradesman father ruled a vast country estate called Addington Court and played at being a farmer.

"Can you swim, Sergeant?"

"No, sir," said the sergeant seriously, "and neither can any of that riffraff except the big Swede, Strawbridge!"

It relieved Graham to hear the sergeant refer to the six privates and the drummer-boy as "riffraff" and use the contemptuous army term "Swede" to describe Strawbridge, the goose-farmer. Somehow it took his mind off the appalling reality of their situation, a body of eight men and one boy isolated on the enemy's side of a deep, swift-flowing river, with a hundred thousand Frenchmen pouring down from the mountains to stamp over their bodies in a rush for Lisbon and the sea.

"Very well, we shall march southeast and follow the bank!" Graham said shortly. "Tell the men and check their ammunition." Then, with a tiny spurt of relief, he remembered Captain Sowden's map and added, "Wait here, I'm going to search the captain's valise," and he hurried off down the street, disappearing into the cloud of gray dust that still shrouded the bridge.

Fox went over to the men and barked them into some kind of formation. Critically he let his gaze run along the short rank, and what he saw neither pleased nor encouraged him. He was a professional who had been in uniform since he was fifteen, and the group cowering under the jail wall were amateurs, most of them first-campaign men without the least idea how to survive in this kind of situation or measure up to the seasoned veterans of Napoleon at this moment descending the pass in their tens of thousands. Lickspittle and his crony Croyde were a pair of condemned felons whose presence here had cheated some seacoast hangman of his fee, for they had been taken in a fight with revenue men and given the choice of enlisting or decorating a gibbet. They were a hard-bitten, truculent pair, and he had already seen each of them flogged for looting and brawling. They hated military service as they hated all authority and were kept in check only by the fear of the provost's firing squad. But now, Fox reflected, there was no provost and they would undoubtedly desert at the first opportunity, so he said, addressing them directly. "The French advance guard is led by dragoons and lancers. They are fast-moving scouts and never take prisoners. If either one of you is thinking of surrendering, forget about it. They'll collect your firelocks, strip you naked and then hack you to pieces!"

He moved on a pace, addressing the remainder of the squad. "The ensign knows of a ford higher upstream and we're going to march for it now. If we keep together we shall be across the river in twenty-four hours and your one chance of living through this is to keep closed up. Any stragglers will be picked off by the dragoons. One of them just killed Captain Sowden at three hundred yards' range!"

He could see that Privates Watson, Lockhart, Strawbridge and Morgan were impressed, but Watson, the man with soot ingrained in his sallow skin, was grinning, as though anticipating some kind of lark. The boy Curle, however, looked as if he might burst into tears at any moment and Fox thought, not for the first time, of the Government's absurdity in enlisting children utterly unable to withstand the rigors of a campaign outside the walls of a garrison town. He stood for a moment in front of the boy, regarding him gravely, almost paternally. "You, boy, what's your name? Speak up, sonny! What do they call you?"

The boy threw up his chin, mastering his tears.

"Curle, Sergeant! My mother was cantinière in the Fifty-first!"

Fox raised his eyebrows and looked at the child with interest. If his mother was a cantinière, then it meant that the boy had been born in the Army and was therefore a veteran, despite his extreme youth.

"You were at Busaco?"

"Yes, Sergeant, I was wounded there." Suddenly the boy seemed to find all the confidence he needed and, dropping his drum, he raised his wide sleeve, displaying a red, half-healed gash about three inches in length.

Lickspittle laughed outright, but the sergeant glared at him.

"It's a damned sight more than you'll ever have to show!" he snapped and pretended to examine the graze carefully.

"It was a Frog bayonet!" said the boy eagerly. "It ripped me sleeve, see!" He pointed to some rough stitching an inch or two above the sleeve buttons.

"Did you kill him?" said Fox gravely.

The boy smiled shamefacedly and shook his head. "He was dead when he did it. Sergeant Murphy shot him through the head, and when he rolled over, his bayonet come at me like a . . . like a spear! It bled, though, it bled awful!"

"Good boy!" Fox said gratefully and suddenly felt cheered. He made them all empty their cartridge boxes and piled the cartridges on an abandoned table nearby. The count showed a total of one hundred and four, which, together with his own ammunition, added up to about fifteen rounds apiece. Carefully he counted out seven piles and told each man to help himself. Curle carried no arms and Fox told him to abandon the drum.

At that moment Graham reappeared. He had not found Sowden's body, much less his valise, for both were buried deep under a vast pile of debris blown there by the exploding mine.

Fox said, "They've got about fifteen rounds apiece. You won't have a musket yourself, sir?"

"No," said Graham, "nothing but this," and he touched his ornamental sword hilt.

Fox hesitated a moment and then he swung his knapsack to the ground and flicked open the flap, pulling out a heavy brass-mounted pistol, a powder flask and a shot bag. "I got these from a cuirassier in the mountains, sir!"

He handed them to Graham, who took them with a nod and stuck the pistol into his belt. Fox again glanced toward the mountains, and this time the pale afternoon sun caught the gleam of a casque and threw it back like a winking signal. He lifted his arm, pointing, and Graham, looking northeast, saw what looked like a long, rolling shadow in the narrow valley between the peaks. At the same time the deserted town seemed as still as a tomb and, cocking an ear, he could hear a faroff murmur like the sea. He knew he would have to get used to asking the sergeant direct questions.

"The main body, how far off would it be?"

Fox sucked his cheeks and seemed to measure leagues with his eye. "Eight—ten miles," he said and Graham noticed that for the first time he dropped the "sir," as though by asking a question Graham had surrendered the leadership.

"And their cavalry scouts?"

"Yon was a thruster," Fox said, jerking his head toward the little platform from which the dragoon had fired. "You always find them among the light cavalry. A youngster, mebbe, who won't last very long!" And suddenly he smiled and Graham felt immensely grateful for his strength and the vast store of experience that lay under the battered shako like a reserve of ammunition waiting to be used. Fox went on, "He'll have ridden back to the squadron by now, telling them how clever he was and how the bridge was blown. We could spare a few minutes to hunt up rations. If we don't find the ford we shall want all we can carry!"

Graham nodded. He was getting himself in hand now, steadying himself upon the two handgrips represented by the sergeant's presence and his own raw pride. He said,

"Very well, Sergeant, tell the men to search the houses. I'll wait here with the boy. He'd best save his strength for the journey."

Fox returned to the group under the jail wall, and a moment later the six men fanned out, moving in and out of the wretched dwellings surrounding the plaza. The boy Curle crossed toward Graham, still dragging his drum, and when he reached the ensign he saluted.

"Sergeant says to leave the drum, sir," he squeaked, and Graham noticed that the child's mouth was set in a sullen line. "I didn't ought to leave me drum, not now I carried it this far!"

Graham smiled, remembering the village children at Addington, ragged little scarecrows who used to run behind his pony calling for ha'pennies.

"The sergeant's right, boy," he said. "We've got a long march ahead of us and it isn't likely you'll be asked to beat the charge!" Then, seeing the boy's crestfallen look, he poked among the mass of rubbish in the street until he found a half-filled sack containing household utensils. He emptied it and gave it to Curle. "You can be quartermaster," he said, "and all the rations can go in the sack."

The boy's sullen expression vanished at once, as though he saw in this assignment a kind of promotion. Whipping out a clasp knife, he stabbed two holes in the hem of the sack and threaded his crossbelt so that the sack hung on his shoulders like a big knapsack. The swift action seemed to give him stature and he drew himself upright, standing almost to attention.

Graham, one eye still cocked toward the mountains, saw the men drift back toward the center of the square, chivvied by the active Fox, who peered into their haversacks to see what they had found. It was not very much— two strings of onions, a half-gnawed loaf green at the edges, a small jar of tobacco and a few worthless odds and ends. What little food there had been in the town had been wolfed down by the rearguard or carried away by the fugitives. Over the mountains blue-gray clouds were gathering, and soon the wind rose, gusting down the street and lifting tatters of debris as it passed. Fox came back, carrying the spoil, and they stuffed it into the drummerboy's sack.

"There are two men we'll have trouble with anon," Fox said, in a low voice. "The jailbirds will have to be watched. The other four are good enough, especially that man Lockhart. He was a gamekeeper and is reckoned the best shot in the regiment. We'd best be moving now, sir." He hesitated a moment and then, with some difficulty, went on, "It might be as well if you said something to them first, sir. Coming from you it will do more good. There's no provost to scare 'em, but they'll march and fight better if they understand the situation!"

Graham nodded, sharing the sergeant's embarrassment as he walked over to the six men now standing in a little group in front of the most important-looking house in the town. The sergeant moved slightly ahead, barking, "Squaaad—'shun!" and bringing them to attention. Curle hung on the officer's heels, as though he were already an NCO not required to stand in rank with the men.

Graham cleared his throat, wishing heartily that he had grown a beard or at least a moustache during the voyage in the transport and the few short weeks in Lisbon. It would, he felt, have given him some kind of excuse to hector a group of men all older than himself in years and experience. He said harshly, "We shall march southeast along the riverbank until we find a ford. Perhaps we can wade or maybe we shall find a boat of some sort. Sergeant Fox will shoot any man who attempts to straggle. If we keep together we shall catch up with the rearguard tomorrow. No one is to fire without my command and if any one of you finds food it is your duty to surrender it at once."

The squad remained silent, their eyes registering the dull acknowledgment of men who had heard officers address them in these terms many times and took but little account of it. Graham studied the file, trying to memorize their features—Watson's narrow, chirpy face, the heavy stolidity of Strawbridge, the half-mocking shiftiness of Lickspittle and Croyde, the somber blankness of the Nonconformist Morgan and the easy confidence of the marksman, Lockhart. "We shall march in single file," he added. "Sergeant Fox?"

"Sir?"

"I shall lead with Private Lockhart. Space the men in twos at intervals of twenty paces and bring up the rear yourself."

"Sir!" And as Fox wheeled about and began pairing the men Graham could have sworn that there was a twinkle in his eye, as though he were watching a child take its first, staggering steps across a floor and make a grab at the nearest piece of furniture.

Because he felt himself flushing, Graham moved off smartly, Lockhart a pace or two behind with his musket carried on the crook of his arm as Graham had seen his father's gamekeepers walk the Addington rides when pheasants were rearing. The man was obviously the best of the bunch and it was reassuring to have an expert marksman beside him when they passed directly under the rock platform from which the dragoon's shot had come. They went on down to the narrow beach and followed the wide curve of the river for more than a mile, the mountain wall getting steeper all the time and the dark river on their right stabbed with slab-sided rocks upon which the current broke and eddied. Then, quite suddenly, the river narrowed and storm clouds centered on a massive wall of rock right ahead, so vast indeed that its bulk gave Graham the impression that he was marching into the mouth of a huge cavern. The beach narrowed until it was less than a yard wide and then disappeared altogether as water rose over his calves. At the same time there was a ceaseless booming, like Atlantic breakers pounding Lisbon bar, and as he edged his way around a protruding rock Graham saw the source of the noise and would have cried out in dismay had he not been aware of Lockhart at his elbow.

The river at this point was a roaring torrent swelled by a tributary spilling directly out of the mountain cleft and cascading down over rocks more than a hundred feet high. The din was deafening and the place so forbidding that Graham shuddered, gazing hopelessly at the waterfall and beyond, where the gully of the lesser river was hemmed in with close-set timber, cork and scrub oak, trunk upon trunk crowding to the very edge of the stream.

There was no crossing it. On the far side of the junction a vertical cliff contained the main stream, and a direct ascent of the water slide would present impossible difficulties to men carrying muskets, packs, canteens, sidearms and ammunition. Graham stared at the rocks, trying to find some kind of cleft or chimney where the force of the descending water was lessened, but such handholds as presented themselves were wet and slimed, offering no promise to inexperienced rock climbers. He saw Lockhart doing his own survey, studying the thick growth of scrub and giant fern immediately above their heads, and then the second couple edged their way around the cliff face and all four were crowded onto the narrow ledge under the overhang.

Graham shouted at the nearest newcomer, the Welsh preacher Morgan. "Tell Sergeant Fox to join me!" he bellowed, and when the man cupped his ear he repeated his instructions and waved his arm.

Presently the man seemed to understand and passed the message to his companion, Watson, who at once wriggled out of sight around the bulge. Graham saw Lockhart shouting to him and saw him struggling with the flap of his knapsack. He did not hear what the gamekeeper said, but, as he watched, Lockhart succeeded in opening the leather flap and his hand emerged with a length of rope, a cord of about ten or twelve feet. He pointed to the ledge about twelve feet above them and made a crouching motion, indicating that the ensign should take the rope and climb upon his back, but at that moment Fox edged into view and behind him the boy Curle, his ration bag swinging in his teeth to give him more elbow room. Fox sized up the situation at once and pointed to the boy. Lockhart passed the rope to Fox and then turned, pressing his face to the rock and straddling his legs, at the same time cupping a hand to give Graham a foothold.

It came into Graham's mind as he hoisted himself onto the man's shoulders that they were all engaged in the kind of game played by a group of boys released from school. Behind them the cascade hissed and roared and the main stream seemed to boil under the weight of the descending water, soaking them with spray and almost alive in its determination to pluck them from the ledge and plunge them into the current. His groping hands sought and found a crevice and he hung on, clawing the naked rock while the drummer-boy hoisted himself from Lockhart to Graham and thence, to Graham's relief, into a mass of trailing roots a couple of feet beyond. The boy's hobnailed boot skinned his cheek, but a moment later Curle's weight was gone and, glancing up, he saw the boy knotting the rope to roots as thick as a man's wrist. Fox, crouched beside Lockhart, was pointing upward and Graham understood his signal. Using Lockhart's shoulders as a springboard, he leaped upward, grabbing the rope with one hand and a root with the other. For a moment he swung, his feet kicking at the rock wall, and then, exerting every ounce of his strength, he hauled himself into the round hollow where the boy was squatting.

They came up slowly and painfully, the massive Strawbridge replacing Lockhart as mounting block. First Lockhart, then Watson, agile as a monkey, then Lickspittle, then the clumsy, cursing Croyde, then Morgan and finally Sergeant Fox, who seemed to have had some kind of dispute with the big countryman but finally scrambled onto his shoulders and was hoisted into the hollow. Up here the roar of water was deadened by the crowding undergrowth, and by shouting into one another's ear they could just make themselves heard. But there was little need to discuss the new dilemma, that of hoisting the huge, lumbering Strawbridge a distance of more than twelve feet on a short length of rope.

He stood there looking up at them, his expression placid and pleasant, as though his bulk presented no problem to seven men and a boy huddled together in a hollow made by an uprooted pine, with a roaring torrent on one side, a dense mass of scrub above and the swift-flowing main stream below. His gaze was fixed on Graham as though persuaded that he had done his part as springboard and now it was for the officer to think of something.

It was Graham, in fact, who took the initiative. He collected all the crossbelts, knotting them together and lengthening the rope by another seven feet. Then he made a pad of greatcoats, wedging it under the rope to guard against fraying. Leaning over the ledge, he conveyed to Strawbridge by dumb show that he was to use the last crossbelt as a stirrup, and when this was done he spaced the men along the rope as far as the root to which it was anchored. He was excited now, his fears and anxieties temporarily forgotten. He leaned far over the ledge and when the men began to heave, hoisting Strawbridge up the cliff face by inches, he made a grab at the countryman's crossbelts and hung on, his knees and elbows scrabbling on the rock for a hold. There was a moment when he thought they would never hoist the man to the top. He swung four feet below the ledge, gyrating slowly on the makeshift rope, his expression still calm and trustful as the men behind Graham strained and slithered among the mush of mud and dead leaves that filled the hollow. Then, as they took the strain once more, Strawbridge began to rise and Graham improved his hold, the sergeant kneeling on the small of his back to keep him from pitching forward into the river. Bruised and battered, his bleeding cheek ground into the rock, Graham hung on and at last Strawbridge flung up a hand that was caught by Fox and between them they managed to drag his dead weight over the edge of the hollow.

With his lungs bursting and blood streaming down his face Graham lay beside the prostrate countryman, sobbing for breath, and behind him the men gave a little cheer. Then, as their wheezing subsided, Watson made one of his Cockney quips that came to mean so much to them. Pointing to the inert Strawbridge, he said derisively, "What did I tell yer? Pregnant, he is, and it's gonner be twins!" and everyone but Morgan laughed at this small joke and began to scrape some of the mud from their uniforms and faces. To Graham, lying face downward on the rock, Watson's jibe somehow was a password that gave him right of entry into a new world where men were measured by what they did rather than by their social caste. Although he was to come to know each one of these men with an intimacy that would have been impossible under different conditions, it was Watson, the man with lines of soot ingrained into his sallow skin, who symbolized the spirit of unity that was to emerge from this unlooked-for experience.

CHAPTER TWO

The Church

$\sim\!\!\infty\!\!\sim$

GRAHAM FORGOT many of the experiences that came his way during the next thirty days, but he never forgot the four hours' march that followed the squad's ascent of the cliff face above the river.

They could not remain where they were, crammed into a small crater and denied sufficient room to move without risking a miniature landslide that would spill them into the water. On their right was the thundering waterfall, and on their left, not more than three miles away, the town that was now almost certainly occupied by the French advance guard. Behind them was the river and above them a dense mass of scrub leading, presumably, to the edge of the escarpment and the valley down which Masséna's army was advancing. They had no choice but to climb upward through close-set timber and a wilderness of uprooted trees and loose stones, their advance progressing at the rate of about a mile an hour. Graham led, fighting his way through the tangled undergrowth and calling back warnings of lightly poised boulders, any of which would have carried them away like a row of skittles. Up they toiled through the long afternoon, Sergeant Fox chivvying the rear and Strawbridge half carrying and half dragging the boy Curle, who twisted his ankle in the first stage and could barely put foot to the ground. Graham heard Lickspittle and Croyde muttering and cursing and Watson wheezing for breath, but still, by some miracle of buoyancy, the Cockney found it possible to crack a wry joke about the toughness of the briers or the plodding progress of his companions.

About an hour before dark they reached level ground where the woods thinned a little and Fox, with his ear to the ground, detected the rumble of artillery caissons in the valley, where the timber gave way to a wild stretch of moorland studded with giant rocks. Looking across the slope toward the next peak, Graham was reminded of a picture he had seen in one of his father's books representing an astronomer's conception of the craters of the moon. Presently, when they had pushed to the very edge of the undergrowth, they could see that Fox's surmise had been correct and that the road below was black with French transport wagons moving at a crawl toward the fold in the hills where the town crouched below the horizon.

Graham said, "We must bear left and go on down until we can find the smaller river again. If we can get across that we can work our way to the main stream and find the ford that the cavalry used during the advance!" He made it sound very definite, as though he personally had knowledge of the crossing and was not relying upon the sergeant's guess.

They moved off again, finding the descent somewhat easier, and when it was almost dark they struck the tributary again, a narrow, twisting stream boiling along between slab-sided masses of rock and not more than fifty feet across, but too deep and swift-flowing to ford. Then, in the last moment of half-light, they saw the tiny beach and cave, and less than twenty yards downstream the fallen tree, a giant pine almost bridging the river.

They went over gingerly, Strawbridge carrying the boy on his back and Fox, roped to a jagged branch, steadying the file in the center. The cave was a godsend. It offered shelter and the chance of a fire, for down here, in the depth of the woods, it seemed unlikely that a French patrol would stumble on them. Fox set the exhausted men gathering firewood, but the boy was too spent to climb the

rocks at the cave mouth and was hoisted inside by Strawbridge and Lockhart. Watson had kept his tinderbox in a
sealskin bag with his stub of pipe and few shreds of
tobacco, so that they soon had a fire going at the back of
the shallow excavation. The wood was damp and the cave
soon filled with smoke, but they were able to make some
attempt to dry their clothes, and presently Lockhart and
Watson busied themselves with the preparation of soup
made of onions and the moldy bread they had brought
from the town.

"We could do better than this by morning," Graham
heard Lockhart tell the Cockney. "We could set some
traps, for there'll be a thousand coneys hereabouts unless
I'm much mistaken!"

"Set some traps, then," Graham told him, and Lockhart, followed by Strawbridge, took flaming billets and
went down to the river again just as Fox returned from a
reconnaissance along the unexplored bank.

"There is a cattle path yonder," Fox told Graham,
"and this beach is probably a drinking place for the beasts
grazing on the plateau above. It leads in the right direction, due south by my reckoning."

"We can try it in daylight," Graham told him shortly.
"Call the men together for their meal and I'll see what I
can do with the boy's ankle."

Fox seemed to hesitate and then, in a low voice, he
said, "Them jailbirds are hoarding, sir! They've got brandy
and maybe something else. Will you hold a pistol to them
while I make a search?"

Graham glanced around the cave. Lockhart and Strawbridge were outside setting traps, Watson was tending the
soup and the Welshman Morgan was carefully cleaning
his musket. It was the first time he had realized that
neither Lickspittle nor Croyde was present.

"Where are they?"

Fox jerked his head and Graham followed him out into
the open and down the bank to a spot where the two
felons were sitting side by side on a fallen trunk.

"Open your knapsacks!" Graham said, leveling the weapon at Lickspittle.

The men looked surprised, then resentful as Fox kicked their knapsacks aside and began to strew their belongings on the shingle. There was just enough light to examine the contents and Fox grunted with satisfaction when he found four hardtack biscuits and a hambone with about a pound of meat adhering to it.

"The ensign could order me to shoot you for this," Fox said. "What else have you got?"

Croyde looked murderous for a moment, and then, jerking up the flask, threw back his head and applied it to his lips. Graham tore it from his hand, placed his thumb on the neck and shook it. It seemed to be about half full of spirit. He said slowly, "You can go your own way, both of you. If you get back to our lines I'll have you both shot, but I don't think you would get back alone, the French would take you sooner or later. What is it you want, to act with us or travel alone? This is your last chance and I'll give you a minute to decide!"

He sensed the sergeant's approval of this ultimatum. They stood with their backs to the rushing stream, watching the two men exchange glances. Lickspittle seemed inclined to brazen it out, but Croyde was confused and almost tearful. Sensing this, Graham ignored the smaller man and concentrated on Croyde.

"Well?"

Croyde scratched the side of his head.

"I'll stay with the file, sir. Matt will, too, for we'd never find our way out o' this place alone and we'd be strung up by they dragoons." He turned desperately to his companion. "We would, Matt, I'm telling you!" When Lickspittle declined to answer he plunged his hand into his greatcoat pocket and pulled out a quid of tobacco, thrusting it toward the impassive sergeant. "Take it, Sergeant, it's good Navy issue. I got nothing else, I swear to God I 'aven't!" And he suddenly swung round and tramped back toward the cave.

Lickspittle stood up slowly. He did not seem in the least cowed by the desertion of his crony and when he spoke there was a grinding contempt in his voice.

"We might as well have been topped or transported," he said, "and I told him that many times. It would have been finished with, wouldn't it? A man can only die the oncet!" And then he too turned on his heel and went back to the cave.

Fox hurled the quid of tobacco to the ground and crushed it under his boot. "Damned scum!" he said. "Is it right they should make good soldiers bed down with the likes o' them? I've said so once and I'll say it a thousand times."

"I don't suppose they would," said Graham, "if they could get enough honest fellows to take the shilling!"

"That's true," replied Fox thoughtfully, "but there's reasons for men steering wide of the color sergeant when he comes drumming for recruits. When a man joins the colors he turns his back on most things as make life worth living! Start young enough, like me and yon drummer-boy, an' it's bearable, maybe. We've never known nothing better, neither one of us, but a man with a trade, a man who wants his own hearth and his woman in bed beside him o' nights, ah, that's mighty different, sir! What would a man like that gain by following the drum into a Godforsaken land like this?"

"You could have got your discharge long since," Graham said, struck by the bitterness in the man's voice and the savage line of his mouth. "They sign a man seven years at a time, don't they?"

"What else would I do now?" said Fox, and suddenly he sounded less bitter than pathetic, like a cripple comparing his prospects with those of the able-bodied.

"Have a swig from the flask, Sergeant," Graham said, smiling, but the sergeant shook his head.

"I never touch spirits, sir, I seen too much madness come of it!" And, seeming anxious to break off the conversation, Fox followed the path to where the faint glow reflected on the rocks outside the cave.

When supper was done and every man but Fox had had a gulp of Croyde's brandy, the sergeant posted Lockhart as sentry and the rest of them lay down to sleep. Graham gave Lockhart his watch and orders to wake the men in rotation, but despite his own aching tiredness he did not feel sleepy. His lacerated cheek was throbbing, but it was not the smart that kept him awake but the strangeness of his situation, cooped up in a cave beside a tumbling Portuguese river with a group of men who at sunrise that morning had been no more than a file of blank, stupid faces but were now, by some extraordinary chance, linked to him and his future more closely than were his brothers at home or the junior officers with whom he drank and gambled and boasted in the depot at Hythe. Propped on his elbow watching the dull glow of the dying fire, he felt an intense curiosity about each of them as an individual, how they came to be there, where they had been reared as children, whether they had wives or children and, above all, what they thought about him, a young coxcomb unweaned in war and clearly uncertain of his responsibilities. They would, he thought, have been much happier with the sergeant, who spoke their own language. If, in the end, they were rounded up by the French and cut down, or marched off to starve in some prison fortress, they would not blame the lucky shot of the dragoon but the green ensign who had led them astray and deprived them of the one source of security that they had ever known, the regiment.

He studied them as they slept, marveling at their ability to relax in the pungent atmosphere of the cave with nothing but a canteen of onion soup in their bellies. Watson was lying on his back snoring, the spluttering flames playing goblin tricks among the begrimed crevices of his face. Where, Graham wondered, had the man acquired such a fearsome complexion, a face seamed with the filth of years and one seemingly that had never known soap and water—yet surely he must shave sometimes? Did he scrape his ugly little face with a dry razor? Was the skin so tough and bedaubed that it had lost all sensitivity? His gaze wandered to Strawbridge, whose face by contrast was round and pink. How did Strawbridge acquire those massive limbs and strength that enabled him to plod over uneven ground with a fourteen-year-old boy on his back? Not on army pork and hardtack surely, more likely from generations of countrymen who had lived all their lives in the open air, developing giant physiques by the exercise of monotonous daily labor.

Beyond Strawbridge lay Fox, the sergeant, as soundly asleep as any of them, which was odd seeing that Fox, when awake, never ceased to look tense and calculating. Perhaps this was a rhythm acquired by a professional who had survived half a dozen campaigns, an ability to slough off the tensions of the hunted animal the moment it found the security of the burrow. Yet the man could be gentle as well as brusque and resourceful. He had been polite and helpful with Graham from the outset, hiding his contempt and irritation under a mask of deference accorded not so much to Graham but to the epaulettes he wore. It was Fox, of course, upon whom each of them depended, but Fox, a mere sergeant, would never admit this, not even to himself. Always he would hint at decisions and then pretend that Graham had made them, for this was how the Army was organized, orders filtering down through graded channels until they reached the cul-de-sacs of brains such as Croyde's and Lickspittle's. Graham pondered the imponderables of the file. Was the smaller, less tractable of the two felons a fool or a yokel? Not in the sense that Strawbridge or Watson was, for at least Lickspittle had possessed brains enough to challenge the established order of things and risk his neck in order to make a guinea or two by evading the law! And he had done more. He had evaded the penalty of getting caught with arms in his hands, for he was still alive and in good health when, by all the rules of the game, he should have been hanging in chains on some seacoast gibbet alongside his friend Croyde.

The boy Curle groaned in his sleep as he turned and scraped his injured ankle on the rock floor. The sprain, Fox had assured them, would be cured in a day or so if Curle was made to walk. Fox had cut up his own spare shirt to make a cold-water bandage and had applied it with a skill not often seen among the supposedly trained ambulance orderlies. Graham had commented on this and Fox had shrugged, explaining that sprained ankles were as common as lice and that no man was permitted to leave the line of march on account of one. He was helped over the next few miles and then he recovered. Provosts followed the rear of the column to ensure that he did.

Remembering Curle's uncomplaining submission to Fox, Graham glanced at the child's face as he slept. He did not look fourteen or anything like fourteen, but younger and infinitely more vulnerable than Graham's youngest brother, Geoffrey, who was nine and was still treated as an infant by the estate workers. How was it possible that a child as frail as Curle could survive an active campaign, march twenty miles a day on the barest minimum of food and most likely a few hours' sleep in the open? Yet there were many such children in Wellington's army and Graham could only suppose that the weaklings died in infancy and those who survived grew as tough and indestructible as men like Fox.

He looked at the composed face of Morgan, the camp preacher, and the thought occurred to him that these ranting, Bible-quoting Dissenters had always proved themselves in the field, ever since Cromwell had recruited his solemn-faced troopers who regarded Almighty God as their personal patron. Graham wondered how Morgan, the Methodist, viewed the men with whom his King had now been at war, more or less continuously, for nearly twenty years. Did he bayonet them as unbelievers and atheists or simply because he was paid to do so and was encouraged by his religious beliefs to give value for money?

He heard a boot grate on the stones outside and remembered Lockhart, the sentinel. Of all the men in the file Graham felt closest to Lockhart, because he moved and spoke like the gamekeepers on the estate at home. He was clearly a countryman, just as Watson was a gamin of the cities, but he was not the type of countryman represented by the bovine Strawbridge. His ingrained respect for the officer class was a legacy of training in civilian life, yet he possessed, within this circle of deference, a measure of independence revealed in his dourness and the way he carried himself along with big, swinging strides.

Despairing of sleep, Graham got up and went to the mouth of the cave. Lockhart was there, leaning on his firelock and staring into the blackness across the stream. Graham could see nothing, but he was aware that the gamekeeper knew by instinct exactly what was going on out there under the scrub crowding down to the water's edge.

"Have you heard anything?" he asked and the man shook his head.

"Nothing to be feared of, sir, just the coneys. I've a notion the traps I set will yield us something. A man could live offen this kind of country, depending he had fire and seasoning, that is!"

Graham strained his ears and heard a vague scuffling sound issue from a clump of briers upstream of the beach.

"We've got one be the forelegs," Lockhart said with quiet satisfaction. "I'll get it soon as I'm relieved, before a vixen happens by and skins it!"

"Go now and I'll keep watch," Graham told him, for suddenly the prospect of cooked meat made his mouth water. He took Lockhart's musket and bayonet, and the man went silently into the bush, emerging a moment later carrying a small hare warm to the touch.

"Skin and joint it now," Graham said. "I'll stand sentry until Watson relieves you."

But the man shook his head vigorously. "Officers mayn't stand sentry while the likes of us are on hand, sir," he said severely, and, dropping the rabbit, he took his musket and went inside the cave to wake Watson.

The little sweep came out rubbing his eyes and looked rather startled when he saw Graham standing there. Graham reassured him, smiling in the darkness.

"Lockhart has just caught a hare, so we shall be sure of breakfast in the morning!" And he was rewarded by the little man's engaging grin as Lockhart reappeared with a canteen, collected his hare and took it across to the fire. When they were alone again the Cockney coughed and Graham, sensing his embarrassment, said, "How long have you been with the Fifty-first? Were you with them at Busaco?"

Thus directly addressed, the Cockney's natural amiability mastered his embarrassment and he began to talk to Graham as though for the moment they were almost equals. "I done two years, sir. Come out with the first lot, I did! I had a crack at 'em that first time at Vimmyro, that time we packed 'em back 'ome with the Navy, but I dodged the last lot, told orf fer 'ospittle guard at that convent, I was. Died like flies in there they did, but we was looked after orlright. All the rum we could drink and bushels o' good straw to lie on. Wisht they left me there, that I do, if you get me meaning, sir!"

The man's nasal accent and his habit of slurring words and phrases made his conversation almost as difficult to follow as a foreign tongue, but Graham recognized "Vimmyro" as Vimeiro, Wellington's first victory in the Peninsula, which had resulted in the defeated French being shipped back to France under the terms of the armistice. Graham reflected that there had been an uproar in London when the terms of this agreement were made public. People who had never seen a Frenchman declared that

Wellington had won a great battle and thrown its fruits at Bonaparte's feet.

He said, "Before you were a soldier, what did you do?"

The man looked surprised, as though Graham should surely have known. "I was chimbleysweepin' down Bermondsey way. That is, the master sweep 'ad 'is place there, but he was sent aht every day, right aht into Kent sometimes, an' even slep' aht, so as to start early! There's a peck o' chimbleys in some o' them big places. One of 'em took us near a week, I remember!"

So that explained the ingrained filth in the man's face. It was soot, grimed into seams and layers in the course of countless scrambles up flues, commencing probably in early childhood. Graham tried to remember if he had ever seen master sweeps and their apprentices at Addington Court, assuming that the chimneys must have been swept from time to time, but realized that until this moment he had never associated the task of cleaning chimneys with a man's livelihood.

"You actually climbed the chimneys as far as the roof?" he asked, and Watson glanced at him warily as though he had a suspicion that the officer was trying to make a fool of him. He decided that this was not so, that the man did not even realize that chimneys had to be swept.

"Till you c'd stick a brush out the top," he confirmed. "The master, 'e waits in the yard to see the brush come out and if 'e don't it's a bloody good belting for the 'prentice when he comes dahn out of it! Mind you," he went on more confidentially, "we sometimes fooled the old bastid wi' longer rods, pokin' 'em up from partway up, but you never did that till you was certain sure he'd had his quart o' four ale and was larkin' wi' the wimmin about the place. A sweep's lucky, yer see, sir, for a sweep don't never 'ave no trouble gettin' the wimmin runnin' after 'im. You'd have 'eard o' sweeps kissin' brides at the church gate maybe, sir? Well, that's the way it is, tho' some sweeps I know warn't so lucky after all, not when they lorst 'emselves in chimbleys an' never found the way out agen. An' there was others, poor sods, 'oo tried their luck in dead-end flues an' got stuck and was hoisted out cold an' blue in the face like!"

As he rambled on, obviously enjoying the recital, Graham was able to visualize the background of Watson. He saw him trudging along behind an equally begrimed master, a man lavish with the use of belt and abuse, who relegated nine tenths of his work to urchin apprentices and sometimes helped to drag them half dead from an airless flue high up in the rafters of some great house. He began to understand the source of this man's essential cheerfulness and toughness, now that he was released into the comparatively lax discipline of army life and was free to breathe fresh air and feel rain and sun on his face. He thought, No wonder the little rascal enjoys his soldiering! It must be infinitely preferable to the life he had as a child, working all day in dark chimneys, thrashed by some drunken sot of a master, then home to bed in a filthy hovel on an empty stomach! But he did not say as much to Watson, for so far their intimacy was unbalanced, a guarded expansiveness on the ranker's part and undisguised patronage on the part of Graham. Yet, for all that, Graham's heart warmed toward him as it had already warmed toward Lockhart and Curle and, to a degree, toward the tight-lipped Sergeant Fox.

He said briskly, "Very good, Watson. Wake Morgan after an hour and then get what sleep you can. We've a long march ahead of us tomorrow!" And he handed Watson his watch and went back inside the cave, where Lockhart was already asleep, the skinned and jointed hare soaking in his canteen. In a few minutes Graham had joined him in sleep.

The cattle path found by the sergeant led southwest, climbing the wooded escarpment mile after mile, steep in some places but for the most part a great deal easier to travel than the previous day's road. About midday the leading pair arrived at a crossing and found a mash of horseshoe scars in the mud of an intersecting path. Fox pronounced the shoes to be French and said that no more than a troop had passed this way within the last forty-eight hours, but Lockhart, who also examined them, declared the marks to be more recent, adding that the shoes were on the small side and were therefore made by light cavalry.

Graham realized they were now faced with two choices: to backtrack on the hoofmarks, assuming that the trail would lead to a village where food and perhaps local directions might be found, or take the safer course of pushing on to the top of the escarpment and working around the shoulder of the mountain in the general direction of the big river. This time he did not ask Fox's advice, and the sergeant offered none. Not only was Graham gaining confidence but the men seemed in far better shape than on the previous day. Lockhart's hare had provided a modest meal when boiled with the hambone taken from Lickspittle's haversack, and young Curle was getting along satisfactorily with the aid of a stout ash thumbstick that Strawbridge had cut for him. Graham gave orders to turn right and follow the horse tracks. The route was a more direct approach to the river, and the chances of finding food higher up the mountain were remote.

They moved cautiously through the brush in the same extended order—Graham and Lockhart as advance guard, the rest of the file in the center and Fox bringing up the rear. Soon the woods fell away, and early in the afternoon they emerged into a little valley where a small town composed of a single street and a square around a church sprawled beside a river running between flat meadows.

They looked down on the huddle of stone buildings from the cover of the last patch of timber. It seemed utterly deserted, but this did not surprise Graham, for they were still less than twenty miles east of the British line of retreat and General Craufford had issued orders that every dwelling over a wide area was to be cleared and anything that might prove of value to the French destroyed. There had been a great deal of resentment of this order among the Portuguese, some of whom preferred to take their chance with Ney's looters rather than abandon everything they possessed, but the Commander in Chief's orders had been carried out ruthlessly and this part of Portugal was now little better than a desert. Discounting the lunatics in the jail, Graham had not seen a single civilian for five days.

Fox would have gone on down the dirt road to reconnoiter, but Graham stopped him, preferring to risk one of the others, and it was the Welshman Morgan who made the survey, returning thirty minutes later with the information that the town was empty of inhabitants and had obviously been pillaged by cavalry.

The rain had held off during the day, but now, in the late afternoon, it came on to drizzle and the prospect of bivouacking under a roof was inviting. They moved carefully through the rubble of the single street and reassembled outside the church, an imposing building for so wretched a town and built, Graham would have thought, in the twelfth or thirteenth century as an adjunct of the local monastery, the ruins of which they could see higher up on the southern slope.

They were on the point of dispersing in search of food when they heard a thin, high-pitched wail issue from the dark interior and then, as they swung around cocking their firelocks, a low, sustained howl quite unlike any sound Graham had ever heard, in that it was neither human nor animal yet carried within it a note of lamentation that reminded him vaguely of bagpipes.

The eerie sound alarmed the men more than would have a rattle of musketry. Strawbridge, his eyes rolling, let fall his musket and clutched instinctively at the diminutive Watson, whose tongue shot out as his sharp eyes darted first at Fox and then, almost piteously, at Graham. Graham, himself startled and uncertain, was relieved to see the sergeant smile.

"Yon's nothing but a keening woman," he said briefly, "and I'll wager her man is laid dead inside!" And he swung around, hitching his musket on his shoulder, and strode across the threshold into the church. They followed him, first Graham and then, tentatively, the others, crowding between the tall columns of the nave and looking toward the altarpiece, where light entered from the high chancel window.

What they saw surprised even Fox, for immediately below the altar rail was a raised tombstone, a heavy block of stone that had been used to seal the entrance to a vault. The slab had been partially moved aside, revealing a glimpse of the dark interior. Crouching beside it was a young woman aged about twenty-two or -three, with a handsome oval face, fair and very smooth complexion and a mass of reddish-gold hair hanging loosely about her shoulders. Graham realized at once that she was not Portuguese but a camp follower, for her skin was too fair for any woman in this part of Portugal and her eyes were pale blue, quite unlike the metallic blue of some of the women he had seen during his stay in Lisbon. She was wearing a green dress that was obviously looted, for it was made of some rich brocaded material and, although ripped and travel-stained, looked as if it had once been the property of someone of rank. Across her shoulders was the red homespun cloak worn by most of the camp followers at the base and recognized by Graham as a quasi-uniform. Her military status was further revealed by the pipe-clayed belt she wore about her waist and the heavy brogues on her feet.

She did not appear to notice their entry, but when she turned and saw them she gave them no more than a glance, throwing back her head so that her throat muscles moved as she uttered another long, dolorous cry, at the same time beating a kind of desperate rhythm on the slate cover of the tomb. The file watched, fascinated by the fierce, impersonal grief of the woman's demonstration, then Fox advanced, touching her shoulders.

"Where's your man?" he demanded.

She looked at him steadily, standing upright and casually dusting the folds of her dress, at the same time inclining her head toward the far side of the tomb, where the light from the window did not penetrate. Graham walked around her and peered into the dark corner below the altar rail and saw the corpse of a Highlander stretched upon the floor, his eyes closed and his hands folded in the conventional attitude of the dead. He had been a big, rawboned man and even in death he looked fierce and quarrelsome, the golden stubble of his beard catching a pinpoint or two of light and his mouth set in a savage line as though he had died with hate in his heart. Beside him was his firelock with the bayonet still attached and in a little pile close by were some of his accouterments—a cartridge box marked with the numerals "43," a black, feathered bonnet and a knapsack made of untanned goatskin.

"Question her," he told Fox. "Find out if there are any more of the Forty-third in the town!"

The file stood around in a wondering circle as Fox began to interrogate, and after a moment or two she seemed to shed her grief like a garment, answering his questions clearly and willingly in a broad, singsong accent that Graham at once recognized as Welsh, the Welsh of someone to whom English is a secondary tongue but who has no difficulty in using it when necessary. She had a pleasant voice, her words striking the ear like soft chords played at a distance, and when she talked she looked animated and responsive.

Her presence in the church was soon explained. She was the camp wife of a Highlander numbered among a half company sent ahead early in the retreat to clear the town, and the others had moved out two days ago. When they were making ready to leave, she told them, her husband, Donald, had been seized with a kind of fit that set him foaming at the mouth, but this had not dismayed her overmuch, for he was subject to such attacks and carried a cordial in his pack for use in such emergencies. She had administered the cordial, but this time the attack had been fatal, and with the help of another woman, the wife of the sergeant, she had carried him here to lie in hallowed ground. When the others moved on she had remained, "thinking to keen a little for respect" and bury Donald in a tomb where his body would be out of reach of the carrion. The lid of the tomb, however, had proved too heavy for her and she had been able to do no more than shift it slightly. She was on the point of taking his arms and equipment and following the line of retreat when a squadron of French lancers had ridden into the town from the south, cutting off her retreat and bivouacking in the houses for the night. She was under no illusion as to her fate if they found her, so she took refuge in the belfry loft. They had entered the church but had not disturbed her man's body. Early that day they had left, traveling north, and now she was preparing to follow the tracks of the Highlanders toward the big river.

She told her story in a matter-of-fact way, and it struck Graham that she did not appear to have been dismayed by her husband's death or the risks she had run by her isolation. She was obviously a woman well accustomed to the hazards of war, the type of camp follower who would soon choose a successor from among her late husband's comrades and trudge along with him, cooking his meals, mending, washing his clothes and possibly bearing his children until he was killed in action or completed his term of enlistment. Already he was familiar with such women, there were about two to every company of infantry in the British Army in the Peninsula, but he had never yet spoken to one. Sometimes, when he had watched them tramping along in the company of the men, he had marveled at their hardihood and the swinging rhythm of their stride while burdened under what seemed to him a monstrously heavy load for a woman to carry over rough ground. He noticed that this particular follower had the same stockiness of build combined with a kind of natural grace when she moved or gestured. She was completely at ease in the presence of men, treating them as a woman at home might regard other women at washtub or stove. He noticed something else too, the freshness and clarity of her complexion, suggesting splendid health and immense vitality.

He said suddenly, "Bury her man, put him inside the tomb and then scatter and search the houses for food. We shall bivouac here for the night!"

The woman looked at him curiously and suddenly smiled as though grateful for the command. She walked across to the corner where the Highlander lay and without glancing at him lifted his pack and musket, hitching the weapon to her shoulder as though it weighed a few ounces instead of several pounds, and standing aside while Strawbridge, with a single heave, spun the heavy slab on its stone mountings and revealed a deep aperture in which a coffin was already laid. She watched with interest but not much concern when Lockhart and Morgan, ineffectually assisted by the capering Watson, lifted the dead Highlander and lowered him ungracefully atop the coffin. Watson seemed to find the occasion very diverting, and his half-smothered chuckles irritated Graham. Then, as Strawbridge prepared to replace the slab, Morgan held up his hand and began some kind of chant in a tongue that was foreign to them all save the girl, who glanced up sharply at the first words, then clasped her hands together in a kind of ecstasy that revealed her complete understanding of Morgan's jargon. A moment later she joined in and Fox, suddenly impatient, made a chopping gesture with his hand, cutting the service short and breaking the brief spell under which the group had fallen. Strawbridge replaced the slab and they drifted back into the open, Graham and the woman remaining on the church steps, the others scattering across the square and using their musket stocks to break open the doors of such of the miserable dwellings as were locked.

The sound of their activities drifted across the squalid little plaza and Graham, alone in the widow's presence, felt slightly embarrassed. He said gruffly, "You had best join the file until we find a crossing and catch up with the rearguard. We were left behind when the bridge was blown in Coimbra!"

The woman smiled, tolerantly it seemed to Graham, and he noticed her small white teeth and full red lips. She was, he thought, younger than he had first supposed, for nothing else could explain her freshness and the suggestion of personal cleanliness belied by her filthy attire and the coating of mud on the expanse of shin revealed by the hitched-up dress.

"Ah, so," she said softly in her melodious voice, "you will be glad of another musket." She raised her head and sniffed, adding casually, "The French are not far away!"

She said this politely, yet without the tone of respect due to his rank and she did not, he noticed, use the word "sir," which he would have expected from a private's drab.

At that precise moment, without the slightest warning, the blow fell on them. Within seconds the little square was full of running, shouting men and the silence shattered by the drumming of hoofs and the rattle of equipment as two compact bodies of horsemen came thundering down the street, heading directly for the scattered redcoats on the far side of the plaza.

Graham was too astounded to do more than leap back into the shelter of the porch. As though he were watching a *tableau vivant* from a distance he saw what was happening before his eyes, but for a full minute his brain failed to register peril. He saw isolated members of the file emerge from houses and run toward him, moving at what seemed to him incredible speed, their boots raising a flurry of gray dust as the two knots of horsemen raced down on them with leveled lances.

Fox and Watson reached him simultaneously, flinging themselves through the porch and seeming to halt, turn and bring muskets to shoulders in a single, synchronized movement. Then Lockhart rushed in from the left and Strawbridge from the right, and a second later, as the two groups of lancers met and reined back, came Lickspittle and Croyde, with the drummer Curle less than a yard behind.

Only Morgan, the Welshman, remained isolated, and as the file struggled to group and adopt firing positions Graham saw him burst through the milling horsemen in the center of the square and run with long, loping strides toward his comrades. He did not get more than halfway. One of the lancers dragged his horse around in a narrow half circle, crouched low in the saddle and spurred forward, his long weapon entering the infantryman's back and emerging at the breast so that Graham saw Morgan lifted and hurled forward, pitching on his face as the horseman wheeled and expertly freed his lance. The poor wretch he had so neatly speared half rose, staggered a few steps and then fell on his face not more than a dozen strides from the porch.

The man who killed him lived less than a moment to enjoy his triumph. Before he could swing back into line the camp follower's musket roared in Graham's ear and the lancer threw up his hands and toppled backward from his saddle, his horse swinging hard right and dashing past the group with one boot wedged in a stirrup and long reins trailing. Several of the others fired, but no other hits were scored, for the cloud of horsemen tore down the street in a swirl of dust and in a moment the only evidence of the engagement were the two casualties, Morgan with blood running from his mouth and the lancer flat on his back, his absurd lopsided shako crushed under the back of his head and one stockinged foot resting on a high-booted leg.

"Reload and no man fires without my command!" shouted Fox, and, turning, Graham saw the Welsh girl

slotting a ramrod into her musket and looking across at
the dead lancer with grim satisfaction. Fox addressed
Graham, the pitch of his voice returning to normal as his
glance darted up and down the street assessing their position and the strength of the enemy. "God curse me," he
muttered, "that I should be caught like that for not having
the gumption to picket each end of the town!"

"Morgan reported the town empty," Graham reminded
him, and the sergeant nodded grimly, adding callously,
"Then good shuttance to him for a useless fool!" Then,
taking command of the situation and making no attempt
to defer to Graham, "There's no more than a troop of
them and we can hold out here unless they dismount and
come at us through the back of the church! Strawbridge!
Croyde! Go inside and barricade any rear entrance. Use
that slab from the tomb if you have to, use pews, boxes,
anything, but make sure our rear is safe. Lockhart, cover
the right. You others face center, there are no more of
them to the south, every man of them joined in the charge
because they thought we were easy pickings! Watch out,
they're coming again!" And as Graham's hand groped for
the hilt of his sword, "Don't draw, use the pistol, man!" as
though the ensign had been a particularly obtuse private
of the line. Graham had been on the point of asking how
many lancers had galloped across the square, but the
sergeant swung away, forcing Lickspittle and Watson
down on one knee and taking his place behind them with
musket leveled. Already the girl was crouching behind
Lockhart, her musket barrel steadied on his shoulder.

The lancers came trotting back into the square in files
of three, perhaps thirty of them in all, with a boyish officer
riding a superb light bay out on the flank. They seemed to
Graham a very professional-looking detachment in their
smart green uniforms and lopsided shakos, small, lean
men with faces strangely alike under regulation moustaches
and side whiskers. He was relieved to note, however, that
there were no carbine buckets on their saddles but in place

of them a pair of pistol holsters emblazoned with the gold letter "N."

He said anxiously to Fox, "Why don't they dismount and take up positions in the houses opposite?"

But Fox said they were not accustomed to fighting as infantry and would almost certainly attempt another charge before relying on tactics favored by dragoons. He recognized them as Piré's lancers, Polish veterans who had harried him over the mountains into Coruña nearly two years ago. He did not take his eyes off them as he spoke but watched them wheel into line, the young officer taking up a slightly advanced position on the left flank.

At that moment Strawbridge and Lickspittle came hurrying out of the church and the latter reported breathlessly that the exit from the side chapel had been barricaded.

"Very well," said Fox quietly, "then look to your front. Lockhart, cover that youngster out on the flank. If you can bring him down we might get a moment to sort ourselves out."

He had not finished speaking when the officer lifted his saber, and the next instant a double line of horsemen were thundering across the square, the dust rising in swirling clouds, the afternoon sun catching the points of their leveled lances as the wings raced around on the trotting center. Graham glanced at the file wedged together in the open porch, and although not one among them showed anything but resolution he did not understand how Fox thought it possible that a small body of marksmen could withstand the impact of such an avalanche of excellently maneuvered cavalry. Yet it was so, for Fox had been weaned on defensive tactics, and the men under him, poor enough material in most respects, were nevertheless the best-trained marksmen in Europe. The sergeant shouted the command when the lancepoints were barely twenty yards away. As the volley crashed out the scene was shrouded by the swirl of dust and powder smoke, and when it cleared the lancers were already cavorting across the square in every direction. Through the drifting smoke

Graham saw two riderless horses bolt into the funnel of the street at the south end.

Soon the wind tore gaps in the cloud of smoke and Graham saw that in the open space before them, where Morgan and the first lancer lay, was a horse with its legs threshing and its body contorting, while dotted here and there, on either side of the dying animal, lay five men, three clearly dead and two others on their hands and knees, one of them badly wounded in the chest but the other no more than dazed by the fall, for before the fastest of the infantrymen could reload he scrambled up and crossed the square at a stumbling run, diving into one of the houses opposite. At the same moment the wounded man collapsed on his face and lay still.

Lockhart had gotten his man. The young officer lay nearest the porch, his saber advanced and still attached to his wrist by the sword knot. Lockhart, glancing at him dispassionately, said he had shot him through the body and seen him fall.

"Five with nine balls! That's promising if no more," said Fox cheerfully, and Graham noticed that under the stress of combat the man's nature had undergone an abrupt change. All his dourness had disappeared and in its place was the ebullience of a schoolboy engaged in some kind of prank at the expense of authority. He went around banging the men on their shoulders, his eyes sparkling with excitement, and Graham saw the boy Curle looking up at him with adoration in his eyes. For himself he felt curiously deflated and cut off from the group, almost a spectator to the encounter, and he looked with contempt at the clumsy pistol he was holding. He could not even remember discharging it when the sergeant had screamed the command.

The woman said as she reloaded, "They won't come again until dark and then on foot!"

The sergeant nodded, posting Lockhart and Lickspittle as lookouts and motioning the others to withdraw into the church. As they moved off, a random pistol shot struck the molding of the arch over their heads and a thin shower of chips rained down.

"We were lucky they weren't dragoons," Fox said. "A dragoon troop commander would never have charged in the first place but shot it out from the houses."

"They'll try that now, I imagine," Graham said, but Fox shook his head and said that the woman was right, they would stay under cover until darkness and then close in on the church in ones and twos, relying on saber and pistol.

The prophecy seemed to dismay Strawbridge, who said, in his thick yokel's accent, "Worn 'em 'ave 'ad their rations an' ride off now, Sergeant?"—a thought that had occurred to Graham.

Fox made no reply, and Graham saw his brows draw together as though pondering the wisdom of admitting the full extent of his anxieties, but finally he sucked in his cheeks and touched Graham on the arm, drawing him deeper into the gloom of the big building and leaving the others nearer the entrance. As they moved away the woman detached herself and joined them uninvited and the three of them stood in a group near the raised tomb in which the Highlander had been laid.

"We can get out of here without them knowing," she said calmly. When Fox stared at her unbelievingly she added, "There is a crypt below with a passage leading up on the hill! My man went down there, searching for rings."

The sergeant looked at her with interest. "You are sure of that?"

The woman shrugged and Graham got the impression that she despised them all, even Fox. "Over there," she said, pointing, and because the light was bad Fox took out his tinderbox and, stooping, plucked a handful of rushes from the floor, twisting them into a torch.

They moved across the chancel and into a side chapel where there was an iron ring bolt on the floor. The woman raised a small square slab and pointed to a flight of steps.

"There are no more dead down there," she said glumly. "We went down and searched before the others moved on. Sometimes these fools bury their dead with rings and trinkets. My man had a gold one out of a tomb in a town back yonder but sold it for a shoulder of mutton. The meat lasted us all the way down here."

She spoke as if she thoroughly approved her late husband's common sense, and it crossed Graham's mind that the ragtag and bobtail of the British Army were an odd, incongruous rabble in some respects, for here was a woman who had risked her life to bury her husband's corpse in sacred ground but found no shame at all in confessing to grave robbery. She seemed, in fact, far more interested in the possibility of rings stripped from the fingers of the dead than in the prospect of escape offered by the crypt.

"Wait here," Fox said, and holding his rushlight high, he ran down the steps and disappeared. He was gone only a few moments, emerging like a demon from the pit. "She's right," he told Graham, "the passage leads away uphill and there's light at the far end of it." He replaced the small slab and stood thinking a moment, his hand rasping on the stiff stubble of his chin. "You must lead the file out through here the moment it is dark," he said. "I and one of the others will stay on and hold them off. That way you can get clear and can wait for me back in the hills. That's no kind of country for cavalry and they won't follow armed men up there. We can be deep in the woods by the time they discover we've gone!"

It occurred to Graham that he should remain behind himself and order the sergeant to lead the file through the exit, but on the heels of this notion came the certainty that Fox would refuse to obey him and would defend his action by reminding Graham that as the only officer among them he was under an obligation to command the main body. He said doubtfully, "How long will you wait?"

Fox replied tartly, "That depends on Johnny Frenchman! Perhaps half an hour, perhaps not so long. I shall fire two shots in quick succession when I'm withdrawing and you can give covering fire from the hill. Maybe they will think there are more of us up there."

"If the enemy are firing how shall we recognize your signal?" Graham asked, and flushed as the woman exchanged a glance with Fox.

"One must not confuse musket shots with pistol shots, sir," he said quietly, and Graham's cheeks burned as they returned to the porch.

It was almost dusk and a faint orange light silhouetted the mountains behind the town buildings. The lancers seemed very quiet, too quiet for comfort, Watson said, displaying a string of oatmeal biscuits taken from the saddlebag of the dead horse.

The sergeant bit into one of the biscuits and spat the flakes on the ground with an exclamation of disgust. "The light cavalry have no commissariat," he told Graham, "so they carry these wherever they go, poor devils!" Graham detected a genuine sympathy for the French in the voice of a man whose general had last week threatened to hang a quartermaster's sergeant for failing to deliver his quota of beer and beef at the end of the day's march. Then, addressing Watson half jokingly, the sergeant said, "If you risked your life for French hardtack you deserve to get a bullet through your thick skull!"

"It warn't me as did it," said Watson, still grinning, "it was the young 'un." He pointed to Curle, who had taken not only the saddlebag but a white sheepskin cloak strapped behind the saddle and one of the lancer's pistols and shot pouch.

"They banged off half a dozen times, sir," the boy told Graham, "but they couldn't hit me on account o' the carcass!"

Graham ordered an issue of one biscuit apiece and

among them they finished the last of Croyde's brandy, passing the flask from hand to hand. In the first moment of darkness Fox made his dispositions, selecting Lockhart to remain behind with him and retaining four of the muskets, the loading and priming of which he superintended personally. Then, feeling half a deserter, Graham led the way through the church and down into the crypt, having provided himself with a rushlight flare that revealed a narrow passage sloping gently uphill.

The atmosphere was cold and damp as they moved along in single file. The passage was a good deal longer than Graham had imagined, all of two hundred meters he would have guessed, emerging under the wall of the half-ruined building they had noted on the hill when they entered the town. Leaving the file near the exit, he crept into the open, moving carefully over a mass of fallen masonry and looking across the roofs of the houses to the plaza. All seemed very quiet down there and after a moment's pause he told Watson, as leading file, to bring the others outside, then move around the angle of the half-demolished wall to the bare hillside that sloped steeply upward behind the buildings.

They were almost clear of the stones, with heather under their feet, when the firing broke out, first one or two isolated shots, then a long, ragged volley. Looking over his shoulder, Graham could see a series of tiny flashes, followed by a flowering of small, winking lights as a confused uproar came from below.

The men seemed inclined to hang back, but he prodded them into moving higher up the hill, where the heather was buried under loose shale and Graham knew they would be safe from pursuit by mounted men. At the top of the slope the ground leveled out among a group of boulders and here he ordered a halt, listening intently for the two-shot signal that would signify Fox's withdrawal.

They waited more than half an hour, growing more and more anxious every minute, and finally Strawbridge plucked his sleeve and whispered, "They'm commin, sir, I can yer 'em! List now!' and held up his hand. But although Graham strained his eyes in the darkness he could see nothing and hear nothing until the swift rustle of the woman's dress on his right told him the camp follower was standing directly in front of him on the very crest of the hill.

"Someone is climbing the slope now," she said, and almost at once a dim figure, bent almost double under a cluster of firearms, flung himself over the crest into their midst. It was Lockhart with all four muskets and he was desperately short of breath.

"The sergeant's done for," he gasped. "I seed 'em come at 'im when I got through the passage. They was waving torches all round him!" And then, somberly, "He was a rare one for a fight, was Sergeant Fox! We downed two of 'em before he tells me to run and I don't doubt but he got another with his bayonet come to the last, sir."

Nobody commented on his news and there was a heavy silence broken only by Lockhart's heavy breathing. They waited another few minutes, but no more sounds of fighting came from below, only a snatch or two of song and once a gust of laughter. Then, with misery in his heart, Graham gave the order to move along the escarpment toward the woods that he remembered as clothing the southern slopes beyond the town's end.

CHAPTER THREE

The Camp Follower

~~~⌐⌐ゐ~~~

THEY WERE unable to march far. The ground was too broken and the temptation to take the down slopes too strong for dispirited men stumbling along in the dark. Yet Graham realized their only chance of safety lay in sticking to ground where cavalry could not follow, so presently he called a halt, determined to move no farther until the moon rose.

They gathered in a hollow between two enormous slabs of rock and Lockhart described what had occurred at the church after the main body had moved out.

Fox's surmise had been accurate. There was no attempt to rush the position; instead the lancers tried to close in from both sides, keeping close to the walls of the buildings left and right of the church and crossing the square on their bellies, using the carcass of the horse and the six dead men as cover. He had winged two on his side of the porch and was confident that Fox had scored a hit on another coming up on his left. "I heard him yelp!" he said in his broad Sussex brogue, "so I knowd Sergeant vound a mark." Then, after the first attack had petered out, the sergeant ordered him to leave and take the four muskets with him. Lockhart admitted that he was dumbfounded by the command and went so far as to protest, but Fox had ordered him into the church, promising to follow within minutes.

"I waited tother end o' that tunnel till I was sure 'ee was vinished," he said, without the least inclination to dramatize the situation. "I had a notion he wouldn't come lest he drawed those green varmints after us! He put that stone trap back, d'ye see, and mebbe they'd fool away an hour or so puzzling where us was tu."

Put like that, there was only one interpretation of the sergeant's act and Graham decided that Lockhart was probably right, that Fox had in fact deliberately sacrificed himself in order to give the file a better chance of winning clear and in so doing had deprived himself of firearms, knowing that muskets were essential in the file's chance of rejoining the rearguard. He went on thinking this for the rest of his life, and so did every other man in the file, for to each one of them Sergeant Fox had died a hero, a man who had voluntarily laid down his life for his friends, but although there was an element of truth in this it was by no means the whole truth of the matter. The real reason why Fox had elected to face twenty-five men with nothing but a bayonet was far more complex. Certainly it had to do with his sense of duty, but it derived more from a streak of obstinacy that had made him such an ideal noncommissioned officer in an army commanded by a man whose recipe for victory in war was one-tenth offensive and nine-tenths defensive.

Sergeant Fox, thirty-three years of age when he died with fourteen wounds in his body, had been fighting the French for seventeen years. He had fought them in Egypt, in Sicily, in the Lowlands, on their own soil at Quiberon and Toulon and in four campaigns up and down the western seaboard of the Peninsula. He recognized no other foreigner as an enemy worthy to engage his professional skill, and although he had probably accounted for more than a score of Frenchmen, some of whom he had killed in cold blood, he felt no grudge against them but rather the respect one purse contender feels for his opponent in the prize ring. Fox's life had been an exceptionally unrewarding one, but there was no element of fatalism in the decision. His choice was dictated by frustration fermenting within a naturally aggressive nature. For seventeen years he had fought the French and for seventeen years considered himself their superior in the field. Yet each victory had ended in withdrawal and more often than not in the shame of precipitate retreat. Fox did not understand how this came to be, but it was so and the memory irritated him. He had beaten the French at Coruña and then taken refuge in the ships of the British Navy. He had beaten them soundly at Vimeiro and seen them ferried away in the ships of the British Navy. Quite recently he had helped to throw them back in disorder at Busaco, yet here he was on the run again, plodding across the mountains to the sea and toward the inevitable British Navy.

As he waited in the dark for the lancers to attack, there came into his head a conviction that this idiotic succession of victory and flight must cease, that he was done with turning his back on inferior troops, that this would be one time when he would stand his ground and see the backs of the Frenchmen for a change. It was a very stupid notion and deep in his heart his professionalism told him as much, but in a curious way he was also tired of acting in a professional manner. For once, and with every fiber of his being, he wanted to think of himself as a fighting man answerable to no one but himself. So he told Lockhart to take the four muskets, because he remembered that the helpless young ensign had nothing better than a pistol and that in any case a musket was very little use for hand-to-hand fighting in the dark. He had his long, needle-sharp bayonet, the weapon he had carried about with him for a dozen years, and with that grasped tightly in his right hand he remained in the porch waiting, feeling as he did so a wonderful sense of elation and irresponsibility, as though, by shedding comrades and firearms, he had cut all the ties binding him to the old familiar life of foraging, trudging, skirmishing, chivvying, encouraging, sustaining and finally slinking down to the beach to waiting longboats and derisive Jack Tars.

He had not long to wait. By now it was pitch dark and the wide street seemed deserted. Listening intently, Fox could hear nothing more than a faint scuffling sound, as though rats were scampering about in the single-story houses opposite, and once or twice his ear caught the jingle of metal, perhaps a spur scraping on a loose stone, although he would have imagined that cavalrymen committed to a dismounted action would have had sufficient sense to remove their spurs before setting out. He sidled back into the depth of the porch, pressing himself flat against the stones and extending his bayonet at full length, its point toward the square. He stood like this for what seemed to him a long time and then, very close at hand, he heard labored breathing and sensed a solidity in the darkness. A moment later a man moved in from the right and Fox realized that whoever it was was only half persuaded that the porch had been evacuated by the British, for the sound suggested a certain amount of irresolution. He remained where he was, keeping absolutely still, and on each side of the porch the Frenchmen probed the darkness. Then, as though a series of tiny bonfires had been lit far down the street, a soft, uncertain light penetrated the pressing darkness, traveling across the plaza and searching out angles where the shadows lay. In the fitful glare of torches Fox saw his man, standing with his back toward him less than a yard away and lifting up his head to call out to comrades who were already clattering down the street from each side, every mounted man bearing a flaming pine torch which he tossed into the porch as he galloped past.

It was, thought Fox in the moment of understanding, a lurid and unlikely scene, men riding with flaming torches, other men shouting as they leaped out of the shadows, the light of the torches catching the steel of their sabers and metal buttons. As the first torch fell at his feet and the Frenchmen whipped around to face the interior of the church, the sergeant lunged, driving his bayonet through the lancer's throat and feeling the sharp tug on the blade as the man fell away. He sensed rather than saw the second man leap in from the right, withdrawing his saber for a short-arm thrust, and he flung himself sideways so that the man overshot by a foot and the bayonet entered his side under his upraised arm, catching for a second on some piece of equipment and then sliding off into the ribs.

The sharp jar of point against bone was the last conscious sensation in the sergeant's life. He did not feel the blow that crashed down through his shako into his skull or the pistol ball that tore into his breast at point-blank range, only a rush of feet and a chorus of yells against an improbable background of winking lights and blundering horses. Then they were over and past him, rushing into the church with torches flaming and sabers flashing, running here and there among the pews, calling to one another for more light and more speed.

It was not until a group of them gathered in the porch looking down on the dead man that they realized the rest of the file had gone, how and where they could not imagine until more torches were brought and they found the stone trap in the chapel and followed it as far as the old monastery. Then the French troop sergeant decided that the stragglers were beyond pursuit and called off his troopers, telling them to light fires in the open street and set about making horse litters for the wounded. He paused for a moment to look down at the dead lieutenant, whose insistence upon a second charge in daylight had cost the squadron an extra five casualties, and then he walked over to look at Fox, who they said had held the porch alone with nothing but a bayonet and had sent two more troopers into the shades before he went down under the final rush. Swiftly, when no one was looking, the Frenchman raised his saber in salute. It was a compliment that he had not paid his own dead.

Graham had never considered following any career but that of a soldier. As a second son he had resigned himself to seeing estate and fortune pass to his elder brother, and when he was a child lead soldiers and toy swords had

been his playthings, military glory his dreams. His ideal-
ized conception of war had survived the officers' training
course at Hythe and the experience of the voyage in a
cramped transport, but during the long march north from
Lisbon his notions of a soldier's life had undergone some
radical changes. Until then he had seen himself as an
inspirer of wavering men standing fast against a resolute
foe, or advancing in faultless formation across a background of meadows and standing corn. In this stirring
setting there had indeed been a few reminders that sometimes soldiers got killed. One or two corpses had lain
about at his feet in composed and graceful attitudes, and
in more introspective moods he had himself received a
clean flesh wound which did not, however, prevent him
from continuing in action. The nagging responsibility of
the long march over the previous two days had tarnished
this idyllic picture somewhat, but it was the encounter
with the lancers that had obliterated the picture. The
corpse of the Welshman Morgan lying in front of the
porch had looked not graceful but obscene, with blood
flowing from the mouth and the eyes glazed in terror,
whereas the body of the lancer shot down by the camp
follower had looked grotesquely comic, with one stockinged leg flung over the high boot and the shako crushed
under the head.

Sergeant Fox could have told him that even the least
sensitive soldier carries to his grave the sense of horror
that accompanies the spectacle of the first men killed in
action, but Fox himself was now lying among the debris
of battle in the plaza and Graham was alone with his six
survivors and the problem of finding a way through the
mountains to the British lines. As yet it was this problem
that obsessed him, but beyond it, tucked away almost out
of sight, was the repellent specter of fear, fear of wounds
and pain, of disgrace and ignominy, but above all fear of
death at the hands of the savage little men who had
speared Morgan and flung him in a bundle at Graham's
feet. Until that moment he had been able to think of the

French as opponents in some kind of sportive contest, but now he saw them as murderous savages who howled, slew and trampled men under their horses' feet. The knowledge that somewhere out in this endless tract of granite and forest were a hundred thousand such men, any one of whom would destroy him with the utmost unconcern, was chastening. It brought his picture of war into a sharp and painful focus, so sharp and so painful that he was glad to seek refuge in pondering the broader issue of finding a way over the lower ridges of the Sierra and across the seemingly unfordable river to Lisbon.

He realized that what he needed most desperately was a map and he thought with rage of the folded map he had seen in the possession of Captain Sowden, cursing the precipitancy of the engineer who had deprived him of this treasure by heaping Sowden's corpse with rubble. He knew that in the absence of maps he must rely upon memory and instinct, but his recollection of the topography of southwestern Portugal was nil, and instincts that he had once thought of as highly developed were in fact as untrained as those of a puppy lost in a fairground. Resentment prowled about inside him, finding some kind of outlet in the helplessness of oafs like Strawbridge and guttersnipes like Watson, whose capacity for finding a way out of the mountains was even less than his own. In a kind of savage desperation he remembered the Highlander's widow, now trudging along behind him and chattering away in her singsong voice to the irrepressible Watson, and he thought, Surely she must have some kind of geographical knowledge inside her head. He made a mental note to consult her at the earliest opportunity.

When the moon rose, the march continued with stumbling uncertainty. They found a track of sorts that seemed to lead across the shoulder of the mountain in a general southwesterly direction, but at every stage it lost itself among masses of giant boulders, and after three hours' tortuous progress he called a halt at a point where the path led them to a comparatively level stretch marked by a couple of shepherds' huts built of flat stones and roofed with reed.

The moon was high now and the mountainside was flooded with silver light, revealing on one side the towering slopes of the peak and on the other a steep, rock-strewn valley, filled with blue-black shadows where timber flourished. Far away, no more than an indeterminate gleam, was what might have been the river, but whether it was a tributary or the main stream Graham had no notion whatever.

He said gruffly to Lockhart, "Tell them to bivouac here and no fires! Post a sentry and ask the woman to come with me!"

He moved along the ridge toward the smaller hut, feeling that for the moment at least he must isolate himself from the men until he could form some kind of plan that would conceal from them his utter helplessness. He paused in the entrance to strike his flint, and the tiny flame revealed a circular interior bare of everything except two or three trusses of damp straw. His calves and thighs ached horribly as he sat unbuckling his sword belt and laying aside Fox's heavy pistol and ammunition pouch. He felt so dizzy that for a moment he thought he was going to faint, but he pulled himself together as the woman's figure moved across the entrance, cutting off the light, and he heard the swift rustle of her ridiculous green dress as she sat down beside him, drawing up her knees and hugging them in what seemed to him a curiously relaxed movement, as though she had entered a civilized home and taken a seat by the fire.

She said flatly, "You are lost?"

His first impulse was to snarl a denial, but almost instantly the realities of the situation reasserted themselves and he said in a tone of resignation, "I have no map and I have been in Portugal less than a month. Do you know what direction we should take to find the left bank of the Mondego and cross it after the rearguard?"

"There will be no crossing down here," she said

thoughtfully. "Higher up there are many bridges and a few fords, but none this far south. The river is wide when it nears the sea. On the way north in the summer we did not cross it until we reached Coimbra. The cavalry did, I believe, but only a few leagues south of the town. We must be a long way south of the place where they crossed, and anyway"—he could sense her shrug—"cavalry will cross where infantry drown!"

Somehow he was able to extract a crumb of comfort from her cheerless statement, for at least it proved that she had some knowledge of the terrain, and for the first time since Lockhart had gasped out the information that Fox was dead he felt that he was not alone. He said quietly, "What do the men believe? Do they think we shall find a way out of here?"

"They still have you to lead them," she said, with a note of surprise, "and you are an ensign!"

The naïveté of her remark made him want to laugh, yet in a sense it disappointed him, for he would have expected her to have satisfied herself regarding his unfitness for the task of leading men out of this wilderness.

"The sham battles we fought on the Downs in England were not this kind of battle," he said. "If I had a map or compass I could make a shift at getting these ruffians back to the regiment. All I can do at the moment is guess. Can you help me to guess?"

At that moment the moon sailed out from behind a bank of cloud, its light flooding through the aperture and striking her face slantwise so that she looked for a moment exactly like one of the stone goddesses beside the lily pond in his father's Italian garden in Kent. He was astonished at the classical regularity of her features, but even more by her expression of serenity. He knew, in that instant, that his life and the lives of those other men would depend upon this woman whose instincts were so much more developed than theirs, and he wanted instant assurance of this. He said urgently, "Forget that I am an officer! This is no time for the courtesies of rank. It is different for the men. To them I must remain the leader and if they have no trust they will break away and try to make their way back individually. The sergeant was very insistent about us keeping together, and he was a good soldier. They must believe that I know the way home and that I have a plan, but you know that I have no plan. If you think you can find the way back it is you who must lead through me, it is you who must make up for the map and the compass, do you understand?"

She got up and without answering walked into the open, holding the folds of her dress with both hands like a woman crossing a muddy street. Wonderingly he followed as she moved across the heather to the edge of the escarpment and stood there, her head raised like that of an alerted animal, scenting the keen, rain-laden breeze from the valley.

"Well?" he said expectantly. "What can you tell me?"

"The west is there," she said, pointing, "and the big river runs through that valley to the south," and she pointed once again, swinging her body around in a slow, graceful movement.

"How can you be so sure?"

"I can smell the rain," she told him, "and the rain comes from the west. Besides, I can see the river in the moonlight. If it were not the big river, then it would not gleam, for the small rivers run through deep ravines with trees growing close to the banks!"

"Suppose we followed the slopes of the mountains until we could go down into the valley, would the French have occupied all the crossings?"

"I told you, there are no crossings below here," she said patiently, "therefore there will be very few French, only an odd foraging party. Masséna and the main body are already on the far side of the river. He would have rebuilt the bridge your people destroyed and crossed over by now. The French are very good at bridge building. They are a clever people, yes indeed!"

He was impressed by her confidence and the certainty

with which she seemed able to draw credible conclusions from her experience.

"How long have you been in this devil's country?" he asked suddenly.

"Since the beginning," she said. "Donald was my third husband. Bryn, my first man, was killed after we landed to fight General Junot. Then I took Briggs, his file companion, but Briggs died on the road to Corunna. He was a sickly man and could not forage enough to keep himself alive when the snow came. I waited with him two days until the dragoons were at our heels. Then I went on to the boats and took Donald after we were put ashore and refitted at Portsmouth."

He noticed she used the verb "took" in the sense that a woman at home might say "married" and that she did so without self-consciousness. It was clear that she regarded these liaisons as binding but terminated by the death of a partner, recalled only as one of the file might remember a piece of jewelry or a pair of boots looted during a march. She gave no sign of mourning the man killed in 1808, or the wretch who starved to death during the terrible retreat to Corunna, or even the Highlander Donald, laid in an alien tomb a few hours ago. From the way she spoke of these associations it was obvious that she regarded them as a by-product of war and no more momentous than her present situation.

"How old are you?" he was moved to ask, and for the first time since he had encountered her in the church he saw an element of surprise register on her placid face.

"How old? Perhaps twenty-two or twenty-three, I am not sure. It is something I have never thought about. How old are you, Mr. Graham?"

"Nineteen. I celebrated my nineteenth birthday on the transport."

"Ah so," she said, in her Continental manner, "you are old for an ensign. All the ensigns in the Forty-third are younger than that. They do not shave, although they pretend it is necessary when they are in garrison and have soap and time to spare!"

He would have liked to remain there a long time talking to her in this way, for her voice and placidity relaxed him, coaxing the ache from his calves and the confusion from his brain. She was like a sister to whom a small boy could run for solace and reassurance, and he wanted to confide in her unreservedly, not merely as a guide but as a comrade. He said, with an effort, "It is as I said, you will have to help me in every way. Suppose we find the riverbank unpatrolled and are able to dodge the forage parties, how can we get across?"

"It is not possible to answer that question until we are there," she said, again as though she were reasoning with a tiresome child rather than an officer. "We may be lucky and find a boat that fishermen have hidden in some creek or thicket. Or we could cross swimming behind floating logs, as we did twice during the march to Corunna. Or we could do better, perhaps, and make a raft if we were fortunate enough to find a house and draw nails from the beams. But let us first get to the river. Then we will think about crossing it, Mr. Graham."

He said, on impulse, "Don't call me 'Mr. Graham' when we are alone, but address me as 'sir' when the men are present."

Suddenly she smiled and faced him, throwing back her head so that he saw her not as an oracle but as a young and attractive woman capable of quickening his senses. "Ah so! And when we are alone, Mr. Graham?"

"My name is Keith," he said, blushing, and went on quickly. "We are a Scots family living in the south."

" 'Keith,' " she said, savoring the word. "That is a good-sounding name. 'Keith Graham'—it is Celtic! I knew you for a Celt when you came into the church back yonder, but it is strange, being so, that you had never before heard a woman keen for her dead!"

She seemed to regard this as a fitting conclusion to their conversation for she turned on her heel saying, over her shoulder, "It will be safe to light a fire inside the big hut. I have salt in my knapsack and there is the French hardtack and onions. I will bring you some soup when it is made. You had better post one man in advance and the other a hundred meters down the track. There are goats on this hillside and a goat would keep us fed all the way down to the river."

He followed her back to the others, now sprawling in and around the larger of the two huts. Lockhart had taken it upon himself to mount guard farther down the track, but the others had stripped off their equipment and Watson was already asleep, his head pillowed on the massive thighs of his comrade Strawbridge.

"Relieve Lockhart and take turns watching the path," Graham said, addressing Croyde. "Tell Lockhart to move along beyond the far hut and keep a lookout for something for the pot. You others"—he stirred Watson with his foot—"get inside and sleep, but first check your priming and share what cartridges you have equally! The woman is going to light a fire and make soup."

Croyde got to his feet and shambled off reluctantly, and soon Lockhart came back, exchanged a brief word with the woman and moved on with his long, loping stride to the small promontory where Graham and the woman had talked. As he went into the smaller hut Graham could see him silhouetted against the sky, his firelock held loosely across his lean body. The straw inside the hut stank of ordure, but within a minute of flinging himself down upon it Graham was asleep.

He awoke with the sound of a distant shout ringing in his ears, and it seemed to come from the slope across which they had traveled during the night. He grabbed the pistol and rushed into the open, to find it was now full day, with the rays of the sun slanting down between the naked peaks and scattering diamonds across the wet heather. As he stood there, bemused in the strong red glare, the yell was repeated, but this time it was on a higher note and he recognized it at once as the cry of a woman, coming from a clump of twisted trees growing in a crevice on the valley side of the path. As he began to run, the sentry on the promontory swung around and Graham saw that it was the countryman Strawbridge and that he looked startled and bewildered. At the same moment Lockhart emerged from the larger hut, rubbing the sleep from his eyes and without his musket. He looked stupidly at his empty hands and then dived back into the hut, presumably to collect his weapon, so Graham ran straight on past the hut toward the gully, noting as he ran that the undergrowth lower down the slope crackled and threshed as though it was being shaken violently by the roots. Then, as he leaped into the fissure, he saw a flurry of green, but it took him a few seconds to recognize the movement as a frantic struggle involving the camp follower and Lickspittle, the woman clawing like a mad thing at the man's beard and hair, Lickspittle attempting to pinion her by the arms.

Graham saw that the woman was half naked, that her dress was in tatters and the heavy brocaded hem had somehow entangled itself in one bare arm, constricting her movement and giving Lickspittle the advantage. Under her dress she wore some kind of corset and the remains of a pair of drawers that had once been white but were now little more than wisps of cotton clinging to her knees. Her thighs and buttocks were bare and because he had never before seen a woman so freely exposed Graham checked in his rush and stared, gaping with astonishment. At that moment the woman's thumbs found her assailant's eyes and she pressed with all her strength, causing Lickspittle to cry out with pain and relax his hold so that she was able to writhe from beneath him, regain her feet and kick with great precision, striking Lickspittle's upraised chin and knocking him halfway across the excavation in which the struggle was taking place. As the man rolled clear Graham shouted at her and she leaped back, seeming to notice him for the first time. For a moment she glared at him, her expression as wild and ferocious as that of a berserk animal, and then, before Graham could make a movement of any kind, she snatched at his pistol, cocked it, swung around and let fly at point-blank range.

The roar of the explosion filled the narrow crevice in which they were grouped and the stench of burned powder set Graham coughing so that for a moment he was unable to relate what had happened to the spectacle of Lickspittle's swarthy face disappearing under a mask of blood. Appalled, he stood looking down at the grotesque thing that had been a strong, active man as the woman, hitching the remains of her dress about her, brushed past him and swung herself back onto the path, passing Lockhart and the boy Curle, who had run over from the hut, Lockhart with his musket at the port, the boy holding a saber that seemed almost as long as himself.

"Great God!" he screamed after her as she quickened her stride. "You didn't have to kill him, did you?"

It had all happened so quickly that Graham still found difficulty in believing that it had happened at all. One moment he had been asleep, the next poised on the edge of the track looking down on the struggle, a witness to an act of savagery that had reduced a man to the inert bundle at his feet. He stood looking down at the thing that had been Lickspittle, trying to relate it to the rascal who, a few seconds previously, had been engaged in what was to him no more than a rough and tumble with a camp harlot, and as he stared at the shattered face a sensation of extreme coldness passed over him, bringing with it a sense of shock more distressing than that which had assailed him when Captain Sowden had been killed by the dragoon or Private Morgan speared by the lancer. As the shock receded, however, he thought with revulsion of the woman who had slouched past him, tucking her bedraggled dress under her filthy corset and then, all his senses outrage, he scrambled back to the path and ran in pursuit, shouting in a voice shrill with indignation.

He called, "Stop! You hear me? Stop, I say!"

She stopped at once, turning slowly to face him with the expression of a woman accosted by a tiresome stranger when she was in a hurry. He drew alongside as Watson and Strawbridge emerged gaping from the hut.

"Great God!" he screamed at her again. "You didn't have to kill the man! I would have told the others to thrash him and drive him out! Couldn't you wait for the French to kill him?"

She dropped her gaze and he made the mistake of thinking it was done in humiliation, but almost at once he realized that this was not so, that she was in fact studying him from his boots to the crown of his head, as a curious person might study a strange animal safe behind bars.

"I kill any man who tries to take me by force!" she said calmly. "It is always that way with us and if you doubt me then go and ask the men. They will tell you it is so, that we have our rules the same as you people have yours!" And then, as though this was more than sufficient justification for murder, she crossed to the smaller hut and disappeared through the entrance with a final defiant lift of her shoulder.

He stood quite still, thinking not about the attempted rape or the death of Lickspittle but about the implication of her remark, her acknowledgment of two different nations—the officers and gentlemen, the other ranks and their rabble—and somehow her statement enlarged the whole nature of this nightmarish adventure and his terrible isolation among these men and these desolate peaks and valleys.

It was true, of course, that there were two nations embroiled in war under one flag, but he had never appreciated the width of the gulf that separated them or the hopelessness of finding a bridge to span that gulf. It crossed his mind then that their sole hope of collective survival lay in some kind of alliance between the two nations, a unity that would endure as long as they were isolated and establish between them a mutual trust and confidence. He understood then that he must make his peace with the woman and followed her into the hut, where she was already busy with needle and thread on the rents in her green gown.

She was sitting tailorwise on the straw, unashamedly naked save for the tight corset she wore, and as she bent forward her full breasts strained at the laces of the ugly garment. The remains of her tattered drawers had been peeled off and stuffed into the brogues, remnants to be husbanded against a march through snow and mud. He noticed again how unexpectedly clean and fair-skinned were her shoulders and strong, well-formed thighs and how clear her complexion and eye. It was odd, he thought, that a woman could present such a healthy appearance on the kind of diet to which she had accustomed herself over the years. He would have thought that she would be sallow like Watson, or bloated and pudgy like the big countryman Strawbridge, yet her skin was as smooth as that of the women his father brought to Addington Court and there was a bloom in the face bent over the rags on her knees.

He said levelly, "Very well, what happened before I arrived on the scene?"

"I went there to wash," she said, "and he came over and stood looking down at me!"

"You took off your clothes in front of him?"

"No!" She looked outraged. "How could I have shot him if I had stripped?"

The qualification interested him and it began to dawn on him that the moral code of these people was far from simple. To strip under the eyes of a man, it seemed, was an open invitation, but to wash oneself was so far removed from enticement that it justified self-defense to the point of murder.

"He did not offer you money or food?"

She threw up her head and laughed, so harshly that again he blushed and felt confused.

"He offered me nothing, but if he had I would not have

accepted anything from a man like that! I lay for soldiers, not for the dregs of the jails, Mr. Graham!"

He nodded slowly, for it seemed that everything she said carried within it the seeds of logic.

"You will be grateful to me before we find the crossing," she went on carelessly, "for he was the kind of man who brings ruin and failure to any detachment. I have seen them flogged and I have seen them hanged, but what use is that when more and more of them are drafted into the ranks, when every transport brings another company of them to repair honest wastage? The provost should hang them as they come ashore from the transports, before they have a chance to infect promising men!"

"There is his comrade," he said. "Are you not afraid Croyde might want to revenge himself on you?"

"I am not afraid of Croyde, for there is a man who will soon find someone else to lean upon. If it is not Lickspittle it will be you or one of the others!"

She put away her needle and bit the thread, slipping the tattered dress over her head and rising swiftly to her feet.

"You have no other clothes in your pack?"

"I have enough," she said shortly, thrusting her broad feet into the brogues and stooping to fasten them.

He rummaged in his valise and drew out a pair of clean cotton drawers, handing them to her with a grin. "Take these, it will be cold when we are not on the march!"

She took the garment and studied it, feeling the texture of the material with finger and thumb. She seemed surprised by the gift, so much so that she was unable to find words to express her thanks.

He left her then and went along the path to the spot where Lickspittle lay. The sun was clear of the peak now and the mists in the valley were violet tatters, through which he could see an endless vista of woods broken by outcrops of naked rock. Nothing moved down there, and Lockhart, his musket held loosely across his breast, might have been a figure of stone standing sentinel on the edge of the plateau. Graham felt somebody touch his sleeve and saw Watson, his face puckered with anxiety.

" 'E took 'im, sir! *Croyde* took 'im an' wouldn't let none of us 'elp. Pushed us orf, 'e did, and said he'd do it lonesome. Over there!" and he pointed to where the path ran between two masses of fallen rock.

Graham shaded his eyes and saw the lumbering figure of Croyde moving down the path, with the body held against his breast. Obviously the stupid-looking felon had some feeling for his crony in spite of what the camp follower had claimed, for as Graham watched he laid the body on the ground and began to scrabble among the shale. Graham turned away, telling the men to share the dead man's cartridges and search his pack. They emptied it onto a flat-topped rock and out fell twenty or thirty items of campaign loot—a small brass crucifix, a silver thimble, odds and ends that seemed hardly worth the taking. Graham paused over a small piece of bone about two inches long and saw Watson looking at him with an expression of intentness.

"Can I 'ave that, sir? It might work for me!"

"What is it?" Graham asked, turning it over in his hand.

"It's wot they call a relict, sir, one o' them saint's toes or fingers. I was there when Lickspittle took it from a church when we passed through one o' them towns before we got detached. It was in a kind o' glass case wi' writing underneath but we couldn't read the writing and Sergeant Fox who knew their lingo told us it was a relict! So Lickspittle went back an' took it."

"Why do you want it?" Graham asked curiously, for it seemed odd that a man who was prepared to rob a church should look for security from the Devil in the proceeds of that robbery.

"Oh, I dunno, sir," said the sweep, wriggling with embarrassment. "It's kind o' good luck, maybe!"

"It didn't bring Lickspittle much luck," Graham said, making the first joke of his military career, and was cheered when Watson chuckled as he pocketed the bone.

"Ah, I reckon the thing on'y works on the 'oly sort, like me!" he said, and Graham turned away to hide a smile, reflecting that of all these men Watson had the kind of perky courage most likely to mark him down as a survivor.

He issued orders to pack up and prepare to move off, and as the gamekeeper Lockhart rejoined them he said, "We'll give Croyde a few minutes to bury his friend. When he returns keep a close watch on him and don't leave him alone with the woman!"

"No, sir," said Lockhart respectfully and, looking down the path to where the distant figure of Croyde was still bent over the body, he added, "It will be as well to bury 'un while the French are close. The wolves will get 'un in any case in a night or two."

"Wolves? There are wolves up here?"

"Yes, sir, I've seen tracks!" And he slung his musket and went into the hut to collect his share of Lickspittle's cartridges.

Croyde was not much dismayed by Lickspittle's death and was not, in fact, engaged in burying him, although he made a pretense of collecting pieces of rock so long as he thought he was being watched. Uppermost in his mind when he had claimed the right to dispose of the body had been Lickspittle's money belt, a broad strip of sail canvas worn around the waist. Croyde had been aware of the belt for some time, although he had never handled it and not once had Lickspittle referred to it during the months that had passed since they were taken from the condemned pen at Lewes jail and added to the unlikely-looking bunch of recruits selected for the draft. Croyde had known Lickspittle since they were urchins fighting for existence among the watermen of Deptford, sleeping in empty hogsheads and glad to fill their bellies on the scrapings of the garbage cans and fish stolen from the carts passing between Billingsgate and the quays.

When they had been captured, of course, all their possessions had been confiscated, and thus it was a source of bewilderment to a slow-thinking man like Croyde that his companion had soon set about building up another fortune which, presumably, he carried about with him in the sailcloth belt. He had watched Lickspittle very carefully since disembarkation at Lisbon almost a year ago, and although he had never seen him salt gold away he had watched him dispose of items of loot in billet and bivouac and knew with certainty that Lickspittle had the proceeds of such transactions about his person.

He tumbled the body this way and that without pausing to wonder how and why Lickspittle had met his death. It was something to do with the woman they had found in the church, but beyond that Croyde did not trouble himself. His kind of brain could grapple with only one problem at a time and just now he could think of nothing but the belt. Lickspittle, he thought irritably, wore an unconscionable number of garments. He tore open the tunic, ripped up the shirt and groped beneath the close-fitting woolen garment that Lickspittle wore like a coarse skin. When his fingers touched a bulky protuberance below the waist he gave a grunt of satisfaction, and after running his hands around the small of the back he found the fastening knot and flung the body over on its face in order to get a better purchase on the tough material. It was too strong to rip, so he took out his knife and slit the woolen garment from shoulder to thigh. There was the belt, a flattish girdle about four inches wide, and as he slashed at the string he could feel metal through the canvas and began to gibber with excitement. He cast a quick glance over his shoulder to make sure that his actions were not too closely observed and then crouched forward, stuffing the heavy belt into his breeches pocket. With the sudden acquisition of wealth a new personality took possession of him. He wanted most desperately to count the money on the spot, but he checked himself and made a zealous display of covering the body with fragments of rock and handfuls of gray, moss-clotted soil. When all but one arm had been thinly covered he stood up, sweating with exertion and very conscious of his new self, for it even crossed his mind that it might be a good idea to mark the grave in case he could return at some time and go through the pockets, which he had overlooked in his eagerness to get at the belt. He thought better of this, however, reflecting that it was unlikely that they would come this way again and also that Lickspittle was not the kind of man to carry loose gold in his pockets. Satisfied, he rejoined the file and gathered up his equipment. When it was dark, he told himself, he would find a rock or a bush at some distance from the others and count Lickspittle's fortune. He would then repair the string fastenings and wear the belt as Lickspittle had worn it, snug around his belly.

They moved off in the same extended order, the ensign leading, followed by Watson, then Strawbridge, then Croyde, then the woman with the boy Curle and finally Lockhart marching as rearguard. Graham had studied the route ahead and detected what he thought was a continuation of the track around the wide shoulder of the mountain. Later, he thought, they would move down into the woods, but up here they had every chance of spotting the presence of a French detachment by the sparkle of polished equipment or the movement of scrub that would cause dust to rise. They were safe from cavalry, and the woman said that the chance of French infantry climbing so high was remote. The infantry, she said, marched in large bodies, owing to the presence of guerilla bands, and were therefore almost certain to stay in the valleys. The threat of rain had passed and for an hour or so the sun was unexpectedly hot, causing them to sweat freely as they picked their way along the track and over half a hundred miniature landslides, but Graham marched confidently, for at last he was beginning to derive comfort from a plan. As yet it was not much of a plan, no more than a vague idea of keeping on high ground until a break in the valley woods on their right indicated an approach to the river, but it was a great improvement on marching blind as he had marched during the two preceding days when Sergeant Fox had led.

CHAPTER FOUR

The Crucifix

⤳◦⤶

THEY BIVOUACKED that night in a glade of cork woods halfway up the long slope of the mountain. Lockhart shot a goat about midday, after discussing with Graham the danger of advertising themselves by the discharge of firearms. The goat was an easy target and obligingly stood still between two rocks while they deliberated, weighing the risks of alerting the enemy against the certainty of starvation. They had now covered about thirty miles over the roughest kind of country on a diet of onion soup and one boiled hare, with a few crumbs of French hardtack shared among five grown men, a boy and the woman, and Graham realized that they could not continue to march on this meager fare, that they would need solid diet of one sort or another. So he told Lockhart to shoot, and the ex-gamekeeper killed the goat with his second shot. They would have fallen on it there and then had not Graham beaten them off with the flat of his sword, telling Strawbridge, the big, plodding countryman, to give his pack to Croyde and carry the carcass across his shoulders.

As dusk fell they made their way down to the rim of the woods, where Lockhart found a deep crevice between rocks and they could light a fire without much chance of its being seen from below. It could have been observed from above, of course, but the woman said there was no danger from that direction, for if a guerilla band saw them it would be to their advantage. They could get directions and perhaps a guide, as well as the latest information concerning the whereabouts of the French.

Reassured, Graham posted a sentry fifty meters down the slope and they sat around the fire watching the joints brown and sizzle in the flames. The smell of the roasting meat was unbearably appetizing, and when it was cooked they all ate their fill, tearing at the portions with their hands and sighing with pleasure as they gulped and gnawed.

Graham carried his meat some twenty paces down the cleft. He did not want the men to see his ravenous attack upon the food and he made himself a bed of bracken under the lee of a rock where the crevice was shallow and gave a view of the dark woods below. After he had eaten and washed his face and hands in the rivulet, he sat with his back to the rock, watching the moon soar over the peaks and flood the valley with cold silver light. The moon, he thought, softened the landscape, masking its terrible bleakness and loneliness which had weighed upon him so heavily during the day. With his hunger appeased, the nag of responsibility was less insistent, so that he felt almost confident and content.

Farther down the cleft he could hear Watson's nasal voice addressing the three who were taking their rest spell, and presently a thin wailing sound reached him, Watson playing a tune on his tin whistle which he had tooted several times on the march. Graham had heard the tune before during the voyage out and guessed it was a chanty taught the infantrymen by the sailors, for Strawbridge was chanting the refrain. Graham wondered whether he should forbid them to make so much noise.

He was on the point of getting to his feet when a shadow passed between him and the sky and he saw the woman standing there, looking down at him with her hands resting lightly on her broad hips and her head on one side as though contemplating him with amusement.

"Leave them," she said. "There is no one up here and it keeps them cheerful. It is important that they should think of themselves as an army in bivouac!"

He marveled at her understanding of men at war, and

his curiosity about her increased. He said, "Stay and talk awhile, but when you lie down find a place beyond me in case of Croyde."

He said this lightly and she laughed, a clear, ringing laugh that must have been heard by the men, for Watson's serenade faltered for a moment. Graham realized that they would almost certainly think the woman was now an officer's perquisite and were probably exchanging jokes on the subject. He did not care, however, for the hot food had made him feel drowsy and relaxed.

She dropped down beside him in one of those swift, serpentine movements that were so characteristic of her.

"We made good progress today," she said, "and I think we must be within a day's march of the river. Tomorrow we will climb higher and push south. Perhaps tomorrow night we shall find a break in the forest leading to the beach."

He had no wish to discuss their situation, he was more interested in the manner in which she had acquired this instinctive knowledge of men and mountains.

"I told you my name," he said. "What is yours? Where do you come from and how did you become a camp follower? Was your father a soldier? Were you born in barracks?"

"Ah no," she said, with her Continental inflection, "but I was born in the mountains, the Welsh mountains!" She glanced around her, adding, "They are not so different. At night they look the same!"

She had the knack of seeming to make herself comfortable wherever she happened to be, composing her limbs in a relaxed yet graceful position, with her feet tucked under her buttocks and her weight resting on backthrust hands. When she spoke there was a tinge of mockery in her soft, lilting voice.

"You have seen my mountains, you have traveled in Wales?"

"No," he admitted. "Apart from coming here I have never been north of London or west of Portsmouth. My father took me on short journeys before I was sent to school, but I was only a child and I remember very little of them. I have studied Wales on the map. What part of Wales is your home? Is it the north, where the big castles are?"

"It is very close to one of the castles, a village called Harlech, a wild part of the country with the sea on one side and Snowdon behind. There are not many people there. One can walk all day and see no one but Idris the Shepherd or Evan the Turf. I was a fool to leave it, perhaps!"

She said this as though she was not sure, as though it was something she had often debated with herself over the years.

"How did you come to leave it?"

"Because of Bryn," she said. Simply and suddenly she threw up her head so that the moonlight caught her throat and her thick reddish-gold curls swung down to touch the sprigs of heather at the base of the rock.

"Bryn was your first man?"

"He was a carpenter, the son of Rees the Wood. Very clever with his hands was Bryn-boy. Make almost anything, he could, from the time he could hold a hammer and saw. Fine coffins he made, with his father to show him, but soon he knew as much as Rees the Wood, so they set him making tables, chairs and dressers for the big house in Tan-y-Llan. I was up at the house, you see, and Bryn, he was the man who took me the first—the night of the big bonfires, that was, blazing for miles about on account of the big fight!"

He gave her all his attention, for she had the Celtic gift of storytelling.

"The big fight? What fight would that be?"

"Why, the fight at sea."

"Ah, Trafalgar, in 1805?"

"Don't take no account of years, I don't, but that was the night when the bonfires were blazing in the mountains."

"This carpenter, Bryn, he took you like Lickspittle, against your will?"

She giggled, rocking herself on her haunches so that her heavy mass of hair tumbled across her face.

"No indeed, I was willing! Bryn was a fine man, too proud to waste his life working for the people at Tan-y-Llan. So he went for a soldier over at Bangor, and me too, with his child in my belly."

He was surprised and not a little shocked, having regard to the price she had put upon her virtue that morning, and then wondered at the plight of the pair, Bryn exchanging the peace of a craftsman's lot for the brutal life of the barracks, and she a girl of no more than sixteen, homeless and pregnant.

"You have his child?"

"No, I have no child, Mr. Graham. Bryn's boy was born dead. On the transport, it was, after we sailed for Kingstown."

"You have fought in the West Indies?"

"I have been all over," she said, and the declaration was made almost arrogantly, so that Graham realized that she found fulfillment in this hard, restless life, despising women who cleaned cottages, made beds, cooked meals and bore children in towns and villages at home.

"You had no children by Briggs or the Highlander?"

"No indeed," she said emphatically. "Women who bear children on the march are fools. I saw five score of them fall out on the road to Coruña!" Then, seeming to tire of recounting her personal history, "You follow a family of soldiers?"

"No," he said, smiling to himself, "from a family of merchants. To be a soldier was my own choice. My family think I am mad."

"Ah so," she said seriously, "but it is not always thus; there are good times as well as bad!"

"Did you have good times in garrison?" he asked, and she shrugged.

"Why, yes indeed, many, many good times. In barracks

there is plenty of good meat and when the rum is served out there are sprees, with dancing and singing. There is pleasure also in learning what is behind the mountain and that is something one would wonder about all of life if one stayed at home. One is not lonely either, neither man nor woman lacks good comrades in the Army. All these things are worth the taking and one should be careful not to forget them when there is no meat or rum or when men are too cold or tired to sing!"

"Is that all? A pound or two of beef, a pannikin of rum and an occasional carouse?"

"No," she said, looking steadily at him, "there is something else, but it is difficult to say it in English words."

"Then say it in your language."

She smiled and threw up her chin, rattling off a string of curious words that made no sense to him. The words seemed to bounce about on the tongue and lose themselves between the lips, yet they were musical and enriched her as a person.

"What does that mean?" he asked, fascinated.

She shook her head and replied, "I told you, it is hard to explain in your language, but it has to do with the age of my people and the kind of people they were before the English king came over the mountains to build the castles!"

It was not in any way a satisfactory explanation, yet it helped him to grasp something of her approach to the profession of arms. Graham remembered talking to one of the surgeons on board the transport, an officer attached to a Welsh regiment, and he recalled the man saying that all Welshmen claimed descent from kings. They were a people, he reflected, who had never quite lost their separateness or sacrificed their spiritual independence, and in this they were like the Irish and the Scots who contributed so much to the offensive spirit of the British Army. Recruited, bullied and led by mahogany-faced Englishmen from the shires, they yet infiltrated into the higher echelons of every expeditionary force sent out by England to fight its battles. Crauford, Graham's own divisional commander, was a Celt, and so was Picton, whereas Wellington, the Commander in Chief, was an Irishman. Pondering this, he noticed the woman fumbling in a pouch she wore on her belt, and suddenly she produced a sealskin purse, taking from it a small handful of tobacco.

"You have a pipe?" she asked, and when he told her no she began to roll a cheroot, tearing a page from a small book, the leaves of which were crowded with close print and gilded at the edges.

"What have you got there?" he demanded, sitting up.

"A book of prayers," she said, "but they are foreign prayers and therefore of small use to anyone!" She rolled the cheroot expertly and handed it to him, striking a light with her steel spring and watching him draw the smoke into his lungs.

"It is good Navy tobacco," she said. "Donald's sergeant had more than a pound of it and I was wife to him for the half of it all the way from Busaco."

She made this admission so simply that any sense of disgust he might have felt was stifled and instead he wanted to laugh aloud. He was not, however, prepared for her next statement, for she said, with the same child-like candor, "You want me before I sleep?"

He stared at her sitting quietly with her back to the rock, her hands in her lap, her feet still tucked neatly under her thighs. It was as though she was not simply offering herself as a gesture of comradeship but also as his hostess inquiring whether there was any small service she could render before she blew out the candle and drew the curtains of his bed.

He stammered shamefacedly, "No, no, I don't want you!" And then, with a candor equal to hers, "I've never had a woman! Most of the other cadets went with women in Rye and later on in Lisbon, but I did not."

"No?" She seemed surprised, but mildly so. "And why was that, Mr. Graham? You already have a wife, perhaps?"

"No," he said frankly, "I think perhaps because they were not clean women."

"Ah so." She nodded, rising slowly to her feet. "I think you are wise and there is time. You are still young, Mr. Graham."

He got up and stood facing her, aware once again of a disconcerting rush of color to his cheeks and also of a feeling of personal inadequacy.

"You have not told me your name!"

"It is Gwyneth," she said, and as she pronounced it, slowly and carefully like a school dame teaching a child his letters, he lifted his hand and touched her cheek very lightly with his forefinger. Again it was the act of a child seeking reassurance in physical contact with someone he needed and trusted. She made no acknowledgment of the gesture, but as his hand fell away she turned and walked slowly past him to a spot where the crevice ran out onto open ground. He heard her settle herself in the bracken, and then one of the men sitting around the fire lower down the slope laughed and the laugh was taken up by the others. They were not laughing at him, he was aware of that, but the sound of their merriment increased his shame.

During his spell of sentry-go that same night Croyde satisfied his curiosity regarding the contents of Lickspittle's belt. He was both surprised and disappointed. The canvas lining contained but one piece of gold, a half guinea, the rest of the cache being made up of a half-handful of silver crowns, twenty or more shillings and a few coins of lesser value, in all a total of about five pounds sterling. It was a pity, Croyde thought, that his comrade Lickspittle had not changed his hoard to guineas when he had the opportunity, for the belt was heavy and he was already burdened with cartridges, greatcoat, bayonet, crossbelts, knapsack and musket. He made up his mind to change the money the moment they rejoined the rearguard, even if this meant converting it to portable trinkets of the kind that most of the men picked up during the retreat. In the meantime, however, he would wear the belt just as Lickspittle had worn it, and he spent his period of watch untying and reknotting the strings and fastening them behind his back. Five pounds was not a great deal of money, but it was more than most infantrymen acquired during a campaign. Croyde had become almost reconciled to the total by the time Strawbridge relieved him, and after noting that Lockhart, Watson and Curle were soundly asleep he took from the canteen the largest lump of meat left over from the feast, stowing it in his knapsack between the folds of his spare shirt. Life had taught him that it was folly to leave good victuals for others simply because one's belly was temporarily filled.

They breakfasted on the remains of the soup, and Curle was given the rest of the cooked meat to stow in his sack. Just before the rim of the sun showed over the range across the valley they ascended the slope again and then turned south, following the rough track around the interminably broad shoulder of the mountain even when it led them away from the general direction of the river. Their order of march was the same, Graham pushing on a hundred meters ahead of the next man, Lockhart covering the rear. When the easterly trend of the track became more pronounced Graham fell back for a moment and consulted the woman Gwyneth, who confirmed his opinion that it was less exhausting and also safer to continue along the path notwithstanding its curve rather than descend to the level of the valley, where there was every likelihood of encountering a French foraging party. This was the way the lancers had come, and now that the main body of Masséna's army had had time to cross the river it was probable that the deliberate devastation of the country would force them to search both banks for food and fodder.

About noon the path leveled off and began to descend into a shallow valley where lay a huddle of buildings, something less than a village, for there was no church and no central plaza, just a single street beside the track. Graham stood waiting for the file to come up and studied the valley for movement. There was none save for a thin cluster of wheeling specks a mile or so beyond the last of the houses.

Lockhart came up, shading his eyes, and stared at the specks for a long time before saying, "There's carrion yonder. Those will be mountain vultures or ravens, maybe even an eagle or two!" and when Graham asked what they were likely to be feeding on, Lockhart said that it might be anything, a goat, a mule or even human flesh. "They baint very particular, sir," he said carelessly, "not they ole scavengers." And the file grounded arms and stood in a silent group, looking down on the rock-strewn valley.

"We can go on down," the woman said suddenly. "There is no one living there now."

They approached the score or so of miserable dwellings, to find them deserted save for a starving dog that whined and backed away at their approach. They searched several of the dwellings, but there was nothing worth taking and no scrap of food to be found. Graham's impression was that the inhabitants had been given plenty of time to evacuate and had possessed enough mule teams or manpower to haul away their goods and drive off the livestock.

Then he saw the stone, a large, oddly placed stone in the exact center of the street, and he walked over to look at it. It was a sizeable boulder, pyramidical in shape, and at first glance it looked like an improvised mounting block, but then it struck him that placed where it was it would impede the passage of carts, so he went closer to inspect. Suddenly he cried out, leaping back so violently that Watson, a few paces in his rear, came running and both men stared down at the stone aghast. Protruding from beneath one face of the boulder were a man's head and, opposite, his naked feet.

The dead man's eyes were open and the lips were drawn back in a snarl, revealing broken and discolored teeth through thin wisps of dark beard. It was quite obvious that the boulder had been placed upon him when he was alive and that he had been crushed to death with agonizing slowness. His outflung hands still held some of the gray dust he had clutched and his elbows were pressed into the ground as though he had exerted a tremendous effort to draw himself from under the crushing weight of stone. As the rest of the file came up Graham turned away, white and retching.

"A convoy passed through not more than three days ago," the woman said impassively. "They were Ney's men, most likely, for the Second Corps are a hard-bitten lot and this they did as a warning to other Portuguese. I saw it in the north once, near Astorga."

"How could men calling themselves soldiers do a foul thing like that?" Graham demanded.

But the woman shrugged and replied, "Clearly you do not know what the partisans do to French stragglers they catch. This man died within an hour. Some of the French conscripts watch the sun around the sky before they are dead."

Graham's impulse was to get out of the village as speedily as possible, and for a moment he was inclined to order a retreat to the mountains, but he checked himself, realizing that this was dictated more by personal revulsion than by military instinct. From the higher ground they had seen the track curve back to the south and it was common sense to follow it rather than to take to the woods before darkness fell.

Lockhart stated his conclusions quietly and soberly. "It was a small convoy," he said, "perhaps half a dozen wagons, with a company as escort. They captured such people as were here and took them along as beasts of burden. They would be short of mules mebbe and making haste to rejoin the main body. Yet there was no fighting hereabouts, tho' perhaps yonder, where they scavenger birds be screaming!"

Graham listened and his ear caught the far-off squawk of the birds they had seen from above the village. He made a great effort to sound casual and said gruffly, "Two of you march ahead, one on each side of the track, and fire a shot if the plateau is deserted." He sniffed the air and thought he could detect a faint smell of wood smoke, but he said nothing more, bending his will to master the successive waves of nausea produced by the spectacle of the dead peasant. As Lockhart and Strawbridge marched off down the track he forced himself to look at the man again and as he did so he felt a hand touch his sleeve. The woman was beside him, offering her canteen, and he seized it gratefully, gulping down almost a pint of stream water.

"Come," she said quietly. "Perhaps we shall be seen by the guerillas. If we are so fortunate we will ask for a guide. There are partisans hereabouts, I am sure of it!"

They moved off slowly and Graham noticed that the Cockney Watson seemed as deeply affected by the sinister atmosphere of the deserted village, for he marched with his head bent and for once his tongue was still. In silence they moved along the track, around which Lockhart and Strawbridge had already disappeared.

The chorus of the scavenger birds grew louder as the road began to ascend, and presently the sound of a single shot caused them to quicken their step until the deserted village was two miles in their rear. Then, unexpectedly, the road leveled off and they came to a flattish stretch where the track ran between two stretches of timber, pine for the most part but here and there a solitary oak or cork. Lockhart was there, leaning on his musket, and as they approached he waved his hand, pointing directly ahead. Here, where the woods closed on the track, was evidence of what must have been a sharp skirmish between ambushing guerillas and the French, and it was clear that the guerillas had had the better of the engagement, for dotted about the fringe of the trees were about a dozen corpses in the ratio of more than three French to one irregular. Graham found that he could look at the bodies without emotion. They were almost all young, some of them hardly older than Curle, and the numerals on their shakos showed that Gwyneth's guess had been accurate and that they belonged to Ney's Second Corps, which had lost heavily at Busaco and been brought up to strength with drafts of first-campaign conscripts. There were no arms lying about, only an odd cartridge box and a goatskin knapsack that had been turned inside out and then flung aside by the victors. Two wagons had been pushed off the road and burned, and a third, still smoldering, lay on its side in the center of the track, its near-side wheels clear of the ground.

As the file split up to poke among the wreckage, the woman Gwyneth puckered her brows, looking this way and that as she extracted every scrap of information from the debris.

"Well," said Graham with a crooked smile, "what happened and when? Where are they now, French and guerillas? Why did they fight here and why would a small body of troops patrol such dangerous country?"

"Because they are hungrier than us," she said confidently. "Perhaps they did not have the luck to shoot a goat!"

"But why so far off the route of the retreat? They must be ten leagues east of the main body, even supposing the French are in force this side of the river."

"Masséna will have established a forage depot some distance inland," she said, "and is collecting every scrap of food for the siege."

"What siege?"

"The siege of Lisbon," she said simply. "We are not running back to the boats this time, the British will stay in the fortified lines all winter."

Her announcement made him feel foolish. Under the stress of the last few days Graham had forgotten the

fortified lines he had watched in preparation when he
disembarked a month or so before—vast, concentric rings
of forts and strongpoints girdling the city, whole valleys
blocked with stone walls and fallen trees to make abatis
and light-gun emplacements on every commanding hillock, the whole converting Lisbon into an impregnable
citadel supplied from the sea and garrisoned by the entire
British Army. It was strange, he thought, that he should
have forgotten such an important fact, for it had surely
governed the entire strategy of the British retreat and had
a direct bearing on their own situation. It meant that
between themselves and the British were a hundred thousand Frenchmen squatting in a huge ring around Wellington's pickets and starving while the redcoats munched
pork and bread ferried from the supply vessels in the
harbor. It was a very heartening prospect for men safely
within the fortifications, but it seemed to Graham to mul-
tiply their own difficulties, for how was it possible for a
party of stragglers to thread their way through such a
concentration of enemies, and even if they were success-
ful how could they make their presence known when they
arrived outside the nearest British strongpoint?

The woman seemed to have the trick of reading even
his transitory thoughts, for she said, "We must forget
about the Mondego and head for the Tagus. By this time
the entire length of the Mondego will be occupied by the
French on both banks, but the southern bank of the
Tagus will remain in our hands all winter. If it was not so,
then Wellington could not hold on to Lisbon for a day.
Besides, there will be regular gunboat patrols on the
Tagus, sent there to harass the cantonments. The French
have no ships, not even a rowboat if I know Beaky!"

It amused him to hear a camp follower refer to the
long-nosed Commander in Chief as "Beaky," but his ad-
miration for her as a strategist increased with every word
she uttered. She had an instinct about war sharper than
that of any man he had met, not excluding Sergeant
Fox.

"Why do you suppose the Portuguese did not defend their village against so small a group?" he asked.

"Because they knew the guerillas were in ambush up here," she said, "and so allowed the French to march them off without a show of resistance—all save that poor fool under the stone, that is, and there is one hothead in every community."

"Then why did the peasants not return to their homes after the French were defeated and scattered by the partisans?"

"Because they are better off in the mountains. They have their livestock and up there are plenty of caves. There was powder in one of these wagons and they can harass any detachment that passes within range!"

"Poor devils," Graham said feelingly, but the woman mocked his sympathy with one of her expressive shrugs.

"These people have always starved," she said. "There was never a living to be scratched from this soil."

"Then why do they fight for it?" Graham asked, recalling how the newspapers at home had trumpeted Napoleon's early defeats in the Peninsula and announced that here he was fighting a nation rather than a government.

"Perhaps it is their religion," she said. "The priests are very active in Spain and Portugal. They are always so in a poor country. At home we are not so dependent upon God, Mr. Graham!"

She used his name ironically, but as always her conclusions made good sense, and he was pondering her words when Strawbridge came hurrying from below, having descended the slope to a point where the canvas hood of yet another wrecked wagon showed among the pines. He was breathless and wildly excited, blurting out, "There be dree more of 'em down over, sir, and they varmints vinished off the wounded halfway down the slope. Nailed up, they be, the poor toads, and the birds just hoverin' to veed off 'em!"

Graham looked down the long slope toward the fourth

wagon and was able to visualize the long, straggling retreat of the French, fired upon from both sides of the track and seeking the lower ground as the irregulars broke their attempts to rally.

"How many did you say?" he asked, and Strawbridge replied that he had counted seven more Frenchmen shot on the slope and three others lower down, one of them still alive.

The news set them off at a run, plunging down through the stunted trees and undergrowth to a broad shelf of rock where the shattered wagon had come to rest against a large oak, the tallest tree in the valley. Two dead mules lay close by, and on the way down they passed the bodies of the men shot down in flight. It was on the far side of the oak, however, that they were brought up short, for here were three more Frenchmen, two privates of the line each hanging upside down from one of the lower boughs and a middle-aged officer nailed by his hands to the main trunk, his feet not more than a few inches from the ground.

They stood around in an awestruck group. As they watched, the officer's eyelids flickered and the body twitched so that Graham shouted hoarsely, "Take him down, damn you, take him down from there!"

Lockhart at once began to prize at the blunt nail driven through the man's right hand while Croyde, white-faced, hacked at the rope securing the officer's ankles.

"Shoot him." the woman said calmly. "There is no life left in him!" But Graham snarled around on her and tried ineffectually to wedge the hilt of his sword under the head of the nail pinioning the officer's left hand.

"You let me attend to that, sir," Lockhart said gently. "I'll have him down in a trice."

He managed at last to draw out the nail on which he was working so that the man's hand dropped suddenly and Watson shied away in alarm. The others stood back, huddled in a group, but Graham moved to take the weight of the man's body as the rope fell away and

Lockhart chipped away at the bark to expose an inch or so of metal and get a purchase on the second nailhead. When the left hand was freed they lifted the body clear and Graham, tearing open the tunic, laid his ear to the Frenchman's breast, but could come to no conclusion as to whether the man was alive or dead. The wounds in each palm welled a trickle of blood and Graham took the woman's canteen, holding it to the officer's lips and watching the water trickle down the dark beard.

Then, unexpectedly, the man gave a long shudder and Gwyneth said, "He's dead, Mr. Graham, as dead as the others! Leave him now, he feels nothing."

Graham stood up, but as he did so he was assailed by a wave of giddiness that caused him to stagger and clutch wildly at Curle, who was nearest to him. As through a red mist he saw Lockhart run to catch him and then, as though watching a distant explosion, the whole slope of the mountain seemed to heave up and topple and the scream of the birds overhead rang in his ears as the blinding red screen changed to blackness and he collapsed into Lockhart's arms.

When he opened his eyes he saw the ripped canopy of one of the wagons immediately above, and the woman was rooting in one of the lockers with her back to him.

"What happened?" he asked presently when she continued rummaging. "Were we attacked from above?"

She turned then and closed the locker lid, holding a small keg that appeared to have been dusted with thick white powder.

"No, Mr. Graham," she said evenly, "there is no one here but us. I told Lockhart to bivouac. The French will not return unless they come with a large body and cavalry, and if they do that we can see them miles away. I told the men to light their fire in the open. Perhaps the irregulars will see the smoke and come down from the pass."

"Might they mistake us for French?"

"No," she said. "They will see the sentry's scarlet coat and will recognize us as British before they get within

range." She blew some of the powder from the keg and
applied her strong white teeth to the cork, pulling it free
with a loud plop and sniffing the contents.

"Ah so," she said with a smile, "men always do the
same things in the same way. We found a ditched wagon
a day's march from Coruña and as now the brandy keg
was buried in the flour locker. It is curious a man should
hide it there, for after spirits a soldier will always look for
flour and then he will find both! Here, have some, it is
what you need, I think."

She poured a measure of brandy into a tin cup standing
ready on the wheel casing and he sat up, gulping down
the spirit so quickly that it made him splutter. It was
excellent brandy and seemed to flow into every part of his
body.

"They carried me in here?" he asked, noting that the
wagon was one of those just off the track and not, as he
had at first supposed, the vehicle beside the tall tree. "I
fainted in front of the men?" And then, when she made
no reply, "It was heat and fatigue!" He tugged at the
fastening of his tunic and loosened his stock an inch or
so.

"There is no shame in weakness," she said slowly, "not
weakness of the stomach and bowels. Weakness of the
spirit in the face of the enemy, ah, that is different, I
think, but you have not turned your back on the French
as yet. When you do I will leave you and find my own
way back to the lines!" She recorked the brandy and
placed the keg in the back of the wagon. "You had better
take charge of it," she said, "whilst I bake some bread.
There is enough flour here to last us for two days if we
are careful. It is strange that the Portuguese overlooked it
when they searched the wagon!"

He watched her scoop a few handfuls of flour into a
canteen and lay back, luxuriating in the haze induced by
the brandy. He thought, She's an extraordinary woman,
even for a camp follower. Nothing surprises her and
nothing frightens her! She has the physical strength of two

men and the courage and ingenuity of a battalion! She can neither read nor write and she is not even sure of her age, but she is more fit to lead troops across this wilderness than veterans like Crauford or Picton.

Lulled by the train of speculation sparked off by these thoughts and the brandy, he slept, waking when the light in the narrow clearing was almost gone and Gwyneth climbed into the wagon with a canteen of stew made from the remains of the goat and seasoned with salt she carried in a block in her knapsack. The hot soup increased his sense of peace and well-being, so that he handed her the brandy keg and gave instructions that each man was to have half a cupful. Then he rose stiffly and moved out into the open, noting that dispositions had already been made by Gwyneth or Lockhart, with Croyde standing sentinel at one end of the track and the drummer Curle at the other. The others were crouched over a small pile of stone, squatting on their haunches like a trio of savages watching the stewpot.

Watson looked up grinning as he approached, saying, "It's a Dutch oven, sir, and that woman is baking real bread, so she says! Lovely smell, ain't it, sir?"

Graham sniffed the pleasant, satisfying odor and was reminded of the vast kitchens of Addington Court, so that for a moment he knew homesickness. He noticed that a fire burned in a little hollow immediately beneath a carefully placed cairn of stones and that the men were feeding it lovingly with small chips of pinewood. In the last moment of light he looked back the way they had come and saw Gwyneth handing Curle his brandy ration and waiting with arms akimbo as the boy lifted the cup to his mouth. She overlooks nothing! he thought and picked up his valise, carrying it to the wagon farthest from the group and looking over the tops of the young trees to the ledge where they had found the crucified Frenchman.

He was still musing there when Watson approached, holding a pine branch as a torch and carrying an assortment of papers, some rumpled and torn but others comparatively well-preserved.

"I collected this lot from them bodies, sir," he said diffidently. "The big Swede reckons I ought to 'and 'em to you, as none of us can't read wot's writ on account o' their lingo, sir." He did not add that the papers would have been equally incomprehensible had they been written in English but grinned like a begrimed, impudent schoolboy confiding in a friendly teacher.

Graham took the papers, but when Watson saw Graham trying to spread the sheets on his knee he plunged his hand into his breeches pocket and pulled out about an inch of tallow candle, which he lit and set down on the wagon seat.

"There was a lot more of it," he said apologetically, "but I 'ad a bite or two of it when I was feelin' 'oller inside, after that fight we 'ad back at the church. Keeps a man goin', it do, but it's 'eavy on the stummick!"

Graham made a pretense of studying the papers. There were several personal letters and two parade states* marked with the imperial "N" sandwiched between laurel leaves. In the space marked *"Designation"* he made out the words *"14ᵉ de la ligne, Deuxième Corps"* and in heavier type *"Situation des présents sous les armes"* and a handwritten list of names with various annotations, above the signature *"M. Darrieu, capitaine."* He could make nothing of the letters. He had been taught French at school, but not well enough to enable him to translate pages of crabbed handwriting in the light of a stub of candle.

"You did right to bring them," he said to Watson, who was still hovering close by, and once again Graham was aware of a feeling of personal inadequacy. A trained officer who had kept his wits about him, he reflected, might have been able to extract some useful information from such a find.

"They don't give us no idea where our regiment is,

* A parade state is a list of available troops and matériel.

sir?" asked Watson hopefully, and Graham told him they were purely personal letters but added that he was hopeful of making contact with the irregulars in the morning and that doubtless they would provide a guide as far as the British lines. He knew that Watson would at once relay this to the others and strengthen the impression that he had the situation in hand.

He sat there a long time after Watson had returned to the fire, watching the rim of silver moonlight spread across the valley from behind the great bulk of the peak. The men seemed to have been sobered by their experiences during the day, for they conversed in low tones and there was no singing. Presently, because he felt no inclination to sleep, he took advantage of the improved light to wander along the track to the boy Curle, who saluted smartly as Graham approached.

"Go back and tell the others I'm relieving you," he told the boy, "and get all the sleep you can."

"Yessir." Curle replied briskly, and Graham smiled at the child's eagerness to pass as a man. As Curle sheathed his enormous saber he added, "We shall get clear of this in a day or so and when we get back I shall recommend you for courage. You have set a good example to the others. Curle."

The boy seemed to enlarge in stature and Graham heard him hiss with pleasure. Then, with another salute, Curle marched back to the fire, but Graham felt no answering satisfaction, only a nag of depression centered not so much in his feeling of helplessness as in an awareness of the uselessness of a war fought on behalf of bigoted peasants who answered cruelty with cruelty, so that the wheel of horror turned faster and faster in and about their bleak, savage mountains.

As he thought back on what he had seen, despondency pressed down on him like an immense weight, like the stone on the breast of the peasant, so that he leaned heavily on a single pine that sprouted on the edge of the clearing, where his wandering steps had led him, a hundred yards or more beyond the glow of the campfire. He was standing there, feeling utterly desolate, when he heard the soft swish of the woman's gown and saw her step into a patch of moonlight, holding herself erect with her strange dignified posture that was something between the walk of the eternal peasant and the tread of a wild creature of the uplands.

She said, in her musical, singsong accents, "You must put it all from your mind, Mr. Graham! Only this way can you play a man's part in our business, for, see now, it is not good to change places with the dead in your thoughts. That way is death itself, but before that, madness, you understand?"

Her words, spoken almost in his ear, brought instant relief, as though he had been struggling in storm-tossed water and had been lifted by a wave so that he could see the lights of the harbor. He realized that this was exactly what he was doing, enlisting with the dead, with the man under the rock and the officer nailed to the tree, and that this way lay failure to justify himself as a man and a leader of men. He was aware of this even as she spoke, but he knew also that words of encouragement were not enough, that what he needed at this moment was the sure, physical contact of her body. Yet it was not easy to leap the barriers of his background and training, of his status as an officer or his shyness of a youth without experience of women, so he remained tense, his fingers pressed against the rough bark of the tree. When she put up her hand and touched his he shivered like a man with a fever.

She was in no way rebuffed by his withdrawal.

"You must not be afeared of me, Mr. Graham," she counseled earnestly. "It is to make you a man fit to lead that I can do, for now you are a boy like the little drummer yonder. If you take me you will feel yourself a man, and think of better things than a man nailed to the tree. I tell you this, Mr. Graham, because you must think a man's thoughts if you are to lead us to Lisbon!"

Her voice, he thought, was like the murmur of a mountain rivulet laving his self-doubts and misgivings. He lifted his right hand and touched her wrist, finding it cool and firm under the tatters of the sleeve.

The touch of her flesh had an immediate effect upon him, releasing him instantly from the bonds of diffidence that had restrained him. He swung around to face her and then, pushing himself from the tree, he lifted her clear of the ground, his mouth seeking her tumbled hair and his eager hands slipping from shoulders to breasts and then, as she writhed in his grasp, to her broad hips and buttocks. He was checked for a moment by her unexpected resistance, but before rage could rise in him she flung back her head and cried, "No, no, there's no joy in it that way!" And she broke free and drew him across the glade to a spot where the moonlight was cut off by the towering rocks and where ferns sprouted waist-high in the thin soil washed down by the rains.

He was astounded by her deliberation, so much so that he willingly surrendered the initiative, and when they were lying on the ground under the shoulder of the buttress she drew his head down upon her breast and pressed it there, her hands stroking his hair and cheeks. He wondered briefly about the men around the fire that he could see winking in the distance and then forgot them and with them all else in the comfort of her soft breasts and the infinitely soothing caress of her hands.

For what seemed to Graham a long time they remained like this, his impatience spent, yet within him a deep yearning for fulfillment, so that presently, growing bolder, he reached up and touched her breast, exploring the hard nipple with tremulous wonder and turning his head slightly to kiss it through the threadbare material of her dress. The kiss was an act of homage, yet somehow, and perhaps because this was his first positive act since she had drawn him there, it adjusted the balance between them and she said, unemotionally, "Ah so, you shall be master now if you are quiet inside. I am not to be taken roughly,

you understand?" And with the same air of purposeful-
ness she extricated herself from his embrace and
unhooked the tattered dress, spreading it between them
with unhurried movements, then slipping out of the cotton
drawers he had given her on the night they escaped from
the church. Everything she did was deliberate and method-
ical, even her tacit instruction of their consummation,
and although in different circumstances he might have
found her ascendancy shaming, this was far from being
so, for he came to her like a supplicant seeking a blessing
and the act itself was gentle and infinitely sweet, without
trace of impatience on her part and without vice or clumsiness on his. He was glad then that he had been afraid to
visit the Lisbon brothels or buy the raddled women who
plied their trade outside the Sussex training depot, for this
was a richer beginning than was vouchsafed most men in
that he possessed her as a person and not an instru-
ment.

She did not signify the completion of such possession by
disengaging herself and donning her discarded garments.
Instead, she reverted to the mood of their first embrace,
holding him in her arms and letting her hand run down
his face from temple to chin, over and over again until a
drowsiness stole over him, and it was he who put a term
to the occasion by rising to his knees and gazing down at
the outline of her round face framed in wildly disordered
hair and saying gently, "You are good to me, Gwyneth,
good and kind and beautiful, so beautiful that I will never
forget, you hear me?" He wished that the moonlight
would reveal more of her that he might worship her with
his eyes, and the ache to do this was so strong that he
went on hurriedly, "This place we are in, it was hell
before you came, but now it is as beautiful as your
body!"

He could not see her answering smile, but he knew that
he had pleased her by the compliment.

"Ah so, it is just as I said," she told him lightly, "you
are thinking a man's thoughts and you will never be a boy

again. In the morning when it is light you will know what is best for us all and the men will know that you have changed!"

He felt a tremor of shame and said quickly, "They know you are here, that we are making love?"

She laughed softly but without derision, saying, "They would be boys themselves if they did not, Mr. Graham! Perhaps the drummer thinks we are gathering wood for the fire. but the others, they will see the difference in you and it will be good for them, because we are a small band with less than a hundred cartridges between us and have many leagues to march before we are safe again."

She rose and picked up her dress, slipping it over her shoulders and stepping into her incongruous drawers. Suddenly, with the drawing on of her shabby clothes, she became a camp follower again, obsessed once more with the serious aspects of life, keeping watch and remembering perhaps the bread baking in her improvised oven.

"I will send Lockhart to stand sentry and you can sleep in one of the wagons. I must attend to the baking now!" And as if dismissing him from her mind she turned and walked into the moonlit glade and down the track toward the fire.

He was in no hurry to follow her or to sleep, but remained alone in the glade waiting for Lockhart. His thoughts. as she had predicted, were a man's thoughts and his grasp of the situation was a man's grasp. a deliberate weighing of risks, an estimation of unpredictables—the weather. the food supply, the likelihood of a French punitive column's arrival, the nearness and approachability of the irregulars. He considered all these things as a soldier and no longer as a panic-stricken youth shrinking from responsibilities that he yearned to put upon other shoulders. The fear had left his belly and the uncertainty his brain. When he thought of the woman now there was an exultation in his heart that communicated itself to his loins, so that already he wanted to possess her again, yet he was able to smile at his impatience. Lockhart found him smiling and handed him a hot flat cake that looked something like the French hardtack that Curle had taken from the lancer's saddlebag but was very much more pleasant to the taste, although he could detect the bite of the gunpowder Gwyneth had used in order to spare her precious salt. He bit into the cake and pronounced it good.

Lockhart nodded, saying, as to himself, "Arr, it were lucky she crossed our path, she's a cut above any of the drabs I've come acrost in camp!"

Graham wondered briefly if Lockhart envied him his intimacy with the woman, but decided not, for Lockhart was a man who did not concern himself overmuch with women.

"We shall remain here for the day, Lockhart," he said decisively. "I think the irregulars will make contact with us before the French come back!"

"Aye," said the gamekeeper grimly, "mebbe we can give it a day if the weather doesna break." And he cocked a knowing eye at the sky above the peak as Graham hunched his cloak around him and strode back to the bivouac.

CHAPTER FIVE

The Renegade

❧

GRAHAM SAW the first of the irregulars a few moments after dawn. Refreshed by the soundest sleep he had enjoyed since the march began, it seemed to him that all his senses were alerted, for although the man on the rock remained quite still and must have been more than a mile from the bivouac, Graham saw him clearly and pointed him out to Lockhart. Soon after, the other men gathered, staring up at the saddle between the two distant peaks, the summits of which were still shrouded in mist.

The air was very keen and there was a dash of sleet in the wind blowing from the southwest, sending great scudding clouds across the serried ranks of pines and carrying with it the tang of the Atlantic. The man on the rock was obviously a sentinel and had probably had their campfire under observation all night. When sighted, however, he made no kind of move to inform his comrades but remained where he stood, leaning on a long-barreled gun, his cloak bellying behind him.

Graham's first thought was to consult the woman, who was still asleep in one of the wagons, but on second thought he preferred to take the initiative and walked down the track to a point about three hundred meters below the twisting fissure that led up to the irregular's observation point on the saddle of the rock. Even here he was still too far off to make himself heard, so he stopped and went through an elaborate dumb show aimed at establishing his identity, sweeping his arms in a wide circle to suggest friendship and then pointing with exag-

107

gerated emphasis to his scarlet tunic. Presently the man was joined by another, a squat, barrel-chested figure in a full-skirted coat and a wide sombrero, and from where he stood Graham could see the armory of weapons in his belt.

He redoubled his efforts, shouting into the wind, "We are British! We are friends!" But when he realized that his words would not carry the distance he returned along the track toward the bivouac.

He had covered perhaps half the distance when he looked over his shoulder, and what he saw made him whistle with surprise, for the long fissure in the rock, which had been deserted a moment ago, was now strung with climbing men, more than a score of them, descending with the assurance of trained mountaineers, their weapons slung about their shoulders. It was such an unusual spectacle in that lonely corner of the mountains that Graham thought of the illustrations in his father's edition of Defoe's *Robinson Crusoe* which he had browsed through on hot summer afternoons during school holidays. The file now descending the rocks looked exactly like a string of pirates depicted in that book, having the same devil-may-care apparel and weapons, knives, swords, blunderbusses and long-barreled pistols hung about them in profusion. He noticed also that at least half the men wore the green uniform of the Portuguese *caçadores* whom he had watched training under British officers in Lisbon, and this set him wondering whether the men were part of a body of Allied troops who had been left behind to harass French communications.

Satisfied that they were advancing friends, however, he rejoined the file and told Lockhart to smarten the detachment's appearance, hoping that this would in some measure make up for their lack of numbers and obvious isolation. During the previous days he had gone to some pains to ensure that the men's arms were in serviceable condition but had paid no attention at all to their general turnout, and the march through the mountains and ravines had played havoc with their uniforms and equipment. He watched Lockhart parade them in line and then crossed over to the wagon occupied by Gwyneth.

She was sitting on one of the lockers, engaged in the surprisingly feminine task of braiding her hair, and he greeted her cheerfully, saying, "We have made contact with the partisans. They are coming down the mountain at this moment!"

"Yes," she said, "I saw them and I hope they are local men."

"What difference is it who they are, so long as they are opposed to the French?"

She gave him a swift sidelong glance, supporting her mass of hair with both hands.

"It matters a great deal, Mr. Graham," she said, "for if the group is local then you will have the benefit of Beaky's reputation hereabouts, but if they are men who have hung on the French march all the way from Spain and are led by one of the Navarrese or Castilian guerillas, then you will soon discover that they are interested in nothing but plunder. They would as lief rob you as the French, although they have orders not to kill Englishmen."

"You are certain of this?" he asked anxiously.

She gave one of her swift rueful smiles and said, "Come into the wagon. It will not be good for the men to know that I give you advice. From this point on, it is you who must give the orders."

He climbed into the wagon, where they were screened from the file by the canvas curtains. She said earnestly, "Listen, now, I know these people. One and all they are brigands and there is hardly a soldier among them! There are several *caçadores* yonder, but the fact that they are loose in the mountains means that they are nothing more than deserters. To get help from them you must impress them with your authority, you are someone of importance, you understand?"

"They will believe anything I tell them?"

"If you believe it yourself, Mr. Graham! It would be very foolish to admit the truth, to say we are stragglers cut off crossing the Mondego. You must think of something better or they will take our muskets and cartridges and go."

"What else can I tell them?" he demanded, his elation ebbing, but she made a gesture of impatience and went on. "You are behind the lines on the orders of General Crauford and are here for the purpose of estimating the enemy's strength. You have completed your mission and all you need from them is a guide or a route to the Tagus, where you have a rendezvous with the gunboats. If you do not report in three days, then your kinsman Crauford will send out a strong force of cavalry to search for you."

"My kinsman? Is General Crauford my kinsman? Why should I stop at Crauford? Why am I not a favorite nephew of the Commander in Chief?" he said, smiling.

She shook her head and said seriously, "If they were persuaded you were a relative of Beaky they would probably sell you to the French. Now go and be high-handed. These people expect harshness from men of rank."

She half pushed him from the wagon and he sauntered over to the men, who were looking with considerable curiosity at a bizarre cavalcade approaching the bivouac from the easterly bend in the track.

"Eyes front!" he snapped and Watson almost let fall his firelock, but the habit of obedience brought them all stiffly to attention and Graham stared fixedly at the line of scarecrows, checking an impulse to laugh as the first of the Portuguese approached, the man he had first observed on the rock.

"*Inglesi?*" the man demanded, and Graham gave a stiff little bow, at the same time raising his hand as if he were greeting the emissary of an unpredictable tribe.

"Ensign Graham of the Fifty-first Regiment of Foot, at present detached from the brigade of Lieutenant General Crauford," he said, trying to give his voice a parade-ground ring, but the partisan did not seem impressed and walked slowly along the rank, sniffing, one hand on the hilt of his sword-bayonet and the other industriously engaged in picking his nose.

Graham at once took exception to the way in which he looked at the file, as though he were inspecting a batch of newly arrived slaves and assessing the profits it represented, but the file did not seem to resent his scrutiny. Watson smirked and the mouth of Strawbridge split in a broad, gap-toothed grin. Then some of the other partisans approached, chattering and gesticulating in a way that further irritated Graham, who had the traditional British contempt for foreigners.

He said roughly, "Where is your captain?" When the scout shrugged, Graham barked, *"El supremo! Capitano!"* Whereupon the man pointed casually at the swart pot-bellied individual whom Graham had also seen on the rock. He turned to this man and bowed stiffly, repeating, "Ensign Graham of the Fifty-first Regiment of Foot. I am in need of a guide as far as the Tagus, where I have a rendezvous with His Majesty's gunboat *Panther!*"

As he heard himself uttering this rigamarole his temper cooled and he was conscious of a certain degree of embarrassment not altogether devoid of amusement. Out of the corner of his eye he saw Watson blink rapidly, as though amazed by such reassuring information, but the fat man only yawned, and as he did so Graham was assailed by a strong whiff of garlic which increased his distaste for the group.

At last the man transferred his attention from the file to Graham and said, in almost perfect English, "Are the British mad? Seven of you, twelve leagues inside the French lines? If you had passed this way two days ago they would have marched over your bodies!" Then, as though such trivialities bored him, "Where is the woman?"

Graham, who was already beginning to regret that they had met the irregulars, replied coldly, "The woman is the wife of one of our officers, sir! She was sick and left behind at Coimbra. I expect her to be accorded the same courtesy as myself by a representative of the Portuguese Government!"

The man darted a shrewd glance at him, contracting his black brows and running a pudgy forefinger up and down his nose. Then, as though to reassure his visitors, he smiled, put out his hand and administered a series of short pats on Graham's shoulder, saying very affably, "It is most fortunate you met us, my friend, the more so as I exercise some kind of authority over this rabble. Permit me to introduce myself, Hervé de Dieu Castobert, related by marriage to the best blood in France, to the Rohans of Villeneuve-St.-Bar and to the Rochefoucaulds of Amand-sur-Mer, in Brittany. I tell you this without pride. however, for most of my kinsmen are at present enjoying the hospitality of your King whilst I, at an age when most men look for slippered ease, have elected to carry the fight against the Corsican and the regicides into this God-forsaken country!" And having thus delivered himself, the renegade embraced Graham, favoring him with two more whiffs of garlic, this time at distressingly close range.

Hervé de Dieu Castobert had explained his presence in the Peninsula to so many chance acquaintances during the last two years that he had long since convinced himself that he spoke no more than the truth when he claimed that he alone among his family upheld the honor of the exiles by his presence in the theater of war. He was that kind of man, half buffoon, half adventurer, with a dash of the buccaneer and the medieval mercenary complicating an already complex character. Liar, boaster and gambler, he incorporated within him most of the vices of the French feudal families whose degeneracy had brought France about their ears, but he possessed also a redeeming streak of obstinacy that had kept him in the field when most of his relatives had scampered abroad. It was in the reeking villages of La Vendée that Castobert had learned the art of irregular warfare. Long before the cruelties of the Peninsular War became a byword in Europe, Hervé de Dieu Castobert had been roasting French republicans alive and pegging out prisoners for the birds and wild dogs that followed the path of the Vendéans and their equally savage opponents. He had played a part in the futile Quiberon expedition and afterward emigrated to Boston, but when the imperial armies had crossed into Spain he had at once returned from America to offer his services to the Spanish junta. After the collapse of the regular Spanish armies he took to the mountains as a guerilla under Mina of Navarre, from whom he learned fresh techniques of harrying enemy columns as well as several refinements in the art of torture. The withdrawal of Wellington's army in the autumn of 1810 gave him an opportunity to enroll in the regular Portuguese forces, but he was not a man who took kindly to disciplined warfare, where commanders expected him to follow a predetermined strategic plan, and preferred to operate as a partisan, swooping on small, slow-moving transport columns and undermanned garrison posts. He was already hated and feared by the French, who had put an outrageously high price on his head and promised themselves the pleasure of flaying him alive if and when he fell into their hands, but his standing among the irregular bands operating between the lines of Torres Vedras and the seat of the French government in Spain was high, for he was a bold and cunning tactician and his personal courage was beyond dispute. He had on occasion liaised with high-ranking British officers who found him useful in enforcing their strategy of stripping the country bare of supplies and population.

His gluttony at table and vicious mode of life had aged him in appearance, but the grossness of his figure had done nothing to diminish his furious energy. During spells of inaction he was restless.

Within an hour of meeting Castobert the Englishmen were astonished by the energy of so gross a man. Hour after hour, with scarcely a halt, he led them up steep mountain paths and across roaring torrents to his head-quarters behind the lower peaks of the Sierra, and Graham felt that his heart would burst in an effort to maintain the rate of progress. Watson, gasping at the tail of the column, was wishing himself dead, and Croyde, weighed down by his belt, silently cursed his late comrade for encumbering himself with the belt. Yet they kept on, slipping, staggering and cursing, with only the less bur-dened woman marching erect behind the chattering Portu-guese.

At length, to Graham's relief, they topped a narrow ridge between two faces of rock where they could look down on a little valley five hundred feet below. A group of huts and smoking campfires marked the semiperma-nent headquarters of Castobert's band.

Graham, too exhausted to comment, sank down on a rock and looked down on the encampment with forebod-ing while his guide, sweating freely but otherwise undis-mayed by their exertions, swept his hand in a half circle and vouchsafed a little information regarding the future of the file.

"You will be safe enough from Masséna here, my young friend," he said. "We have been recruiting in that valley since Junot entered Portugal more than two years ago, and no Frenchman save myself has ever entered this camp except as a prisoner."

"You keep prisoners down there?" Graham asked in astonishment, but instantly regretted the question, for the renegade uttered a short, neighing laugh and went on, "We keep them a day or two if we are otherwise engaged. Then we dispose of them at our leisure!"

"By torture, I assume," Graham muttered, and realized how much he already hated this arrogant partisan.

Castobert shrugged, neither offended nor surprised by British squeamishness. "The Portuguese rabble are enti-tled to their sport," he said. "If we have plenty of powder we use the stragglers we catch for target practice, but if not there are other ways of demonstrating our loyalty to the old order. Nothing happens down there that did not happen every day in France during the Revolution!"

Graham wished then that he had taken more pains to study the background of his country's unending war against Napoleon. As a boy he had heard his father deplore the excesses of the French terrorists, but his acquaintance with a representative of the Old Regime made him doubt whether the Bourbons deserved the general sympathy extended to them at home. He said stubbornly, "It is not my intention to remain attached to your band for more than twenty-four hours, m'sieur. It is imperative that I keep my rendezvous with the gunboat *Panther* on the Tagus. How far is the Tagus from this valley and how best can I approach the river without running into enemy detachments?"

"We will discuss that after we have eaten," Castobert told him, and with a wave of his hand he set the column in motion again.

As they descended into the valley Graham's disquiet increased. One or two of the narrow, grass-grown patches they had traversed between the peaks of the Sierra had been pleasant, inviting places, but this was not one of them, perhaps because it was high above sea level where the vegetation was gray and stunted. A stream traversed the encampment and on the eastern side of the valley was a small pinewood crowning an outcrop of rocks, but the rest of the little basin was walled in with naked granite rising steeply to the sky. The mouths of caves showed here and there, but the spot was so remote that the partisans had built themselves cabins and on the open ground campfires were smoking and men and women were moving about preparing the evening meal. Graham looked all around the valley for an alternative exit and at length spotted a zigzag path rising from the rock plateau immediately behind the pines, crawling uncertainly up the steep face to disappear in the canopy of mist that hung low over the valley. Without his understanding why, the path became for him the focal part of the camp and he noted everything about it, its nearness to the largest of the cabins, its tree-masked approach, its steepness and narrowness as it followed the broader contours of the mountain. A column of men, he thought, would be obliged to use such a path in single file and one man might hold off any number of pursuers providing he had ample firepower. It struck him as odd that he should be considering the means of retreat while entering the camp of an ally, but there was something about the place and the men who inhabited it that encouraged him to anticipate the worst.

When the column reached level ground he drew Lockhart aside and said quietly, "Don't let the file disperse and don't on any account lay aside your arms!"

Lockhart nodded grimly, as though he shared Graham's suspicions. Graham then turned to look for Gwyneth, intending to ask her if she had discovered anything useful about the band during the march, but she seemed to have disappeared, so he directed the men to make their own fire on the far side of the shallow stream and bivouac under the lee of the small wood. If they had to leave in a hurry, he decided, it would be better to be stationed near the entrance to the path he had noted.

He had expected that Castobert would invite him to share a meal, but the guerilla chief seemed to have lost interest in his guests. When Graham inquired his whereabouts of the man in the long cloak and sombrero who had first sighted the file from the rock above the track, the man pointed to the largest hut, about a hundred yards down the valley. Before going there Graham walked through the wood and looked at the path. No one was guarding it and it did not seem to be as steep as it had looked from across the valley. He stood pondering a moment and finally made up his mind, recrossing the stream and crossing toward the chief's headquarters.

He found Castobert already at table, sucking his way through a large bowl of stew and attended by a mountainous gray-haired peasant woman whom he addressed as Catrina. The woman was even more grotesque than her master, an absurdly small head topping her enormous bulk, and a pair of dark, furtive eyes set in her face like currants in a wedge of dough. The food, and the wine at his elbow, seemed to have mellowed the renegade somewhat, for he said, between gulps, "She is as ugly as the Devil's sister, but she cooks like ten thousand angels! Judge for yourself, milord!"

Graham recalled then that every British officer was accorded a title by the Portuguese, but he was aware that Castobert must know better and could only suppose that he used the word ironically. Still uncertain, he sat down opposite the Frenchman as Catrina waddled in with another bowl of stew, in which large pieces of meat were floating. The stew was highly flavored with garlic, and the renegade's table manners left a great deal to be desired, but notwithstanding this Graham ate ravenously, forcing himself to pay the cook a compliment, which Castobert drove home with a jocular punch as the woman passed within range.

"You hear him?" he said, in the same ironical tone. "Milord is praising your cooking, Catrina! That is a great compliment, you understand? For a long time now milord has been enjoying the best of everything!" And he tilted his head on one side as though anxious to record his guest's reaction to the gibe.

Perhaps it was the remark or the man's studied bestiality, or possibly a sudden quirk of fear amounting almost to panic. Whatever the reason, Graham made his decision. Rising quickly, he pushed aside his plate and said, very deliberately, "I am obliged to you for your hospitality, m'sier, and if you will lend me a guide as far as the Tagus I shall commend you to General Crauford on my return to Lisbon. In any case, we march at first light, so I bid you good night, sir!"

Castobert was unable to conceal his surprise at this demonstration of firmness, yet he mastered it within seconds, leaning back in his chair and grinning. When he spoke again his tone was conciliatory.

"Listen, my young friend, the Tagus is more than twenty leagues from here and the French have already occupied Santarém on the river. If you keep your rendezvous with the gunboat you have an arduous journey ahead of you, for your only course is to cross the river a safe distance north of Masséna's pickets. Given luck, such a march will occupy you seven to ten days, depending upon good weather and how capable you may be of steering a course by the stars!"

Something told Graham that in his eagerness to make a fool of him Castobert had inadvertently spoken the truth. He said firmly, "Then it is your duty as a representative of His Majesty the King of Portugal to supply me with a map."

"Perhaps," said the Frenchman, his unpleasant grin widening as Graham's cheeks reddened, "but with the best will in the world, milord, I could not help you in that respect. I have not seen a map in two years. If you insist upon continuing your march, then you must smell your way across the mountains as I do. In any case, you will leave the woman behind!"

Graham made a tremendous effort to speak calmly.

"The woman marches with us," he said, meeting Castobert's eye and holding it when he failed to stare him down.

After a moment or so the Frenchman conceded the contest and looked down at his plate, his hand rasping slowly across his jowls as though he was weighing his guest as a calculated risk in the same way as he pondered the wisdom of a descent on a French convoy. He did not, however, appear to resent the Englishman's challenge, but rather balanced it against the known and unknown factors, the younger man's skill as a swordsman, the chances of being called to account for treating the English as enemies, the gain, if any, in complying with this little gamecock's demands for assistance. At last he seemed to have made up his mind.

"You are not in a position to bargain," he said pleasantly. "You are five half-starved men and a boy to my three score cutthroats. I have only to raise my voice and any one of them would tear you in pieces. Yet I would have you believe that I am reluctant to give such a command. My business here is to kill Frenchmen and I would not deprive you of the chance to live, in order that you may kill still more when Masséna is forced to retreat into Spain in the spring. Do not encourage me to overcome this prejudice, my young friend. Camp here tonight and take your five scarecrows over the range at dawn. If the woman is as ripe as she looks, then it is possible that I will be in good humor tomorrow and may be persuaded to give you detailed directions as to your route."

"The woman marches with us!" Graham repeated, and his hand moved along his sword belt until his thumb rested on the butt of Sergeant Fox's pistol.

Castobert saw the movement of his hand but made no effort to rise. Instead he tilted his chair, clasped his hands behind his head and regarded the Englishman with benevolence.

"You would fight for her, for a camp drab? And you barely old enough to need a woman?"

"I would fight if it was necessary," Graham said, "and my men also. The woman is on the strength of a British regiment, and when we march she marches!"

"So?" Castobert kept his eyes on Graham's hand. "But up here we do not settle our differences with firearms and you would have to make good such a claim with a blade! You, my friend, not your men!" And suddenly he let his chair fall forward and hoisted himself to his feet. "There is still sufficient light, I will tell the men to make the circle!"

"It would be wiser, m'sieur, to find out what has happened to Pedrillo!"

Gwyneth was speaking from the door, and both men

swung around to face her. She had crossed the threshold unobserved and was now standing with her hands resting on her plump hips, looking directly at Castobert. She was neither angry nor defiant and clearly in no way intimidated by him. Her voice had the same lilting quality that Graham had noted when he had listened to her explaining her presence to the file in the church.

For the first time the renegade showed active interest in the discussion, but even now he seemed supremely sure of himself and he said, as his lips moved in a surly smile, "What do you know of Pedrillo?" Graham realized that he had been dismissed from the contest, that it was now a duel between the woman and the partisan.

"You will be a man short when you call your muster rolls," she said. "That is, if you brigands have muster rolls, which is unlikely, I think, for there is nothing I see here to tell me I am among soldiers! As for Pedrillo, he is now well on his way south with a message for General Crauford, the kinsman of the officer you are threatening, but I do not think you will do more than threaten, because although you are a dirty ruffian you are not as stupid as the men outside!"

Castobert took a single step toward her and when she did not give ground but continued to look directly at him Graham drew his pistol and cocked it. The click of the hammer was the only sound in the cabin as they remained facing one another on three sides of the table.

Then Gwyneth went on. "I chose Pedrillo because he seemed to me the least stupid of the band, having just enough brains to desert with a gold guinea in his pocket and the promise of four more when he reports the whereabouts of this detachment. Perhaps they will have an interpreter at General Crauford's headquarters and perhaps the General will ask Pedrillo about a partisan leader who decoys British soldiers into the mountains because they have with them a drab for the generalissimo's bed and half a dozen new British muskets for his armory! If Pedrillo talks as freely to the British as he talked to me there should be a sizeable price on your head, and if Pedrillo will do this for one gold piece, what will the rest of your rabble do for a hundred?"

Graham thought he had never seen a man look so astounded. By the time Gwyneth had finished, Castobert's jaw was agape and his several chins writhed under the stress of words he was unable to utter. There was a large vein on his temple and about it a pulse beat, causing him to put up his hand and touch it and then, as his brain absorbed the implication of her elaborate threat, a rage that was almost visible seemed to storm through his body. For what seemed a long time they remained like this, Castobert gaping at Gwyneth, Graham leveling his cocked pistol across the table, and the woman regarding the partisan with the hint of a smile puckering the corners of her mouth.

"You play chess, Capitano?" she said at length, when Castobert stopped struggling for words that would not come. "This is checkmate, but you will think of a move sooner or later and it will be our business to be gone from here before you do! You will spend the whole night thinking about it, Capitano, whether or not Pedrillo will be encouraged by the promise of four more guineas to keep his bargain, or how likely are the French to catch him and string him up when he tries to pass their lines. It is an even chance, I would say, for Pedrillo knows the country and the French do not, but one thing is quite certain, you yourself will never catch Pedrillo now. He has had several hours' start and the woods are very thick down in the valleys." She turned abruptly to Graham. "You can put up your pistol, Mr. Graham. He will not dare attack us yet, he is far too uncertain of his men to risk his life for a woman and half a dozen rifled muskets!" When Graham uncocked the weapon and thrust it back into his belt she seemed to dismiss the partisan altogether and busied herself scooping up the remains of the bread that lay beside Castobert's empty plate. "Come," she said, turning on her heel, "the file will have eaten now and the Capitano has plenty to engage him until morning." And she went out with Graham following, and still Castobert continued to stare, the pulse in his forehead winking like a small beacon under the flush on his broad suntanned face.

They exchanged no word as they went down the bank and crossed the stream to the British bivouac, but after Lockhart had challenged them in the gloom, and Graham had stepped over the sleeping forms of Watson and Croyde, he said gently, "How much of that was bluff, Gwyneth? You had no money to give to that deserter Pedrillo."

"No," she said, "but Croyde has money. He took Lickspittle's belt before he buried him and carries it round his belly. It was I who told you to contact this scum and it was bad advice, for they are not local men but carrion who have come over the mountains from Spain thinking of nothing but loot. That man Castobert is a brigand and he fights the French only because he owes them a grudge. I saw him looking at me and I saw his men fingering our muskets and it was enough to tell me we are in bad company, Mr. Graham. They would not crucify us perhaps, but they would shoot us down for the cartridges we carry. This I told Croyde to persuade him to give me the guinea, but even that was a foolish thing to do, for if any one of those scoundrels saw his money belt they would kill us at once and then fight among themselves for what Croyde has about him!"

"I told Castobert we would march in the morning with or without his guide."

"Yes," she said, "and you were willing to fight him on my account and that is something I shall not easily forget, Mr. Graham. It is a long time since any man paid me such a compliment! He would have run you through, however, for he is almost certainly an expert swordsman. All the French emigrés are good swordsmen. It is their one accomplishment."

Her instinctive awareness of the situation at any one moment still had the power to astonish him. It was as though she had lived a thousand years in these circumstances, alone in the company of men who were almost children, threading the hills and valleys of a strange land where death was the price of a single misjudgment. Her mind was an encyclopedia of the knowledge required to survive and at each turn of the road she was ready with a clear-cut decision representing the difference between survival and disaster. He felt like an eager student in the presence of an old and infallible teacher.

"Should we leave during the night?" he asked earnestly. "Should we not go at once? I have examined the path and once we were on it Lockhart could pick them off one by one if they tried to stop us!"

"It would be safer to wait for daylight," she said. "We will go if they make a move, but I do not think they will until that brigand can discuss Pedrillo's desertion with the others and guess if the boy is likely to risk his life for the promise of a larger reward. Besides, the men need sleep and you too need rest before climbing more mountains. Lie down, then, and I will watch with Lockhart and in an hour or so I will wake one of the others. They have all eaten their fill and we have something left over for tomorrow." She looked up at the sky and sniffed like a hound. "It will rain during the night and there will be no moonlight worth having. No, we must wait for daylight, Mr. Graham!" And she took a musket from the piled arms near the fire and turned her back on him, resting the long weapon across the crook of her arm like Lockhart and staring down at the pattern of fires where the partisans were gathered in little groups.

Graham took out his cloak and wrapped it around him, blanketwise. As he stretched himself on the ground someone in the valley began to strum a mandolin and the clear, tinkling notes drifted across the encampment to the bivouac. He drew up his knees and slept.

Tam Strawbridge was the sixth child of a Kentish farm

laborer who had never earned more than eight shillings a week, from which total a sum was deducted for milk, potatoes and the rent of the two-roomed hovel in which the family lived on the edge of the Weald. As a child Tam had watched soldiers march over the Downs to their camps at Hythe and Rye and had envied them their scarlet coats and bright, jingling accouterments. When he was sixteen and already approaching six foot in height, he received a thrashing from an irate farmer for stealing beans. The next day he ran off and enlisted, and now, at the age of twenty-one, he was a veteran. He had never regretted his decision. The life was hard, but no harder than that of his father or brothers, and whereas his kin wielded nothing more lethal than a billhook Tam never went anywhere without his shining musket, which he carried as an idle boy carries a hazel stick he uses to swipe at hedgerows. Strawbridge was wedded to his musket, and few men took such care of their wives or lavished upon them the tender thoughts that Strawbridge entertained for his Brown Bess. At nights, in bivouac, he would sit for an hour crooning over her while he cleaned and oiled and polished, rubbing away at invisible stains and testing the mechanism over and over again, making trebly sure that the hammer came back with a soft, pleasing snick and that the long ramrod slotted neatly into its furrow and did not have to be coaxed to bed down alongside the barrel. He could find his musket in pitch darkness, plucking it unerringly from a pile of stacked arms, and when he lay down to sleep he wrapped the lock in a piece of flannel and hugged the weapon to his body. He had treated his original musket with the same tenderness and had wept when they withdrew it at Lisbon, replacing it with the new-type weapon fitted with the rifled barrel and giving far greater accuracy and range, but he soon got used to his new love and forgot all about her predecessor. Officers who knew him paused for a split second in front of Strawbridge when they were carrying out arms inspection, then passed him by and concentrated on the weapons of men like Croyde and Lickspittle to whom a musket was just another piece of baggage. Apart from the meticulous care of his arms Tam Strawbridge was an excellent soldier, strong, uncomplaining and obedient to the last order. He seldom had any thoughts of his own, unless it was how to satisfy his periodic hunger, or what small service he could tender little Watson, his file companion over the last two years. Next to his musket Strawbridge loved Watson, admiring the little man's incredible flow of words and broad, sooty grin, and listening with rapt attention to the Cockney's interminable tales of London life as a chimneysweep. When Watson had finished a story his friend would reward the narrator with a great bellow of laughter. He would have died for Watson, but as it happened he was not called upon to do so; instead he died for his musket.

After Lockhart and the woman had watched for more than an hour they awoke Strawbridge and Watson, and the ex-gamekeeper posted them about twenty yards apart on the very edge of the tiny plateau formed by the fall of rock under the wood. From here, half screened by scrub, they could look down on both ends of the valley and had every campfire under survey. The mandolin player was asleep now and the encampment was silent. As far as Strawbridge could judge, the Portuguese posted no sentries, and after half an hour's uneventful duty Strawbridge began to feel lonely and longed to hear the familiar sound of Watson's voice. He was aware, however, that it would be wrong to desert his post and for several minutes he battled with his boredom. Then Watson hailed him from the bushes, asking if he had a screw of baccy about him, and Strawbridge replied delightedly that he had, just enough for a single pipe if Watson would wait until he foraged in his tunic pocket for loose shreds. Strawbridge did not smoke himself but he hoarded tobacco for his friend, and the half-handful in his tunic dated from their spell of hospital guard at Coimbra. He stood his bayoneted musket against a rock and turned to face Watson, whom he could sense rather than see against the dark mass of the pines. Holding the bottom of his tunic with one hand, he groped in the pocket with the other and marshaled a shred here and a shred there until he had enough for a thin pipeful. Then he moved forward a few strides, found his friend and pressed it carefully into Watson's outstretched hand.

Watson said, "Thankee, mate," and returned to his post farther along the plateau.

When Strawbridge went back to his beat and bent over the rock to retrieve his musket, his hand swept the empty air. Musket and bayonet had gone.

For the space of about a minute Strawbridge was incredulous. Barely sixty seconds had elapsed since he had laid his musket against the rock, and for at least two thirds of that period, while he was groping for the tobacco, he had been standing within two or three feet of the grounded stock. He scratched his head, grunted with dismay and then moved around to the other side of the rock, thinking it must have fallen into the scrub. Going down on hands and knees, he struck his flint, but as he did so he heard the sound of a dislodged pebble farther down the slope and the rattle told him what had happened to the musket. In the few seconds that it had taken him to hand Watson the tobacco one of the partisans must have crept up to the rock, reached over and whipped musket and bayonet into the bushes.

A shudder of rage ran through Strawbridge. Even before the outrageous theft had been perpetrated he had entertained a sour dislike for the irregulars. Watson distrusted them, and all the opinions of Strawbridge stemmed from Watson. Watson had said only that afternoon that Portuguese irregulars were worse than the French, adding his opinion that if Old Beaky would patch up his quarrel with Boney and declare war on the Portuguese and Spaniards it would be a fine thing for all of them. Now Strawbridge realized what lay behind Watson's far-seeing remark. Obviously the Portuguese were utterly devoid of

morality, for men who could creep up on an ally in the
night and steal his musket were capable of any enormity.
Suddenly he began to gibber with rage, running about in
the scrub and calling the Portuguese all the names that
occurred to him—"bliddy snakes," "double-dyed mag-
pies" and "prowling, yeller-bellied crabs." His vocabulary
was limited and Watson could have introduced far more
variety into the flow of invective, but for a mild and very
amiable man Strawbridge acquitted himself well.

He was still prancing about in the bushes, bellowing at
the top of his voice, when Watson appeared, demanding
to know what all the noise was about, but by this time
Strawbridge was so enraged and excited that he was inco-
herent. It was only when he kept pointing at Watson's
musket that the Cockney suddenly realized what had
occurred and at once expressed his opinion of all foreigners in a stream of blasphemy that gave his friend a
moment or two to calm down, so that he clutched Watson
by the sleeve and roared, "I'm agoin' arter un, Billy! I'm
agoin' down there arter un an' if they've 'armed 'er with
their clumsy gurt fingers I'll 'ave the blood out o' their
bellies, so help me God!" And before Watson could utter
a word of caution he was gone, plunging down the slope
with great, loping strides and splashing across the stream
into the heart of the sleeping encampment.

Watson screamed after him, telling him to wait, but he
paid no heed to the warning. When Lockhart, roused by
the uproar, descended from the wood Watson gabbled the
story and Lockhart added his shouts. Within a few moments the others were there, standing in a group on the
edge of the rock platform, all shouting to Strawbridge to
return to the bivouac.

They shouted in vain. Strawbridge, still bellowing
abuse, headed straight into the circle of banked-up fires,
stumbling over sleeping men and plucking at every
firearm he spied, only to fling each of them down the
moment he was satisfied it was not his incomparable Bess.
Rage and excitement dulled his perceptions. Ordinarily he

could have seen at a glance, even by firelight, that the clumsy fowling pieces and blunderbusses piled beside the campfires were nothing like his own polished weapon, but his bull-like progress through the camp aroused sleeper after sleeper, each of whom struggled to his feet and made a grab at his arms under the impression that the camp was being attacked by the French. Then, by pure chance, Strawbridge stumbled upon the thief, identifying him instantly by the furtive speed with which he tossed the musket across to a comrade who came running out of a hut. The swift exchange was made just as the Englishman rounded the corner of the cabin into a circle of firelight, and this time Strawbridge did not need to identify his weapon by handling it but recognized it at once as a gleam of firelight caught its highly polished stock. He rushed upon the man in the doorway like a maddened elephant, grabbing the long barrel with one hand and a handful of the thief's tunic with the other so that they both pitched sideways, striking the doorpost with such violence that the flimsy structure shook along its entire length. Now men were up and running in all directions, adding to the chorus from the edge of the wood by a cacophony of yells and shouts.

In the course of the brief struggle in the doorway Strawbridge managed to wrest the musket from the man by lifting him clear of the ground and thumping his head against the doorpost until he was limp, but as he flung him down and rushed back into the circle of firelight two other men leaped at him, one brandishing a knife, the other swinging a fowling piece by the barrel. Strawbridge arrested the sweep of the knife by holding his musket across his body so that the long blade rasped along the barrel and caught momentarily in his sleeve, but the man with the fowling piece had his wits about him and, crouching low, swung his weapon in a wide arc so that its heavy stock struck Strawbridge across the shins, buckling his knees and bringing him down on the edge of the fire.

At the same moment the struggle enlarged itself as more and more men, most of them convinced that they were engaged in a life-and-death struggle with the French, plunged into the fray, and when Strawbridge rose to his feet he was the center of more than a dozen partisans, all getting in one another's way and every man among them screaming at the top of his voice. Considering that the blow from the fowling piece had all but broken his leg, and that he was now assailed on all sides by men hacking at him with knives, swords and billets of wood snatched from the fuel pile, the countryman gave a notable account of himself. With the butt of his beloved musket he knocked one man into the fire, and when the stock parted from the barrel under the impact he retained his grasp on the metal and broke the arm of a man jabbing him with a bayonet. Then somebody leaped upon his back and he went down again, carrying two men with him and rolling right across the fire at the feet of another group of men who had come up at a run and who flung themselves bodily upon the trio struggling in the embers, jabbing with their knives and calling to one another to stand clear and give them room to use their weapons.

From the rock plateau some two hundred meters away the file watched the wild shadow play that accompanied the death of Private Strawbridge, dragged clear of the fire with a dozen wounds in his body but still clutching the bent barrel of the stolen weapon. When the figure on the ground had ceased to heave and men rose breathlessly to their feet calling for torches, the partisan chief arrived, staring down at the body on the edge of the scattered fire while around him men gasped and groaned and two of the Englishman's assailants were dragged half roasted from the fire.

"One mad Englishman," Castobert said, looking slowly around the circle. *"One,* you hear me?" He glanced across at the group who had succeeded in beating out the blazing clothing of the two partisans and then beyond the fire to the still form of the man whom Strawbridge had brained against the doorpost.

Nobody answered him. The man with the broken forearm rocked to and fro in agony, and a fourth casualty, stabbed in the thigh by an overzealous comrade, dragged himself into the hut, his hand pressed to his wound.

Suddenly Castobert erupted. "The others? Where are the others?" he demanded. "Are they here? Have you killed them all?" And he kicked the prostrate Strawbridge in the ribs.

Someone said, "They are still camped over in the wood. This one came down alone."

Suddenly a single shot cracked out and a partisan came running with news that the English party were leaving by the eastern exit and had fired at Benvenito, wounding him in the leg.

They stood around in uneasy silence, waiting for Castobert's orders. Someone muttered that it would be a simple matter to go up the western path and work around the mountain to catch the Englishmen as they descended into the next valley by daylight, but Castobert seemed not to be listening.

Presently he said slowly, "This one, how many did he kill?"

They told him that three were as good as dead and three others were wounded.

"Six," Castobert murmured reflectively. "One more than a half company of the French accounted for in the hills." Touching the body of Strawbridge with his foot, he added, "Get this one away from here and leave the others to the French. Why should we sacrifice men fighting maniacs?"

One of the partisans stooped and pried the bent musket barrel from the dead man's grasp, studying it with interest.

"It is rifled," he murmured. "With fifty like this we

could shoot a hundred Josephinos a day without ever meeting them in the open!"

When it was clear to Graham that Strawbridge had roused the entire camp and was fighting for his life beyond the campfire in the center of the valley, he would have given the order to charge without a thought of what would happen to them if they descended on to level ground. Perhaps Lockhart sensed this, for he laid his hand on the ensign's shoulder, but before he could counsel him to await attack Watson made his wild dash for the slope, screaming that he would bayonet every partisan in the valley. Gwyenth saved Watson's life, tripping him up and calling to Lockhart to hold him down, and it was while the three of them were threshing about on the edge of the plateau that Graham realized that the woman was right and that to abandon the higher ground and access to the path would be fatal to all of them.

He ran across and seized Watson by the shoulder, pulling him around and shouting in his ear, "Leave him! You can't save him now! Get up the path. Everyone get up the path before they attack!" And he helped Lockhart drag Watson to his feet, shaking him and shouting at him in a desperate effort to make the hysterical man understand the uselessness of joining his comrade. But Watson could not see reason and continued to struggle in Lockhart's grasp, calling them cowards and traitors and bellowing that Strawbridge was the only man among them. Then Graham saw there was no time to waste, for a group of partisans had already begun to mass at the foot of the rocks and their clamor reached the men occupying the plateau. He struck Watson a heavy blow on the jaw and suddenly the Cockney ceased to struggle and shrank against Lockhart, whimpering like a child.

Croyde and the woman were snatching up their equipment, and the boy Curle stood by with a pine branch that he had fanned into a flame. A spatter of small shot struck the branches above their heads, and Lockhart said quietly, "I'll put a shot over among 'em to keep them at a distance!" Shouldering Watson aside, he leveled his musket and fired into the group, which immediately scattered for cover. Then, with Curle and his torch in the van, they withdrew through the copse and began the ascent, Lockhart half dragging Watson, and Graham bringing up the rear, expecting any moment to be overwhelmed by a rush of partisans.

As they emerged from the trees and followed the track's westerly curve they could look down on the encampment now alive with moving figures and bright with replenished fires, but there was no immediate pursuit, or so it seemed to Graham, looking over his shoulder as he climbed. Presently the campfires were pinpoints in the valley and the rain that Gwyneth had prophesied began to fall, striking cold on their sweating faces as they picked their way ever higher among the tumbled masses of rock. Soon the path became steeper and the surface was covered with loose shale that made progress dangerous and toilsome. Curle's torch had burned out by now, but they blundered on for more than an hour until Graham caught up with them on a comparatively level stretch where the overhang of the cliff formed a shallow cave. Here, on Lockhart's advice, they stopped to await the light that was glimmering behind the eastern range, the moist air striking cold through their wet clothes and each one of them far too breathless to talk. Only Lockhart seemed as steady as ever, taking up his position on the edge of the ascent with his musket crooked over his arm in the same carelessly poised position.

As the light improved, Graham looked across at Watson and saw misery in the man's pinched face. He said gently, "How did it happen, Watson? What made him go down among them in that mad fashion?"

Watson growled, "They stole his Bess, that's why! Old Turnip'ead set great store on that Bess. They couldn't have done nothing worse to 'im, the bastards!" He then seemed to make a big effort to pull himself together and

said, "Best mate I ever 'ad, was Turnip'ead! Stick by yer
through thick an' thin he would, not like some of 'em!"
And he glanced at Croyde, who was lying flat on his back
prostrated by the climb.

Graham thought dismally of their diminishing strength
and of his seeming inability to prevent their numbers from
being whittled away one by one. They were nine when
they set out and now they were five, reduced by almost
half in a matter of days, and yet, thinking back, he could
not see how any action on his part could have checked
this attrition. Morgan had been caught in the open by the
lancers, and Fox, of his own choosing, had remained
behind to cover their retreat from the church. Lickspittle
had been shot by the woman, and Strawbridge had committed an act of suicide by challenging an entire camp in
an attempt to regain his wretched musket. There was a
kind of devilish pattern running through their adventures,
a variation of tramping and scrambling interspersed with
short, murderous bursts of action, each episode claiming
another victim. They must have tramped at least a hundred miles since the bridge was blown and had yielded up
a life for every day's march, but still they were lost and
isolated, hemmed in by these interminable peaks and cut
off from their friends by innumerable enemies, among
whom they could now number supposed allies operating
behind the French lines. Graham wondered if an experienced officer could have extricated the file with more
certainty and less cost, but he could not see what alternatives would have suggested themselves to a man like the
dead Captain Sowden. Surely the real author of their
troubles was the fool who had prematurely fired the explosive charge under the bridge. As he remembered this,
rage rose in his throat and he felt a sharp, smarting
sensation behind his eyes, as though, at the slightest
demonstration of sympathy, he would blubber as Watson
had wept for the death of his friend.

Perhaps Gwyneth was aware of this, for she made no
attempt to discuss their escape but occupied herself doling

out portions of the bread she had taken from Castobert's table. He took his share, a mere mouthful, and, masticating it with the thoroughness of a man uncertain of his next meal, he went out to join Lockhart, who was looking back to the path they had traveled and peering into the mist for signs of pursuit.

In answer to Graham's query Lockhart said, "I doubt if they'll come after us this road, sir! Likely as not they'll use the path we come down yesterday and hope to cut us off in the valley, but it's my belief they won't stir so long as the French are below. Praise be to God I winged one of 'em back yonder, I heard him yelp!"

"We shall keep well clear of the irregulars from now on," Graham said shortly. "From the summit we should be able to see the lie of the land. Cover the rear and I'll take the van, and keep a sharp eye on Watson."

"Aye," said Lockhart solemnly and Graham gave the order to march. As the light grew stronger they began to straggle up the tortuous path to the summit, and presently they were completely shrouded in white mist so that it seemed to Graham that they were heading into the mountains of the moon. Then, very abruptly, the path leveled out and at the same time the sun came out, revealing a superb vista stretching for more than thirty miles to the south and west, a country spread out like a relief map, with a series of dwarf peaks glittering in the sun and between them belt after belt of timber hugging the valleys like a dark-green skin. Somehow the sheer vastness of this view brought him a sense of release and his spirit lifted as confidence began to return to him. He stood quite still on the summit, watching the pale sun drink up the mist, and far away to the south, so far that he could not be sure, the sky resolved itself into a harder outline that suggested the sea.

Then Gwyneth was beside him, pointing to a rift in the woods far below, where a bright and continuously rippling sparkle indicated what Graham took to be a torrent. But when he looked again he recognized it as the movement of light on polished metal. Somewhere down there was a metaled road cleaving the woods, and along the road troops were moving, thousands and thousands of men and animals, judging by the width of the arc—a whole army trudging purposefully from east to west.

"The French?" he asked. It was not their presence but their numbers that astonished him.

"Wait," she replied and knelt, laying one ear to the naked rock and lifting her hand for silence.

"At least an army corps, with siege weapons and baggage train," she told him, rising, "for they are strong enough to march without flank guards. That is good, you understand, for it means we can go on down to the edge of the woods and take a close look at them."

He nodded, having learned to accept her infallibility, and one by one they left the ribbon of track, picking their way down a slope that was less steep on this side of the mountains and was covered with scrub almost as far as the summit. They moved forward in a long, extended line, with Lockhart on one flank and Croyde on the other, and as they drew nearer the tall timber they heard a long, continuous rumble rising from the valley below.

CHAPTER SIX

The Torrent

~~~∞~~~

THAT WAS the place where he found the first of his new confidence, as though, by descending from the granite of the mountains to levels where vegetation abounded reminded him of the deep woods and shallow streams of home and restored to him the resilience and bright hopes of boyhood. Down here the air was soft and lazy and the rain from the dripping trees caused a continuous murmur that seemed to Graham very soothing after the whine of the wind in the peaks. He said to himself, as he plodded ever downward, We have only to cross their line of march and strike south into the woods on the far slopes and we shall find British pickets in less than forty-eight hours. I won't lose any more men. Strawbridge was the last and we shall arrive, the woman, the boy and the four of us, in spite of everything. I know this to be true. I shall make it come true! And as he reached the first of the cork trees he threw out his arms, bringing the extended line into a group once more and then into file, with himself leading.

Down here the rumble from the valley below increased to a steady roar. Graham told the others to make camp in a clearing under a giant oak and after a brief word with Lockhart pushed on ahead, threading the dense spread of undergrowth until he reached the lip of an almost precipitous drop of about a hundred feet where the timber fell away to begin afresh on the lower shelf, masking the road. From here he could distinguish individual shouts of the teamsters urging their mules up the incline and the harsh rattle of ammunition caissons above the deeper rumble of heavier transport—guns, no doubt, and perhaps also the siege train that Gwyneth had mentioned. He examined the slope with great care, looking for a way down, and presently he found one where a landslide had exposed the trailing roots of a large tree, making a kind of net that gave access to a straggle of rocks reaching the lower shelf. He worked his way along the cliff and swung himself over the edge, scrambling from hold to hold until he dropped into a clump of flowering rhododendrons, and from here he moved cautiously forward so as to look directly onto the road below.

What he saw amazed him. He had been prepared for a largish body of troops, perhaps a regiment or two, with cavalry and a few field guns, but here was an army, its toiling columns stretching east and west until both vanguard and rearguard were lost in the coils of the road. The spectacle excited and uplifted him, for it struck him at once that here was a unique opportunity to estimate the fighting strength of Masséna's cohorts. The chance of being caught while so engaged was negligible, for yet another drop of over a hundred and fifty feet lay immediately below, and even if the French threw out flank guards they would have to pass along the escarpment from which he had just descended.

The rain that had fallen earlier in the day had done something to lay the dust, and although it still hung in clouds above the columns, he could see everything passing his viewpoint with the utmost clarity. A long column of infantry was marching by, bowed under packs and moving at what seemed a snail's pace, and behind them, just rounding the wide curve in the road, was what looked like a siege train of twenty or thirty mule-drawn wagons. Spaces between the bodies of troops were filled with horse-drawn batteries of ten- and twelve-pounder field guns, and ahead he could see the sun glinting on the casques of a body of cavalry bunched across the entire width of the road.

His first problem, he realized, was to estimate how many troops had already passed, for although the road was comparatively straight on his right, he could not see the end of the column. He realized that he had struck the road at a point high in the advance, however, for if a column of this size had been marching around the foot of the mountains all the previous day Castobert's scouts would surely have brought word of it, and it therefore followed that the march had commenced only at dawn, perhaps four or five hours ago. Troops were now passing him at the rate of about a hundred per minute, marching in columns of four, and a rapid calculation told him that perhaps a corps of men had already gone by. He was tempted to scramble back the way he had come and pass the word to the file to remain bivouacked until he rejoined them, but he did not want to waste the time and effort, so he compromised by worming his way back to the foot of the root ladder, fixing his shako on an isolated stump where it could be seen from above, then hurrying back to his observation point. He guessed that Lockhart's sharp eyes would interpret his signal and understand what he was doing.

He used the letters taken from the murdered Frenchman for his notes, having found a stub of black lead that Captain Sowden had loaned him to make a list of requisitioned articles an hour or so before he died at the bridge. Hour after hour he lay there, noting and scribbling, while Masséna's army filed below, three entire corps comprising about seventy-five thousand men if one took into account the corps that must have passed earlier in the day. He was astonished not so much by the numbers as by the latent power of this army, by its complement of guns and baggage wagons and, above all, by the sense of purpose conveyed to him by the massed infantry and the general condition of the cavalry. This was the army, he remembered, that the British had mauled at Busaco a month ago, but there was nothing about the endless columns to suggest that Masséna had taken the check very seriously.

Perhaps he had been reinforced from the north and somewhere in this devastated country had found fresh transport and mule teams numbered by the hundred. Graham paused in his note-taking for a moment to reflect on what might happen when this splendidly equipped force reached the sea at Lisbon. It seemed very unlikely that Wellington's few thousand rascals and mob of half-trained Portuguese could stop such an avalanche, and as he thought this his horizon widened and he remembered that all his life the French Emperor had been marching and countermarching these same men about Europe, overturning everything that lay in his path. Where, he wondered, did the man recruit and train such splendid battalions? And what use were amateurs like Watson and Strawbridge against veterans who had marched over the bodies of every professional army on the Continent? Where would it stop, this vast onrush of military might? He could remember the upheaval caused in the area around his home during the threatened invasion by the French five years ago, when Graham's portly father had been seen strutting about in the gay uniform of the Fencibles alongside yokels and country gentlemen drilling on the green, but how effectively could a local rabble have checked the advance upon London of the lean pack-laden men now marching below? No more, surely, than Wellington, Crauford and old Tommy Picton could stop them now unless the guns of the fleet took a hand in the business.

Grimly he put away his notes and worked his way back to the foot of the cliff. There was Lockhart, the one reliable survivor of the file, standing on the broad ledge where Graham had made his descent, and when he saw the ensign emerge from the rhododendrons he lost something of his habitual phlegm and waved eagerly. Graham made the climb in the fading light and reached out for the ex-gamekeeper's outstretched hand for the final scramble.

"We was afeared for 'ee," the man said. "Leastways,

they others was, but I guessed what you was at down there! Be there many of 'em, sir?"

"The entire army," Graham told him shortly, "but it's my belief they'll stick to the road. It might be possible to scramble up here a mile or so back, but the partisans will keep away from them so why should they throw out flanking parties?"

Lockhart looked westward along the line of ridges and nodded confirmation. "Youm right about that, sir, and we'm safe enough, so long as us bides up here. There's nowt for the pot, tho', so I'd best try for a coney or two!"

"You can't fire a shot," Graham warned him.

The man smiled and shook his head. "I'll snare 'em, don't fret, sir," he said and led the way through the undergrowth to the bivouac.

The men jumped up when they saw him and Graham noticed the look of relief in Watson's pinched face and the sparkle of excitement in the eyes of the boy Curle. Briefly he told them what he had seen and his information sobered them, so that they stood for a moment in a silent circle, their eyes on the ground. He knew then that he must say something encouraging and added, "Lockhart is going to get something to cook. We can light a small fire in a hollow and tomorrow or the day after we shall cross the road and head south. We should reach the lines by night or the morning after!" He caught Gwyneth's glance and read approval in it, as though she were a mother who heard someone reassuring her scared brood.

Lockhart came back with one small rabbit, and while they were boiling it Graham motioned the woman to one side. She said, without preamble, "A river follows that valley and I should say it passes less than a mile beyond the road. If we get across the road after the French have gone, we still have the river to cross."

"So much the better, there will be no French on the far side," he said. "We can stay close to the bank and work our way upstream until we find a crossing, then push on south to the Tagus."

But she shrugged in her casual way and said, "Wherever there is a crossing there will be French. We must cross where they have found it impossible to get over with baggage and gun teams."

"How could we do that?"

"You say you can swim, and we have a rope. Perhaps we can lengthen it with belts or vines, who knows? Let us give them a clear night and a day to pass and then we can reconnoiter."

She remained crouched on her haunches, deep in thought, and for a moment he did not care to disturb her. It was almost dark now and the roar of the endless columns still reached them from the road. He thought she looked like a savage squatting there, with muscled thighs spread, her head lowered and a tangled mass of hair falling across her face. Suddenly he was shy and uncertain in her presence, knowing that she had temporarily forgotten him and was devoting the whole of her concentration to their problems and the means to overcome them, but presently she looked up.

"It is essential that we succeed now," she said, "for what you have seen Beaky will wish to hear about. You made a careful count?"

"Yes," he said gleefully, "I made many notes on the papers we found on the French and I have it all here, the number of guns, draft animals, baggage wagons and a fair estimate of their numbers. I added one corps that must have passed before we came up with them."

She nodded and then, standing suddenly, smiled. "You are learning very fast, Mr. Graham. We will talk it over after supper!" And she walked back to the fire that Watson had lit in a dip behind the thicket.

The word "supper" flattered the meal they ate that night. There was no bread left and only one of her cakes, but they were able to thicken the soup with the last handfuls of flour taken from the wagon, and the rabbit

provided about one mouthful of meat apiece. Watson was
very silent and Graham thought he was still mourning his
friend. Up here there was no point in mounting a guard,
so he told them to lie down and sleep with their feet to the
fire. The night was fine and mild, much milder than any
they had experienced so far, and when the moon rose he
went through the scrub to the edge of the first escarpment, knowing that she would be there awaiting him.

He found her sitting on a flat rock silhouetted against
the sky, listening to the unending roar from below, and as
he came up she said, "They are marching through the
night. So much the better! They will pass quicker and leave
the road free for us to cross. We must watch all day
tomorrow for the stragglers, for there will be hundreds of
stragglers in an army as large as that."

"Where does he find so many men?" Graham asked
suddenly.

She replied, shrugging, "From every village and hamlet
in Europe. The price he asks the bourgeois for government is their young and strong to fight his wars. It is not
so difficult. Before he came the kings and emperors took
the men just the same, but they did not give anything in
exchange."

He was interested in her defense of Bonaparte and
asked, "What does he give, apart from wounds and med-
als?"

She looked at him unsmilingly. "If he was left alone he
would give a great deal," she said. "He offers roads,
bridges, good harvests, a thriving trade, manufactories,
aye, and something more, I think, judging by what I have
heard from French prisoners in Lisbon. He gives them
something no other ruler ever gave them, a share in his
glory. In our army it is very different, Mr. Graham."

"Tell me, Gwyneth!"

"The French are all one, you understand, the rich and
the poor, the officers and the rankers. There is no flogging
in the French Army and the provosts do not hang a man
for looting. The rank and file are encouraged to loot and

live upon what they find, wherever they may be. They made a revolution in France and it will never be the same for them again. Perhaps one day we shall make a revolution, but I think not. We sing that we are never slaves but it is not really so, because in England property is everything and a man is judged not on what he is but on what he owns. As a child he learns to touch his cap to the squire and bob to the parson. In the Army it is much the same. Those men down there are the comrades of their officers, but no man of our Army could win epaulettes such as those you wear on your shoulders. It is possible to buy them, of course, if one has money, but we can never win them in the field as do the French. That sergeant of ours, the one who died back at the church, he would have been a major or a colonel in the French Army, and you, when you got back with what you have written down today, you too would be promoted and wear gold lace!"

"Perhaps I will," he smiled, but she went on, earnestly.

"No, Mr. Graham, it is more likely that you will be reprimanded for losing your regiment."

He realized that he was always learning from her, and here were things never to be forgotten, the true difference between imperial France and her opponents, the one fighting as a tribe, the others under a rigid caste system, yet he was unable to abandon all his prejudices without argument.

"Napoleon enslaves people wherever the Grand Army marches," he argued.

"He has no other choice," she said simply. "From the beginning he has been ringed by enemies."

The picture of Napoleon fighting a vast defensive war was as new as everything else she told him, but after pondering this for a moment he decided that he did not want to talk about war, did not, in fact, want to talk at all but to draw close to her and find renewed courage and resolution. He reached over the rock and put his arms around her narrow waist, raising them slowly until her large breasts were under his hands and then lowering his cheek until it touched her hair. Peace came to him the moment he touched her, and they stayed thus for a moment. She lifted her hands from her lap, pressing his hands to her body and at the same time moving her head so that her cheek touched the soft stubble of his beard.

"You will remember me afterward?" she said, and he thought he detected a hint of teasing in her voice.

"Yes," he told her, "always, Gwyneth. Forever, you understand?"

"Ah no!" she said and shuddered and at the same moment disengaged herself and broke from him. In an instant she was the soldier again, preoccupied with the passage of the enemy below. He remembered all too vividly what she had said regarding her prerogative in the relationship of man and woman on the march and did not press her. For the moment her presence and the sense of comradeship between them were enough.

"You hear something new?" he asked presently.

"Yes," she said, "they are more scattered now. There are moments when the road is almost quiet."

He stood listening, his head cocked to one side, and the more muted sounds from below told him that she was right. All the weight had gone from the column and it was now the passage of detached groups, not of close-ranked battalions and guns.

Thirty-six hours later they found the belfry with its bell rope intact, more than twenty feet of strong plaited cord, as thick as a man's thumb.

They had remained in camp a night and a day, waiting for the last of the stragglers to pass, and about sunset on the second day Graham watched a squadron of dragoons escorting a string of open wagons filled with wounded and exhausted men unable to sustain the rate of march. When one of the dragoons dismounted to hustle a half-crippled infantryman into the last wagon, he concluded that the squadron was whipping in and that the road behind them was empty. He returned to the bivouac and gave the order to march at midnight.

They did not have to descend the two cliffs, for Lockhart, reconnoitering out on the right, had found a ravine where access to the road was comparatively easy. They came slithering down without incident and in less than a minute all six of them were across and into the woods on the other side, crossing small patches of marsh and belts of scrub, guided to the river by the steady roar of the torrent. Once clear of the woods, Graham turned upstream, taking the opposite direction to that taken by the French. When he moon went down and progress along the rocky bank became dangerous, he ordered a halt in the reeds to await daylight.

Progress thus far had been arduous in the poor light, and they spent a wretched interval without fire or a dry spot to lie upon. Graham could hear Curle's teeth chattering and Watson's soft, persistent cough, but he kept them stationary until gray light in the east showed them their position on a wide curve of the stream. The river on their right was ten yards wide and broken almost everywhere by rapids where the water foamed over innumerable slime-covered rocks. There was no way of telling whether it was a tributary of the Mondego or the Tagus, but from where they stood it looked a formidable obstacle. No timber grew here, and there was no chance of finding or felling a tree and using it as a bridge as they had done on the previous occasion. The land on both banks was dangerously open and a belt of trees on the gentle slope of the farther bank was more than a league distant. Graham knew that for the time being they must stick close to the reeds. As soon as it was light enough he ordered an advance across the oxbow of the stream, heading for a low bluff that ran down from the direction of the road, meeting the river at a point where it descended a water chute.

Every step was an effort, their feet sinking into soft yellow mud that plucked at their worn shoes and sometimes rose higher than the shin. Curle and Croyde each lost a shoe and in spite of repeated attempts Curle failed to recover his. Once Watson sank to his armpits, screaming with fear when he could find no bottom, but Lockhart had had the forethought to noose his length of rope, and between them, floundering on the treacherous surface, they managed to get it under the sweep's shoulder and drag him free. After that Graham turned away from the river and they made somewhat better progress, until they mounted the bluff and looked down on the charred remains of what had been a small riverside community but was now utterly deserted, for it lay close enough to the French line of march to have been ransacked half a dozen times.

The only building more or less intact was the stone-built church, crowned by a tall conical tower, and when they passed the unlatched door and flung themselves exhausted on the tiled floor they saw the rope passing through a hole in the belfry floor. It was a miracle that it had escaped the eye of the muleteers and artillery teamsters.

When they had recovered their breath and made some attempt to scrape the mud from their uniforms, Watson was for swarming up and cutting the rope loose from the cross-trees, but Lockhart stopped him just in time.

"Will ye rouse half the countryside by a tolling bell?" he demanded, and Watson admitted ruefully that there was sense in this and offered instead to go outside and look for the orthodox way to the belfry loft.

"There are no stairs, they used a ladder," Gwyneth said, pointing to a centrally placed trapdoor, "and the ladder has been carried away. Someone will have to climb that buttress and cut at the rope where it comes through the floor."

"We need every inch of that rope," Graham said. "Watson can go outside, climb up and break through the tiles of the roof to the belfry."

"The risk of his being seen on the roof is greater than

the advantage of another foot or two of rope," she said shortly and then men waited, uncertain whom to obey.

Graham felt a spurt of irritation but mastered it and forced himself to weigh the alternatives objectively. The rope, he would say, was thirty feet, but if it was hacked off short they would have to make do with twenty, lengthening it with Lockhart's rope and crossbelts. On the other hand, Gwyenth was right about the risk of being seen by stragglers on the road, or by a partisan lookout on the peaks. The tower was the single landmark in a flat, featureless landscape and anyone clambering on the roof could be seen from the ridges above. He decided in favor of Gwyneth's plan.

"Take a knife and see what you can do," he told Watson, and the little man, using Croyde as a springboard, at once swarmed up the wall and gained a handhold on the tall buttress, where, using his toes like a monkey, he hoisted himself to within fifteen feet of the bell rope. From here on, however, progress was much more difficult. They angled the rope within his reach, but he dare not grasp it for fear of ringing the bell and was obliged instead to feel his way an inch at a time along the crevices of the almost perpendicular wall until he reached a narrow window recess where he was able to support himself with one arm wrapped around the grille. From below, his perch looked dangerously precarious, and when he extended his free arm to gather in the rope Graham expected him to slip and pitch headlong to the floor. He held on, however, and they saw him grin with triumph when he managed by dint of various contortions to anchor the rope under his chin, after which he drew his knife and began sawing away at the tough fibers. Twice the invisible bell clapper complained, its harsh note booming through the tower and causing Lockhart to curse softly, but at last the rope parted and the length came snaking down to them as Watson, grunting his relief, carefully disengaged himself from the grating and began his perilous return along the crevices to the buttress. As he jumped down there was a glow of virtue on his mud-smeared face.

"You'd none of yer got up there but me," he crowed, "which proves yer don't never know what good comes o' learning to climb chimbleys! Thought I'd gone once or twice, I did, but I warn't, was I?" And he capered about the room in childish celebration of his feat.

"It was a good climb," the woman said, and Lockhart added, "Arr, it were that!" and fell to examining the rope with professional thoroughness.

Graham said nothing. They had the rope and now they would have to look for a place to use it, a spot where the one swimmer among them could cross over, dragging the heavy rope behind him. As this thought crossed his mind he saw Gwyneth regarding him with intensity, and the certainty of her concern made him impatient to prove himself as surely as Watson had done in the matter of the climb. He said, "We must look for a ford or the remains of a bridge. If there is neither, then we must find a place where the river is narrower or the current eases a knot or two. We can't reconnoiter by night, so the risk of moving in the open by day will have to be faced."

Lockhart spoke up, firmly but with his customary note of respect. "Beggin' your pardon, zir, that's a job for one rather than six and I'm the one best used to moving without being spotted."

Without waiting for orders, he picked up his musket and went out, the others scattering about the church in the hope of finding something edible. Watson scraped the wax deposit from the shattered candelabra and tried to persuade Curle to nibble a sliver or two of the yellow grease, but the boy shook his head and Graham, having ensured that all the firearms had been cleaned, issued orders to search the hovels and vegetable patches in the hope that the French had overlooked a few turnips or potatoes. They had reassembled, emptyhanded, by the time Lockhart returned with news that he had reconnoitered the bank a mile or so upstream and had found the site of the original footbridge, destroyed by the British during their retreat or perhaps by the villagers themselves when word came of the approaching French. Graham told the men to remain in the church. He was still very uneasy about the possibility of being overlooked from the road and went out with Lockhart to view the site.

The bridge had stretched between two flat rocks, the one on the far bank being several feet nearer the stream than its opposite number, and the iron stanchions to which the wooden structure had been fastened still protruded from the crevices on the bank on which they stood. The river here was about twelve yards wide and ran swiftly through a tiny gorge toward shallow rapids about fifty yards downstream. It was probably ten feet deep where it passed the bridgehead, but because of the height of the banks at this point there were no shallows on either side. Elsewhere the stream broadened to as much as sixty feet but, even there, was far too deep and too swift-running for wading. Lockhart sounded it here and there with a tall bullrush, but in most places the bed shelved very steeply, and Graham soon made up his mind that their chance of crossing lay in getting the rope across the bottleneck and anchoring it on the farther side. Then, with luck, he thought, the file might cross singly, clinging to the rope and being hauled up the bank by whoever had gone over first.

Lockhart said soberly, "No matter how strong a swimmer you be, sir, you'll not make yon bank with a heavy rope attached to 'ee, for when her's wet her'll weigh considerable! Still, mebbe we can get over that if us makes a guide rope to carry the big 'un. Seed it done, I have, when I was a little lad!" He looked more than usually thoughtful as he plodded back to the hamlet.

The landscape was still empty of life and movement. Not a sheep or goat showed on the hillside and even the birds seemed to have deserted the area. It was so quiet and still that Graham made up his mind to attempt the crossing in daylight and, having gained the south bank, to make for the woods on the horizon, where there was good cover and a chance of making bivouac for the night. It was curious, he thought, how new was this prejudice on his part for cover. Always as a boy he had loved moors and gorse-grown hills, preferring them to the deep woods that covered the area close to his home, yet now he was beginning to hate open country, reflecting that from the very commencement of their flight he had hugged trees, scrub-sown crevices and gullies, feeling naked and defenseless in the open. He outlined his plan to Gwyneth and the men, and there was no dissension, no argument at all. Each of them was aware that safety lay only in the deep woods on the far side of the river and each shared Graham's distrust of the open.

Before they left, Lockhart made his guideline, a hodgepodge of twine unwound from the cracked stock of a musket and lengthened by the unpicked hemline of Gwyneth's tattered green dress. All the time the man's blunt, skillful fingers were busy with the task Graham was conscious of the woman's anxious attention, and he said, more to reassure himself than her, "I once swam across the Medway for a wager." But although she threw him a swift glance and Watson whistled approval, not one of them ceased to watch Lockhart until he stood up, looped his line around his elbow and said, "I reckon her'll do, zir, but dornee put much strain on her!" Glad to relieve tension, they made ready to go.

On the way down the riverbank to the spot they had chosen, Graham's fear left his belly, replaced there by a sense of exhilaration that continued to mount until he was standing on the rock above the torrent watching Lockhart fasten one end of the belfry rope to the iron stanchion. He would have thought that the prospect of plunging into the swift current would terrify him, but now that the actual moment was here he grasped at the opportunity of contributing something positive to their salvation. Day after day, throughout the whole of the interminable trek, he had been dismayed by a feeling of personal inadequacy.

First it had been the sergeant who had led and afterward, in all but title, the woman. Every crisis that had been passed since Captain Sowden fell dead at the bridge had been met by one of the others, and each time this had occurred Graham had known shame. It was the bulk of Strawbridge that had enabled them to climb the rock face and pass into the woods, and it had been the sergeant's reckless courage that had covered their escape from the lancers. Later it had been Gwyneth who charted their route and poor, stupid Strawbridge who had facilitated their escape from the partisans. Even the invaluable rope had been secured by Watson's agility, but now at last he was about to do something that not one of them could attempt and the knowledge steadied his nerve and lifted his spirits as he stripped to his drawers and issued his final instructions. He told Lockhart to make all of them undress and roll their shoes and clothes into bundles that could be maneuvered along the downward slant of the rope when it was made taut. The muskets could come across the same way and Lockhart showed them how to make running slings of their crossbelts and attach their weapons and bundles of clothes to the buckles. The men showed a curious unwillingness to strip before the woman, and Watson particularly wriggled with embarrassment, until Gwyneth, making nothing of it, hoisted the tatters of her gown and tucked them into the waistband of the white drawers that Graham had given her. But when he saw her tie her brogues together and hang them around her neck he protested.

"You would do better to put them in one of the bundles," he said, but she shook her head and helped him to fasten the guideline around his waist.

"I have crossed many rivers in this fashion," she said. "Go upstream as far as the line will reach. In that way you will get a few yards' leeway when the current catches you."

He decided to follow her advice and they walked along

the rock for the length of the line, standing a little apart from the others as they took their private leavetaking.

"Will you wade as far as you can?" she asked, and he said no, he would dive, for this would give him a start over the current. Then he turned, facing the stream, and braced himself, but as he did so he felt her hand on his shoulder and looking over his shoulder he saw that her lip was trembling. Her sudden weakness surprised him and he said brusquely, "I'll get across, never worry!"

She replied in a whisper, "Then God bless you, Mr. Graham, for it's a brave thing for any man to attempt!"

At that he hesitated no longer, leaping from the elevated rock with every ounce of his strength. As he rushed down he heard them give a thin, scattering cheer and then the current seized him like a dead leaf and he was turning over and over in midstream with walls of water rushing down upon him in a mood of savage frolic.

There were underwater rocks that he had not suspected and one of them grazed his side as another struck his instep like a blow from a club. Striking out madly, he fought his way to the surface, throwing up his head and beating the water in a frenzy. The torrent was ice cold, but he was so occupied with maintaining his slanting direction that he noticed nothing but its effort to hold him to the center of the current. Twice, as he slid over submerged rocks, he bobbed up shoulder-high, and the second time, spinning like a twig, he caught a fleeting glimpse of the group on the bank. Then his knees buckled under him as he touched bottom and clawed at the edge of the slab-sided platform of rock forming the farther bridgehead, losing it, finding it again and finally rolling over and over into a runnel where the torrent swept over his head but failed to dislodge him.

He rose to the surface dazed and spent, but as he staggered clear he remembered to lift his hand in acknowledgment of the cheer that piped across the river. Only then did he remember the guideline attached to his wrist and in sudden panic he clutched at it, finding it still secure and dragging at him as he crawled higher up the bank.

He was very cold now, his body shuddering as he gulped the moist air, but as soon as he got his breath he began capering and slapping himself like a boy on a frosty morning. Then he heard Lockhart hailing, saw that the gamekeeper was signaling him to pull on the guideline and a moment later heard the bell rope slide into the water, and he pulled it in hand over hand, bracing himself against the rock to counter its drag. There was a single bent spike embedded in the runnel where the bridge had been anchored and he knotted the sodden rope around the metal. As he did so, however, he felt a sharp pricking sensation under his ribs and, glancing down, was surprised to see a film of blood spreading over his thigh. The rock had lacerated his side just above the hip and when he put weight on his left leg it pained him and he remembered the impact of the boulders on his instep. The shock of the water, however, had invigorated him and he made light of his injuries, signaling to Lockhart to loop the first of the bundles on the running noose. The firearms came over easily, propelled by their own weight, sliding just clear of the water, but the transfer of the bundles proved a tricky and tiresome business, necessitating a prolonged series of tugs from Graham's side and sometimes sagging into the stream, from which they had to be jerked free and set in motion once more. Every bundle that reached him was soaked, but he laid them out in a row and shouted to the men to begin their crossing.

Watson came first, managing it very expertly, for he was the most agile among them and his weight was insignificant. He came across like a monkey, balancing on the rope, using his crossed legs as a pulley and making the journey in under a minute. He laughed as he scrambled ashore and turned to shout encouragement to Curle, who followed far less expertly and, to judge by his expression, with considerable anxiety. Then Gwyneth slung herself across the rope, ignoring Watson's spate of advice, not a word of which she could have heard above the roar of the water.

At first she tried Watson's method, kneeling in the slack of the rope and propelling herself forward by her crossed feet, but less than halfway across she lost her balance and swung around so abruptly that each one of them shouted with alarm as they saw her supported by her hands, with her legs deep in the water. Graham jumped in waist-deep, but her voice sang across the space between them as she shouted, "Go back, I'm coming over!" He retreated up the bank as she swung at arm's length, the current tugging at her legs. Then, with a carefully judged action, she drew herself higher, hooking one leg clear of the flood so that it gave her the leverage to begin moving again.

Astonishingly a note of comedy entered the scene. It was droll to see her clinging so, with her ample behind an inch or so clear of the water and her brogues emerging like grotesque earrings from her trailing hair. First Watson began to laugh and then Graham found himself laughing too, as slowly and painstakingly she eased herself along the rope in a series of contractions and expansions, her tresses dipping the water with every foot she progressed. When at last they pulled her onto the bank she said breathlessly, "I was a fool to listen to you, Watson! I should have done better to start out like that!" And she advised Graham to give the rope another turn around the stanchion before Lockhart or Croyde attempted the crossing.

Lockhart was now shouting something that Graham could not catch, and then, to the four gathered on the western bank, it seemed as though the two men on the farther bank were engaged in some kind of argument, for Lockhart made a number of threatening gestures and Croyde squared up to him as though a fight was imminent, but in the end the gamekeeper turned away and spat on his hands preparatory to straddling the rope. He climbed across awkwardly but doggedly, taking more than twice as long to cross as had the others, but he arrived without incident. When Graham reached down to help him to the top of the bank he said breathlessly, "Croyde won't leave that belt he's wearing! I reasoned with the vool, but it was useless. You should have took it from him bevore you crossed, sir, for what's in it belongs to all of us!" He turned to the others as though for confirmation of the claim.

Graham had noted the heavy canvas girdle when Croyde had peeled off his breeches, but he had not recognized it as the money belt that Gwyneth had spoken of back at the partisan camp. He could not understand from Lockhart's grumbling remark whether the gamekeeper meant that the money belonged to the file as loot or, in the more official sense, as part of their traveling equipment, but it did not seem to him to have much importance now, for they were unlikely to need money during the remainder of their journey. He said briefly, "To hell with Croyde's belt. Get dressed, all of you, and head for the woods at the double!" Then, turning, he beckoned urgently to Croyde, who was standing at the edge of the flat rock, presumably trying to pluck up courage to cross.

The ex-smuggler had not needed to be reminded of the belt by Lockhart. He had watched, with the deepest concern, Graham's initial struggle in the flood and afterward the perilous crossing of the drummer and the woman. Although he had a wider experience of the sea than any of them, he hated and feared water, and only the prospect of being left behind among murderous partisans and the French encouraged him to consider trusting his weight to the slender thread stretched over a leaping torrent. He could not swim a stroke and it seemed to him that the rope had stretched a good deal under the passage of the others and was likely to sag below the surface level before he was halfway across.

He had thought about the belt as soon as he learned they were to cross the river on a rope, and his common sense told him that it was folly to make the attempt handicapped by something weighing several pounds, yet it called for more resolution than he possessed to abandon money he had carried thus far. Ever since he had buried his friend Lickspittle the belt had been a source of comfort and security to him, giving him something that he had never possessed, confidence in the future and in his ability to stand on his own without having to lean upon others. He had parted with the guinea because the woman had made it very clear to him that unless the partisan Pedrillo could be bribed they would be murdered out of hand, and he had to admit that events had proved her correct. Prior to becoming the owner of the belt he had never thought very much at all, but possession of money converted him into a contemplative man and it seemed to him, looking back on the incident of the bribe, that the guinea had been well invested, for in some strange manner it had led to their escape from the partisans. Surely this, if anything, proved the power of money, and who but a fool would abandon a double handful of silver pieces on the bank of a river in the wilderness? He stood looking down on the rope and occasionally casting a glance at the gesticulating Graham and the others beside him, who were now dressing themselves preparatory to marching off. He was terrified of beginning the crossing but even more frightened by the prospect of being left behind to fend for himself. Yet he could not bring himself to throw aside the belt, and the longer he hesitated the heavier and more constricting it seemed to become, enclosing his waist like a girdle of chain mail and chafing the flesh of his belly below the navel. His thick fingers toyed with the knots above the hipbone, and the roar of the torrent filled his brain with a tumult of doubts and fears, making him grimace and fidget under the scourge of indecision.

He must have remained standing there for several minutes before he saw the others on the far bank pick up their equipment and turn their backs on him. It was a mere ruse on Graham's part to compel Croyde to make up his mind one way or the other, but Croyde at once interpreted the movement as a concerted decision to abandon him. With a grunt of dismay he laid hold of the rope and inched himself clear of the rock platform, wobbling perilously as his knees and feet scrabbled for a grip, then swinging right around and dangling as the woman had done in midstream. He was aware, however, that the others had turned their faces to the river again and were now awaiting him, and the relief arising from this encouraged him to drag himself clear of the bank so that he looked down on an inverted picture of the boiling water and half-submerged rocks pointing up at him like the snouts of sharks.

His fears regarding the sag of the rope were well founded. Before he had traveled half the distance the water was splashing his face so that he jerked his head higher and higher, clasping the rope with his forearms and bending his body in an arc in a desperate attempt to hoist himself clear of the dragging current. It was then, when he was more than halfway across, that he saw the drifting log bearing down on him. It was not a very large log, just a heavy branch of pine with a growth of dead twigs sprouting from it and a tangle of brier trailing from one of the projections. It was heading straight for him, and in the extremity of his terror he saw it not as a branch weighing a few pounds but as the trunk of a huge tree, capable of smashing into his awkwardly poised body like a giant battering ram and driving him down into the water. The rope at this point was almost touching the surface, and the floating branch was stopped by it, part of the flotsam shooting under Croyde's arched back and tugging at him gently and insistently. As the twigs touched his bare skin he screamed and lost his foothold and for a moment swung by his hands chest-deep in the flood. Then, as the twigs probed and shifted, he remembered the belt. It was as though the piece of debris were a spidery water creature intent on depriving him of his money before devouring him as prey. With the whole of his being he resented and opposed this spoliation, and in an effort to combat the thrust of the branches he whipped his left hand from the rope and struck at the twigs, beating the water and kicking out with both legs in an attempt to assist the current in freeing the horrid thing and sending it on its journey downstream. For a few seconds, while the others pranced and shouted on the bank, he hung by one hand, but while he did so other pieces of driftwood began to pile up behind the spray of branches. Their weight, added to the relentless drag of the current, tore his right hand from the rope and sent him rolling over and over in the brown flood. The weight of the belt dragged him down into ten or twelve feet of rushing water and in the struggle below the surface he once more became entangled in the hateful embrace of the twigs. They saw him rise once or twice as the midstream current seized him and then he disappeared as the pine branches bobbed up and spun in the slow swirl of the bend above the rapids.

Graham, Watson and Curle rushed along the bank shouting, Graham with the guideline coiled like a lasso ready to be thrown the moment Croyde appeared among the white breaks of the water, but he did not reappear—and would not do so until a succession of dry summers reduced the torrent to a trickle and exposed Croyde's skeleton wedged between two rocks like a bolt of metal hammered into the crevices of a wall. That was years after the war, when two boys were looking for trout under the stones, and it was a lucky find for the village as a community. The belt was still there, anchored by weed to the stones, and the money in it was used to buy materials for a strong metal bridge at the very spot where Croyde had fought his losing battle with the piece of flotsam.

CHAPTER SEVEN

The Convent

～◦◦～

THEY HAD watched the drowning of Croyde from the rock basin that marked the western approach to the bridge-head, and when they were sure they would not recover his body they reassembled there, each reluctant to comment upon a fate that might have overtaken any of them during the last hour.

At length Lockhart said, "Well, if any man died on account o' gold, then he did, the blamed vool!"

Watson added callously, "If we could ha' got his corp ashore, then the boy could have 'ad one of his brogues. That was in my mind all along, for the boy's in rare need o' shoe leather!"

The woman said resignedly, "I'd as lief Croyde went as anyone. He was a better man than his comrade, but not much!"

Graham said nothing, for the sense of failure had come down on him again, making nonsense of his unspoken boasts to get home without losing another man. No matter how savagely he reminded himself that it was the man's own greed, hesitancy and crass stupidity that had caused his death, the black mood of the earlier stages of the march pressed on him like a cloud, blotting out the prospect of the distant woods and imagined safety and filling the vacuum of his stomach with bile.

He turned aside, snarling a curse at the boy who trotted forward with pale, eager face, and without waiting to make sure that they had repossessed themselves of their boots and accouterments he strode over the rim of the basin to look across the marshland that lay between the river and the woods. He stood there some twenty yards in advance of the others, ostensibly surveying the route but in fact trying with all his might to put Croyde's death out of mind.

Suddenly he was conscious of a swirl of movement in the reeds, a wide ripple such as might preface the upsurge of wild geese. Yet no bird soared from the riverside growth and for a brief moment he forgot both Croyde and route, wheeling around on the group as they emerged from the hollow, with a cry of warning on his lips.

It was cut short by a sharp exclamation from Lockhart, and Graham saw him bring his musket to his shoulder and lay his face to the barrel, but before he could pull the trigger there was a single report from a patch of reeds on Graham's left and miraculously the marsh was alive with uniformed men, converging on them from all points of the compass. Graham had no opportunity at all to draw his sword or even think of doing so, for the nearest man was less than ten yards distant when he first saw him and within a matter of seconds they were all around him, their weapons advanced, as still more men poured into the rock basin and swarmed over the bedraggled file. As they advanced they laughed and shouted and encouraged one another, like a mob of boys on a playing field. Then somebody took away his sword and another plucked at the pistol in his belt, and behind him, only a yard or so distant, he saw Lockhart on his hands and knees in the marsh with his head bowed and blood pouring from a wound in his leg.

Graham had thought of the appearance of the French hussars as a miracle, the final thrust of the demons who had plagued and persecuted them since the very beginning of the march, now doling out small slices of luck, now pouncing down on them with teeth and claws as their confidence rose a point or two. It had been like this all the way from the big river: the finding of the forest track that

led directly to the lancers, the seeming deliverance by
partisans who had murdered Strawbridge for his musket,
the finding of the bell rope that had destroyed Coryde and
led them straight into a French ambush. Yet the presence
of a hundred dismounted hussars in the tall reeds beside
the river was not a miracle but merely the result of
military prescience on the part of an Irish mercenary in
command of a French flying column exploring the western
bank of the river before marching on Abrantes, farther
south.

The French army had crossed Graham's river on hastily built bridges and had done so less than half a day's
march above the point where the file had anchored their
rope. The main body had then marched directly south to
Santarém, but forage was running out at an alarming rate
and the infantry, prevented from scattering to search for
food because of the density of partisans in the mountains,
were already reduced to two biscuits a day and that with
the certainty of a siege directly ahead. Once across the
river, a trivial obstacle to a man of Masséna's ability, the
Commander in Chief had dispatched columns in every
direction, equipping them with wagons to convey anything
they found to a central depot at Santarém. It was one
such column, commanded by Colonel Michael Dillon,
that had emerged from the woods that morning and
pushed scouts to within a kilometer of the river. It was no
miracle that had filled the marsh with dismounted hussars
but rather the prosaic report of a sharp-eyed troop sergeant who had seen half-clad figures running along the
riverbank and had deduced from this that there must be a
village close by. As a village meant, or might mean,
mules, pigs, grain or even vegetables, he lost no time in
reporting the presence of the file to his colonel.

Dillon was an experienced soldier whose presence in
Portugal led all the way back to the abortive Irish rebel-
lion of '98 when, as a lively young patriot, he had escaped
from Kerry with a price on his head and enlisted in the
French Army as a sublieutenant of light cavalry. The son,

grandson and great-grandson of professional soldiers, he had made rapid progress during the wars of the Empire, and at the age of thirty-five there was nothing capable of surprising him. He had fought under Masséna in the Zurich and Genoa campaigns, had been taken prisoner by the Austrians and freed under the peace terms, had marched down into Bohemia to be present at Austerlitz and afterward across Prussia and Poland to fight at Jena, Eylau and Friedland. Two years ago he had gone down into Portugal with Junot and now he was making his third Peninsula campaign. Because of his experience down here he knew what his French Emperor did not know, the hopelessness of waging war in the Spanish Peninsula with armies of more than a few thousand men, for where a division could barely exist a corps began to starve in two weeks and most armies began to disintegrate a few days after they left their base. Yet Dillon's Irish sense of humor made him a good commander of light cavalry, and somehow, by exercising ingenuity and forethought, he had kept his men moving and his horses shod. An optimist by nature, he looked forward to the inevitable withdrawal into Spain and perhaps his ultimate posting out of this pestilential country to the more cogenial atmosphere of Germany, Italy or, with a great deal of luck, a French training depot. He was a softly spoken man, with a lean sunburned face and a dark cavalry moustache that bristled below a pair of sparkling black eyes, giving him the appearance of a man who found it difficult to take war seriously.

In point of fact he took his work very seriously indeed, and if his careless approach to soldiering belied this fact the men who served under him, and the countless opponents he had drubbed during the last ten years, could testify to his efficiency.

The moment the troop sergeant reported the presence of civilians he dismounted and accompanied the man to a small reed-crowned knoll about halfway between the trees and the river. Here, using the sergeant's shoulder as a rest, he ran out his field glass and trained it on the bank, remaining motionless for more than a minute before snapping the glass shut and issuing orders for the horses to be taken back into the woods.

"They are not civilians, Sergeant Lemartine," he said quietly when the man gaped at this unexpected order. "That is a British patrol and they must have access to a bridge or they would be on the far side of the river."

"I could ride over with a troop and cut them down in ten minutes," said Lemartine, who held the conventional opinion that dismounted operations reduced hussars to the status of sweaty infantry.

"I have no doubt you could, Sergeant," said Dillon even more mildly, "but I cannot extract information from men you have sabered and ridden over!" He lit his pipe, seating himself tranquilly until such time as men came in from the flanks and he could lead the advance in person.

The ambush was brilliantly executed. Graham was the only member of the file who had so much as a few seconds' warning of the onrush, and Lockhart, a few paces in his rear, was the only one to unsling his musket. He was brought down before he could use it, however, and now lay gasping in the mud with blood spurting from a hole in his leg and was likely to bleed to death if someone did not attend to him at once.

Colonel Dillon walked past Graham and glanced at the groaning man. Unable to resist pointing an object lesson to the hussars standing around, he said, "I have always had it in mind to recommend the disuse of firearm slings. Now, if this man had been carrying his musket at the port one of us would be lying alongside him!" Then he saw Gwyneth being escorted over the lip of the basin and added, "Let the woman attend to his wound!" and returned to Graham.

For a moment the two men studied each other, Graham flushed and despairing, the Irishman no more than mildly interested in the bedraggled figure now standing between two grinning hussars. Finally Dillon said, very politely, "You appear to have had a troublesome march, sir. Allow me to offer you some refreshment!" He signed to one of the men, who shouted something to a group of cavalrymen engaged in collecting the British arms and equipment.

A very short hussar came running, carrying a metal flask of the kind Graham had seen strapped to the saddles of hunters when the foxhounds had assembled in his father's forecourt. Perhaps it was the man's essential courtesy, or perhaps a bitter consciousness of his own filthy condition, which seemed an affront to the dandified officer in his parti-colored pantaloons and heavily braided and swinging hussar jacket, but Graham felt a sudden choking sensation in his throat and for one painful moment he thought he would break down and sob like a thwarted child. Their capture had been so sudden and so final. There had been no opportunity to consider the taking of one course or another, simply a general envelopment that made all their strivings over the past ten days futile and ridiculous.

Dillon's brandy saved him and he was able to say, hoarsely, "My men have eaten nothing for forty-eight hours. It would be a great courtesy on your part to give them a few mouthfuls of bread!" But as he said this he saw that his request had been anticipated, for already Watson and Curle were sitting on the ground looking surprisingly cheerful as they munched away at French hardtack. Lockhart was now sitting with his back against a tree stump and Gwyneth, having cut away his breeches and discarded his leggings, had almost finished her bandaging. Graham looked at the little group with pity and the thought occurred to him that perhaps it was fortunate for them that the end had come at last and that they had fallen into the hands of men who fought without bitterness. He said aloud, "We were nine to begin with, not counting the woman. We crossed the river on a rope taken from the belfry yonder, but the village had been ransacked a dozen times and it is not worth the trouble of a search on your part, Colonel."

"You are a detachment, just these few?" Dillon asked wonderingly, and Graham sensed that beneath his courteous air the man was putting a shrewd, searching question.

"We were cut off at Coimbra," he said and the French colonel raised his eyebrows.

"But Coimbra is almost a hundred miles north of here. How in the name of God did you cross our line of march?"

Graham hesitated. Suddenly he remembered the notes he had made on the papers taken from the butchered infantrymen on the far side of the range. Before swimming the river he had stuffed the notes into his boot and they were still there, he could feel them with his great toe, a bulge that would make a long march a painful ordeal.

He decided that the only way to prevent the French from finding the papers was a show of complete frankness, for they would be more likely to search truculent prisoners and the discovery of the papers could easily lead to all five of them being shot out of hand. With the determination to bluff this suave, gentlemanly captor a little of his courage returned and he said, with a smile, "That was the easiest part of the journey, a great deal easier than our escape from our so-called allies in the mountains! We crossed at night, after the last of your stragglers had gone by." He went on to give the Irishman a brief account of their adventures, not omitting their brush with the lancers in the village. The man listened, obviously deeply interested, and when Graham had described Croyde's death an hour or so since he looked at the narrator with respect.

"*Eh bien*, but you deserved to get through to your lines and I apologize for being the one to end such an odyssey! However, perhaps it will be of some small satisfaction to you to hear that when he learned of your presence from the lancers you fought, General Reynier detached two squadrons of light cavalry to beat up the woods beyond the village. We were under the impression that there was at least a company of the Fifty-first in our rear." He rose and addressed a blank-faced lieutenant in rapid French. Although Graham failed to understand what was said, it was obvious that he had given orders to fetch the horses and resume the march. "You will give me your parole until we bivouac?" he asked, with a smile.

Graham glanced at Lockhart, still lying with his back to the stump, and then at the boy Curle, around whom two or three hussars were standing as he gnawed at the biscuit. Their attitude was that of men feeding a starving puppy.

"We are in your hands," he said briefly. "I will give my parole until sunset!"

"A convenient compromise," Dillon said cheerfully, "for it means you can travel in comfort. The wounded man can go in a wagon and the woman can attend him. She is his wife?"

"No," Graham told him, "she is the widow of a Highlander we found in a church, but she is as good a soldier as any man in the British Light Brigade, including General Crauford!"

"Ah, Crauford," Dillon said, with a chuckle. "There is a man who has led us some merry dances all the way from the Spanish frontier. My Lord Wellington will have trouble with that young man, cooped up behind entrenchments all winter! We nearly had him once when he fought with his back to a ravine, but he slipped away. He has the devil's own luck, almost as much as you, my friend!"

They carried Lockhart across the marsh to the fringe of the wood, where a short string of wagons waited beside the remounted column. Graham addressed his first words to Gwyneth since their capture. "Look after him well," he said, "and get him something to eat. These people are not savages and I have given my parole until sunset." He wanted to tell her that the papers were still safe in his boot, but he did not know how to hint at this in the presence of the hovering sergeant.

There was a spare horse for him to ride, and Watson and Curle were mounted behind a couple of troopers. Someone up ahead of the column gave an order and they set out along the edge of the wood, heading south. After they had ridden a mile or so the sergeant trotted up and handed Graham the wing of a fowl, saluting and falling back into line as Dillon edged his horse alongside. He smiled as Graham bit into the meat.

"Eat, my friend," he said gaily. "It will be a long war, I fear!"

An hour or so after they had skirted the woods and moved out onto the plain beyond, Graham saw another column of troops in the distance. Before long the two columns converged, heading for a large stone building on a low hill about a league ahead. Dillon, who had ridden off to confer with the commander of the second column, returned after an interval and told him that this group had combed all the villages on the far side of the woods without finding a thing to eat or capturing a single civilian.

"This is a new way of making war," he said glumly, "and only two men as dedicated as Masséna and Wellington could achieve it. When I was down here with General Junot's expedition two years ago this was a fertile, well-populated country, but now it is nothing but a desert. The entire population appears to have taken to the mountains or moved down into Lisbon!" He glanced at the sun, now sinking over the western plain. "Your time is running out, my young friend, and I have fresh orders to ride on through the night to reach Santarém tomorrow. I shall be obliged to hand you over to Major Fricourt at the convent. You will remain there until orders for your disposal arrive from headquarters. Perhaps you will be summoned for questioning, or perhaps Masséna and Ney have all the information they require. I have given an account of you to Fricourt and the only way I could extend my hospitality to you is if you consented to prolong your parole. In that case you could ride on with me to Santarém."

"That would entail leaving behind the three men and the woman?"

"Yes indeed. Perhaps prisoners are being assembled at Santarém or Abrantes. I can only tell you we have no arrangements for escorting them back into Spain." He looked at Graham humorously, his black eyes twinkling, and added, "This campaign has not produced many prisoners so far. I am told we have fewer than a hundred. It will not be long before protests arrive from Paris. His Imperial Majesty sets great store on prisoners."

"You have been very kind," Graham said stiffly. "Would it be within the laws of war to ask your advice regarding my decision?"

The Irishman nodded gravely and Graham was suddenly aware of a great liking he had conceived for the man, so great that he felt ashamed of the bulge he could feel in the toe of his boot. It was as though by concealing the papers he was betraying the confidence of an enemy who had become a friend. "In my position, what course would you adopt, sir?"

"As a field officer old enough to understand the absurdity of jingling across a depopulated country, I would be inclined to give my parole and sit out the dance in some tidy provincial town, my friend, but how old are you?"

"Nineteen, and this is my first campaign," Graham told him.

The Irishman knitted his brows and drew in his cheeks, as though giving the matter serious contemplation. Finally he looked up and smiled. "That alters things. At nineteen I daresay I would withhold my parole and stay with my men!"

"Thank you, sir," Graham said quietly, and it was

almost as though the man beside him knew all about the papers in his boot.

James Lockhart had always been a self-communicating and observant man, but never more so than during his brief spell in the hospital at the big convent on the edge of the plain. Major Fricourt of the engineers, a fussy and much harassed man, was at present engaged in converting the vast, sprawling building into a fort, and, having more than enough to do, he had been embarrassed by the presence of prisoners when Dillon abandoned them to his keeping and rode on across country to Santarém. The major sent Lockhart to the hospital, locked the three sound men in what had been a wine cellar of the convent, and gave the woman the run of the camp on condition she worked as laundress for the officers stationed at the post. After that he quickly forgot all about them and continued his survey, the problems of fortification being the sole aspect of war for which he was trained and in which he was interested.

The sick among the garrison were housed in what had been the buttery, a high-ceilinged building with two narrow windows facing east and a stone floor on which the patients lay about on straw palliasses. They were indifferently fed on haricot beans and an occasional bowl of broth brewed from the garrison's shrinking supply of goats, supplemented by the occasional mule that had died for want of fodder.

It did not take Lockhart long to decide that the French army now closing in on Lisbon was already on the verge of starvation and had fared little better than had the file during its long trek from the frontier. Every day men were carried into hospital for no more reason than that they were too weak to stand guard duty, and some of the conscripts who had marched down from the French border less than three months before were reduced to skin and bone. Lockhart spoke no word of French and understood nothing of their conversation, but he lay quietly on

his straw thinking and watching until his leg was sufficiently healed to enable him to hobble about in the open.
He had already formed an opinion that it might not be
too difficult to escape from this assembly of scarecrows,
and when Gwyneth whispered to him that Graham, Watson and Curle were confined in the adjacent wine cellar
he decided it was time to make one of his unhurried
reconnaissances and see what prospects of escape
presented themselves.

His wound was painful but not serious. The ball, fired
from close range, had gone through the fleshy part of his
calf and left a neat hole without inflicting permanent
damage. The surgeon, who examined it once, said that it
would heal in a matter of weeks, but even so Lockhart
realized that he personally would be unable to take part
in an escape that meant a march across country, even
country as flat as that surrounding the convent. With the
aid of a crutch, however, he could soon hobble about the
flagged courtyard that lay outside the buttery, and it was
here, some ten days after their capture, that he located a
ground-level grille giving access to the cellars. He limped
over and called through the narrow aperture, but there
was no response. It was not until later the same day that
Gwyneth told him that the cellar was subdivided and that
Graham and the others were locked in the farther section
beyond a boundary wall. He glanced over the wall on the
next occasion when he was alone in the courtyard and
could just see a similar grille let into the wall about ten
yards nearer the corner of the main building. Having
marked the spot, he wasted no further time on exploration
but concentrated upon the large barn abutting the courtyard to the south. Lying on his straw he had recognized
the intermittent chink of metal coming from this direction,
and when he dragged himself around the building out of
range of the single apathetic sentry he found what he
expected to find, an improvised blacksmith's shop with
half a dozen men busily engaged in the routine work of
bayonet sharpening, shot manufacture and the shoeing of

officers' horses. He approached closely and stood near the forge, pretending to warm himself, and all the time his sharp eyes roved among the litter until he spotted a long, tapering file, blunt at one end and sharply pointed at the other, which had been thrown on a bench by one of the smiths working at the bellows.

Nobody took the slightest notice of him or remarked upon his prisoner status. Semistarvation and endless marches across the mountains seemed to have dulled the soldierly instinct of the French, but it remained sharp in a man of Lockhart's temperament. He had no opportunity to steal the file on that occasion, but when next he returned to the forge it was still lying on the bench. Positioning himself with care and leaning his weight on the crutch, he edged the file along the bench until it fell into a pile of shavings at his feet, but he did not, as most men would have done, press his luck to the extent of picking it up then and there. Instead he limped away to draw his ration of beans, and on the third visit to the forge, when most of the men were engaged in quieting a restive horse, he slithered to the floor, thrust the file into his tunic and then dragged himself to his feet and limped back to the buttery, where he concealed his prize in a chink between the flagstones.

Toward dusk he got up and dragged himself along the corridor and out into the guarded section of the courtyard, where only the shoulder-high wall separated him from the second grille. He had made up his mind to risk being missed when the buttery was locked for the night and to use the hours of darkness to seek a way over the wall and perhaps back again before daylight. He did not know how he could explain his presence in the open when the guard unlocked the big double doors in the morning, but it did not seem to matter very much. He was now a cripple and had no intention of embarrassing the others with his presence when they fled south to the river. His duty, as he saw it, was to get the file to Graham and then let the officer make his own dispositions.

There were only a few minutes of daylight left and he used them to survey the wall along the whole of its length as far as what had been the home farm and piggeries, where the forge was now situated. It was built of loose blocks of stone, far too substantial to be pulled down without a great deal of noise, and the sentry post was sited about twenty yards from where he stood pressed against the wall of the main building. Nearer to him was a jumble of outbuildings marking the limit of the enclosure, but beyond the sentry post, where the wall was much lower, was what appeared to be a lean-to shed, a flimsy structure with holes in its reed thatch. It struck Lockhart that if he could get inside the shed he would have limited cover for surmounting the wall, providing he chose a moment when the sentry was at the far end of his beat. He watched the sentries changed and the new guard settle himself in the angle of the buttress as the duty officer and a squad of infantrymen marched up the slight slope to secure the double doors that gave access to the convent. They passed without seeing him, for he too had found a buttress to crouch behind. When they had gone rain began to fall with the enveloping dusk and he remained in the shadow working out his plan of approach: a stealthy circumambulation of the big courtyard so that he could enter the shed from the extreme end of the sentry's beat.

In any event, he managed it with far less difficulty than he had anticipated. The driving rain kept the sentry close to the wall and disinclined to patrol more than a short section of its length. Lockhart kept him under observation as he sidled around the extremity of the main building, his crutch skidding on the rounded stones and once or twice almost bringing him down. By the time he had reached the shelter of the farm buildings he was dripping with sweat and his reopened wound was causing him a considerable amount of pain, but he observed with satisfaction that the sentry had now abandoned his patrol altogether and was hidden behind the angle of the buttress. All Lockhart could see of him was a faint gleam where the light from a room above the main door reflected on his bayonet tip. He waited for a moment and then flung himself across the slush at the foot of the slope and over the threshold of the shed.

Inside it was pitch dark and rain dripped dolorously through the leaks in the thatch, forming pools where the water was unable to drain away. He groped at the topmost stones and was relieved to find that here they were unmortared and easily dislodged. With infinite care he removed and lowered a dozen, reducing the wall to the height of his breast. The lower stones were larger and firmly fixed and he was unable to dislodge them, so he laid aside his crutch, gripped the file between his teeth and hoisted himself across the rubble, dragging his wounded leg and projecting himself inch by inch into the far section of the courtyard.

The passage of the breached wall caused him agony and it seemed to him that he made a considerable amount of noise, but at length he passed the point of balance, tipped forward and fell face foremost into the mud on the far side. From here, half on his belly and half on his hands and sound knee, he dragged himself up the incline and then diagonally across to the second grille.

It was Watson's cough that guided him to the actual spot. Watson had been coughing all the way from Coimbra, and Lockhart remembered its note because it reminded him of a sheep's cough in summer pastures at home. He found the main wall and then the grille and, lying full length in the pelting rain that cascaded from the steep roof, he called softly, "Watson! It's me! Lockhart! You there, Watson?" And he tapped gently on the central bar of the semicircular grille.

The coughing ceased instantly and for a moment there was silence, broken by the sough of the wind and the soft hiss of rain. Then, in a voice trembling with excitement, Watson replied from below—from a long way below, it seemed to Lockhart, who heard him squeak, "It's 'im, sir!

He's aht there callin' down to us! *Lockhart,* sir, an' signaling, be Jesus!"

There was the scrape of feet on stones and Graham's voice came to him. "Is that you, Lockhart? Is the woman with you?"

"No," Lockhart said, "but I've got a file for 'ee and you can cut through they bars in an hour if youm so minded, sir!"

"Wait, then!" There was a prolonged scuffle, followed by a whispered consultation, and then, like a man rising to the surface of a dark pool, the outline of Graham's face appeared, followed by a pair of hands that shot out and grasped the inner bars of the grille. Graham seemed very breathless and Lockhart, wondering why, suddenly realized that he was now standing on Watson's shoulders and that the level of the floor of the cellar was about eight feet below that of the courtyard. This was something he had not realized and it made the business of escape more complicated.

"Give me the file, Lockhart!" Graham said and took it, dropping it behind him on the straw. Then Watson began to cough again and Graham hissed down at him, reaching through the bars and grasping Lockhart by the wrist.

"Where's the woman? Is she still here? And you, how were you able to get here and how is your wound?"

"I don't reckon us c'n waste time on talk, sir," said Lockhart sententiously, "but the woman is washin' fer the officers and havin' the run o' the place. As fer me, I'm goin' on well enough, but I come to tell 'ee you c'n get out of here and the woman c'n give 'ee proper directions to the river. She'll have picked up that workin' along o' they Portuguese. I c'n pass any message you've a mind to give her!"

"Are there no sentries there?" Graham asked eagerly.

Lockhart briefly described the location of the two courtyards, divided by the wall. "On a night such as this," he said, "you could rendezvous down by the forge. There baint no sentry there and you could strike clean away across the moor and show 'em clean heels be marnin'!"

"You could meet us by the forge? Tomorrow, about this time?"

"No, zir, I couldn't, but she could mebbe. I'd be mazed to come along with a leg like this, zir, so you'd best make up your mind to leave me be, they baint a bad lot hereabouts, not fer foreigners, that is!"

"Can you get back to your quarters?" Graham asked.

Lockhart said no but he would wait in the porch until morning and tell the guard he had been locked out while visiting the latrines. "You won't be gone 'till the marnin' after that, so they won't know as I had a hand in the business," he said. Then, as a wave of giddiness swept over him, he sought and found Graham's hand and pressed it, saying, "Good luck to 'ee, sir, and my respects to Sergeant Major Corbett when youm back with the regiment!" And then he was gone, sliding away into the rain and darkness, dragging himself across the slush to the breach in the wall and thence, on his snail-like crawl, around the courtyard to the shelter of the porch.

They found him there in the morning, but he had no need to make excuses for his presence. He was unconscious when they carried him back to the buttery and laid him on his pallet, and one of the conscripts told Gwyneth that the wounded Englishman was dying.

The conscript exaggerated. Lockhart was sick and exhausted after his exertions and a night in the open, but he had an exceptionally tough constitution. After Gwyneth had brought him boards and fresh straw to lie on and fed him a bowl of broth begged from one of the cooks, his fever subsided and he was able to tell her, briefly, of the likelihood of Graham and the others breaking out of the cellar that night and waiting for her behind the forge. Gwyenth extracted this information while redressing his wound. The presence of the sick around her caused her no concern, for none of them understood more than a word or two of English. During the general diversion caused by the midday issue of beans she praised his courage and enterprise, and a faint flush showed under the man's pallor when she said, "I shall report this to your regimental officer when we get back, Lockhart, for it is a good soldier you are and a sorry thing we do to leave you like this. Have you any money about you or maybe a trinket or two I could use to buy you things you need?"

"Nay, woman, I've nothing," he said gruffly. Then, with a twitch of the mouth which was the nearest Lockhart came to smiling, he added, "I were never yon Lickspittle or Croyde's kind, I took the shilling and set about earning it, lass!"

She left him then, but he was in her mind for the rest of the day, more so than were the others, for it seemed to her that it was Lockhart who had more urgent need of her. She did not give her full attention to the breakout until she had ransacked an officer's kit left in an unlocked room and removed from it no more than she needed, a few silver pieces and a double plug of tobacco. If there had been anything likely to be useful to them in the immediate future she would have taken that too, but there was not and, like Lockhart, she practiced a very personal code of morality. The French, within their limits, had been just, and one took from the just no more than was needed.

The touch of Lockhart's hand and the sound of his voice had relit in Graham's heart a flame of hope that had been all but extinguished when Dillon's men had swarmed out of the marsh and taken his sword. Throughout all their adventures in the woods and mountains the sword had been a symbol of his authority and freedom of action, and as long as he could feel the leather scabbard chafing his left leg, or rest his hand for a moment on the heavy brass hilt, there was hope and a sense of purpose. Subconsciously the sword had become for him what Strawbridge's firelock had been for Strawbridge, and what the sweep's tin whistle was for Watson. Watson whiled away the dismal hours piping "The Lass of Richmond Hill" and

"The British Grenadiers," but Graham's sword had not been restored to him, and as he prowled up and down the stone floor of the wine cellar, or around the courtyard during their brief spells of exercise, he found it very difficult to contemplate the present or the future but returned again and again to the moment of capture. The conviction grew upon him that he alone was responsible for what had happened, for in contemplation of Croyde's death he had disregarded the elementary precautions of a fugitive crossing open ground, and the knowledge of this deepened his sense of personal failure. Watson made pathetic efforts to rouse him, but apart from a casual survey of their prison, or an occasional complaint to the blank-faced jailer about the discomfort and dampness of the cellar, he spent the days in moody contemplation of their communal waste of effort from the moment they had turned their backs on the bridge.

On the fifth day of their isolation the sergeant major in charge of a dozen deserters and recalcitrants penned in the adjoining cellar agreed to the Englishmen taking a walk around the courtyard, but Graham was too dispirited to use this opportunity to study the prospects of escape or even note the position of the sentries, for almost without realizing it he had set aside the notion of flight. The door was massive, the walls of close-set blocks of stone and the single window secured with inch-thick iron bars, yet these obstacles did not discourage him as much as the fact that they were now in an area heavily patrolled by French troops. He had learned something of his geographical position from Dillon's remarks. He knew, for instance, that the direction of their march had been fairly accurate and that the Tagus lay no more than a day's march to the south. He was also aware that the north bank of the river was picketed along twenty miles of its length by the main body of Masséna's army but that the southerly bank of the river was in British hands. To cross, however, was an impossibility, for even if they were able to break out and find an unguarded spot there were no boats to be had. Wellington had destroyed or taken away every river craft before retiring behind the lines around Lisbon.

There remained the original plan, the one stemming from Castobert's ironic advice, to march upstream in the opposite direction from Lisbon until they found a bridge or a ford east and north of the French picket lines, but to achieve this they would need food to sustain them for at least a week. When mobile and fully armed forage columns returned to base emptyhanded, how was it possible for fugitives to march thirty leagues across rough country already ransacked by a hundred thousand practiced thieves?

Watson bore his confinement with extraordinary cheerfulness, playing tunes on his whistle, sleeping with his mouth wide open and speculating on the immediate future. He asked himself and the others innumerable questions. Were they likely to spend the winter at the convent? Would they be marched back into France? If they were sent to France, would they be distributed among the prisoners of war in one of the fortress towns or would they end up in hulks as did the French prisoners in England? He had heard of places like Bitche, where large communities were penned together in squalid conditions—soldiers, sailors and civilians swept into the imperial net during forays up and down Europe. But there were other places where living conditions were tolerable, and perhaps they might even be exchanged. Graham did nothing to disillusion him. He was now alive to the appalling difficulties of the French in Portugal and thought it very unlikely indeed that they would detach men to escort a tiny column of prisoners across the length and breadth of the Peninsula, and even if they did it seemed probable that prisoners and escort would starve to death en route.

The health of the boy Curle began to concern them after ten days in the cellar. He had kept up extraordinarily during the march, but inactivity seemed to drain his strength far more effectively than had the rigors of the trek across the mountains. The prison diet of beans and new wine upset his stomach, and sometimes, as he sat crosslegged on his truss of straw, his eyes seemed to fill his narrow face, and their gaze, hopeless but somehow trusting, became hateful to Graham, so much so that he addressed hardly a word to him and abandoned him to Watson when he writhed with colic. Graham compelled him to take exercise when they were escorted into the yard. There, watching him shamble along in misery, Graham made up his mind that he would demand the boy's transfer to the hospital, where Lockhart could accept responsibility for him. Occasionally he thought about Gwyneth, wondering if she was installed as an officer's mistress, or whether in fact she was a prisoner in the sense that they were prisoners. He had no experience to guide him in such matters and, did not know whether women captured in the train of enemy troops were regarded as combatant or noncombatant. His sense of abandonment extended to her and it seemed to him that their close comradeship throughout the march over the mountains and down to the plains was something that had uplifted him a long time ago, belonging to the golden period of his boyhood in the woods and fields of Kent. He was aware that both Watson and Curle in their differing ways continued to look to him for encouragement and inspiration, but he had none to give them. He thought of himself as a failure, and because he had failed them he could now regard their future with indifference.

Then, in the blackness of the night, with the wind soughing through the grille and little spatters of rain driving into the cellar, Watson had gripped him by the shoulder and whispered that Lockhart was there, Lockhart the steady, the imperturbable, the silent, tireless man who walked on ahead with his firelock in the crook of his forearm, his searching gaze sweeping the peaks and valleys for the gleam of enemy metal. Graham's response to the summons was instantaneous. He sprang up like a man told that the house was on fire and heard himself babbling directions to Watson to make a back that he might reach

the grille and project himself from past to present at a
bound. Physical contact with Lockhart was a powerful
restorative, and news that Gwyneth was still free made his
heart soar, for, with this news and possession of the file,
his mental vigor leaped within him.

He said, as soon as Lockhart had gone and he had
dropped to the floor, "Curle shall do it! Curle shall stand
on our shoulders and cut through the central bar! We
shall be out of here by tomorrow night and move north to
the woods and then east, level with the river. The woman
is meeting us and she will have food and directions!"

He could not see their faces, but he could sense their
excitement. Curle was in the act of climbing on his shoulders when Watson had a better idea, reminding them that
the central wine rack was not clamped to the wall as were
all the others. They groped around until they laid hands
on it, and they were able to drag it under the grille so that
its slats formed a serviceable ladder. Graham climbed up
and tested the bar, finding it firmly secured at base and
top but rusted with years of exposure to the weather.

"I could cut through it in an hour!" he exclaimed
triumphantly, drawing the heavy file across its surface.
But then he stopped, realizing that the cutting of the
central bar would be wasted labor, for it was only the
centerpiece of the iron lattice. To make a hole large
enough for even the smallest of them to wriggle through,
it would be necessary to cut the iron clamps at each
corner where the frame was bolted into the stone. Even
then the operation would require immense patience, for
no matter how he turned and twisted in order to apply the
file to the metal, the outer surfaces of the bars could be
reached only by first removing four horizontal spikes.
Four clamps and four spikes meant eight separate cuts by
men working in a painfully cramped position.

He was battling with his disappointment when the boy's
voice reached him, cool and restrained, as though he had
sensed Graham's disappointment. "Might I take a look at
it, sir?"

Wondering at Curle's assurance, Graham climbed down and stood beside Watson while the boy took his place on the ladder and made a careful manual survey of the aperture. Presently he was down again and there was the same incongruous note of confidence in his voice when he said, "We broke out of a window like that before, sir! First we pulled the tops off the bolts, then Lieutenant Peterson used his belt, sir!"

For a moment Graham thought the boy must be wandering in his mind and apparently Watson thought so, too, for he gave Graham a discreet nudge. Trying to sound confident, Graham said, "We can take a closer look at it in daylight. Move the rack back in position."

But the boy laid an eager hand on his arm, protesting, "But it's true, sir, we did escape that way, all but Corporal Sedley, who was too fat to get through! We had to leave him stuck in the hole."

"You mean you were a prisoner once before?" Graham asked, incredulously.

"Yessir, at a place called Lugo, in the north. Montbrun's dragoons cut us off and locked us in a church while they rode off after the Forty-third, but we was gone before they came back for us, sir, all but the corporal, that is!"

"With a *belt,* you said?"

"Yessir, the lieutenant's sword belt, an' it was no thicker'n yours, sir!"

Graham's fingers sought his belt, from which the empty sword frog still dangled, but again it struck him that Curle was lightheaded. He could see no link between his belt and the heavy iron grille barring the window.

"At Lugo during the retreat on Coruña?"

"Yessir!"

"You lowered yourselves out of the window on the belt?"

"No, sir." The boy was impatient now. "Lieutenant Peterson took off his belt an' twisted it round the bars, then tightened it somehow with his scabbard. The bars snapped, sir—that is, one of them did—and there was room enough to climb through, all but the corporal, sir!"

The boy's constant reference to the unlucky corporal stuck in the hole and left to the mercy of the dragoons irritated Graham so much that he could have taken the drummer-boy by the shoulders and shaken him until his teeth rattled. He said sharply, "Never mind the corporal, Curle! Tell us how it was done! You saw it done, didn't you? Think, boy, and tell us how Lieutenant Peterson broke the iron bars with his sword belt and scabbard!"

"Jesus, he means a capstan!"

It was Watson who was excited now, and he flung himself at the frame and hauled himself up to the grille in a matter of seconds, calling over his shoulder, his voice shrill with delight, "He's right, sir, an' we can do the same 'ere, on'y a bit different, because we got a file an' c'n weaken them nuts before we start twisting! We gotter brace too, wi' this rack pressed against the wall, an' the whole lot'll come away like pullin' a tooth, it will!"

He was down beside them again, his hands groping toward Graham.

"I seen it done, sir. The boy's right about it, sir! You ties the belt to something as can't move and slips in a capstan bar, anything as'll twist round and round an' tighten up gradual like! Then she gives all of a sudden but it's like I said, sir, wi' the file we c'n weaken them clamps so as they'll come away easy like!"

They were like three boys now who have found an unexpectedly easy means of reaching a bird's nest. Graham made a loop of his belt, and Watson, after a brief tussle in the dark, managed to detach one of the iron brackets from the wine rack. They made another rapid survey and then went to work on the clamps, taking turn and turn about until their hands were raw and the sweat ran from them. All through the night they worked, the hiss of the rain drowning the rasp of the file, and shortly

before the first glimmer of light showed across the courtyard they had the belt buckled around the central bar
and braced to the heavy rack. There was room for only
one of them to work at the grille and it was Watson who
inserted the bracket, twisting slowly until the belt was
taut, then tightening an inch at a time with his face
pressed close to the grille. The other two waited immediately below, arms upraised to catch the frame if it toppled, but nothing so dramatic occurred. Instead, as Watson continued to apply pressure, the top left-hand clamp
tinkled to the floor and then, after he had tightened and
readjusted his belt, the right-hand clamp came away, so
that the grille was now secured by its lower clamps. Then
Watson ceased twisting and tested its resistance, finding
that strong pressure could bend it downward. When he
reported this Graham said, "Very well, leave it and push
the clamp into position. When they come with the rations
we'll meet them at the door and keep them at that end of
the cellar!"

His palms were stinging where the skin was stripped
from them and in the growing light he noticed that Curle's
hands were bleeding. The boy looked feverish again, and
he said gently, "That was a very good idea of yours,
Curle. Get some sleep, boy, we shall need it if we are to
get to the Tagus by this time tomorrow." Together they
replaced the wine rack and scattered straw under the
window where flakes of rust had fallen. Then they lay
down together near the door and in a moment Watson's
whining snore began to compete with the persistent drip
of the rain and isolated, indeterminate sounds that
reached them as echoes from the stone passage above.
Graham thought, as he drifted into sleep, Surely a man
couldn't wish for better comrades, a gutter rat and a waif,
with the courage of lions and the patience of starving cats
at a mousehole! If ever I get out of this I'll speak up for
them to somebody, to General Crauford perhaps, or even
Beaky if I'm given the chance!

CHAPTER EIGHT

The Tagus

❧

SHE WAS waiting for them in the shadow of the forge, a canvas bag half full of scraps slung on her shoulder. There was little more than one good meal in the bag, but it was something to sustain them throughout the march which she had planned, and which she outlined to Graham in a few whispered sentences after they had crept down the long slope, past the fishponds and out onto the track that curved across the moor.

The Tagus was due south, she said, but they must try and strike it about halfway between Santarém and Abrantes, where the French were billeted in strength. In between these two centers it was possible that pickets and patrols would be thinly stretched, for she had been told that the army was dispersed as widely as possible owing to the terrible shortage of food and forage. Her plan went beyond that, however, for she had extracted two vital pieces of information from a Portuguese woman who had been sent north from one of the river villages less than a month ago. The woman had told her of the underground grain stores placed at intervals all along the riverbank— deep, funnel-shaped excavations where, from time immemorial, the harassed peasants had stored their grain when the district was visited by bandits or requisitioning troops. There were many such pits, she said, all close to the river settlements, and they were marked by a cipher of white stones usually arranged in the shape of a Maltese cross. Some had been discovered and rifled, but if the fugitives were lucky enough to find one they might lie hidden there in reasonable safety until they could make their bid to cross the river. Graham reflected that the woman must have been a rare patriot to divulge such a communal secret to a British camp follower. He did not know that Gwyneth had purchased the information with her sole remaining possession, a topaz brooch she had carried through all her wanderings as her only reminder of the Welsh boy with whom she had left home when a girl of sixteen. The additional information Gwyneth had coaxed from the peasant concerned the gunboat patrols. Every day, she had been told, British naval cutters mounted with brass three-pounders sailed up the estuary and warped inshore to pepper the French concentrations. A famous French general called Saint-Croix had been killed outright by one of their random shots on the day the woman had been impressed into French service, and the river opposite Santarém, Abrantes and Vila Franca was seldom free from these waspish assailants, who sometimes stood off and fired at a range of under a hundred yards, slipping away the moment a French field battery was run up to reply. Their sole hope of ultimate success, Gwyneth urged, lay in making contact with one of these vessels, and the only person among them who could achieve this was Graham, who could await his opportunity to swim out and persuade the naval commander to make a landing and bring them off under the noses of the shore patrols.

It was a daring yet well-conceived plan, Graham thought as they trudged on through the darkness, but it depended upon a combination of lucky chances—the finding of one of the grain caves for lying up, the intervals between shore-posted sentries, the location of a gunboat within swimming distance and, above all, the willingness of the Navy to risk a sortie ashore for the purpose of bringing off an ensign, a private, a drummer-boy and a camp follower. Pondering this, he referred glumly to their diminished numbers, but the woman brushed aside his self-criticism, speaking with a note of authority that suited her assumption of the leadership of this final bid for the lines.

"You have held us together this far," she told him, "and if you can swim a slow current as surely as you swam a fast one back yonder, then we've a good chance of rescue!" She smiled in the darkness, adding, "Man, but I thought you were drowned that time and all the hussars would have had of us was a corpse full of flood water!"

"That and the information I carry in my boot," he said grimly, remembering what it was that caused him to turn his left foot outward in an effort to ease the pressure on his instep. They were still there, those sodden sheets covered with a French boy's scrawl and his own meticulous tally of Masséna's battalions, and he wondered if an officer like Craufurd, who always seemed to know how many cartridges every enemy *voltigeur* carried in his pouch, would laugh scornfully when he presented himself and submitted the information for what it was worth.

They made good progress in spite of the darkness, following the track across the open moor and down through a thin growth of spruce into what appeared to be a semicultivated area. They could smell the sea now, but they had no real means of correcting their direction until they reached the river. Dawn found them seven to eight miles from the convent, and they paused to discuss the wisdom of getting under cover until darkness but decided against it, for their food would not last them another twenty-four hours and nothing seemed to stir in the gray landscape that unfolded below as the light steadily grew stronger. Watson was very cheerful now, but Graham noticed that the boy was wilting, and they had to stop once or twice to wait for him to catch up. Graham told Watson to take his arm and when the sun rose, promising a mild, windless day, he limped on, his bootless foot swathed in a pad made of a waistcoat and secured with strips torn from his shirt. Graham found that the journey did not tax him overmuch, for they had no baggage or weapons to carry.

"If we run across a single armed man we're done for,"
he told Gwyneth, but she shrugged in her offhanded way
and replied, "If we were armed to the teeth we could not
fight seventy-five thousand men, Mr. Graham. At least
that number will be within field-gun range the moment we
catch sight of the river!"

They got their first glimpse of it from a low, scrub-
covered hill an hour or so later, and because the trek to it
had been so arduous and so checkered with sacrifice and
adventure, they paused in a forlorn little group looking
down upon the broad, steel-gray ribbon of water that
divided them from the hazy outline of hills on the farther
bank. From this distance it did not seem as formidable an
obstacle as had some of the torrents and defiles they had
crossed during the march south from the Mondego.

Graham said, in an effort to hearten them, "Across the
river is safety, plenty of beef and barrels of British-
brewed beer! We shall be there by this time tomorrow!"
He turned his gaze left and right, searching out signs of
cover or evidence of town or village. There was none so
far as he could see. The ground was flat and open,
covered on all sides by what looked like extensive
vineyards. It seemed as empty and uninhabited as the
mountains behind them.

They ate sparingly from the bag and then began to
thread their way through the vines, neglected and
unkempt since the forced migration of the peasants in the
days leading up to the British withdrawal into the fortifications. The going was much harder here, for the soil was
loose and there were scores of small obstructions, a wild
tangle of trailing vines and broken-down boundary
fences. They had gone less than a mile from the hill when
Graham heard Watson shout and, looking over his shoulder, saw the woman hurrying back toward Curle, who was
lying on his face, with Watson bending over him. He
retraced his steps to the foot of the slope and Watson said
glumly, "The kid's about done, sir. Stuck it well, he has,
what with no boot to 'is foot! Would it help if I give 'im

one o' mine? This ain't as bad as footing it over them bleedin' rocks!"

"He can't walk with or without boots," said the woman, flatly. "We shall have to carry him."

They lifted him, debating the best method of moving on over the hill to a long, scrub-sown ditch they had observed from farther back. The boy was only semiconscious, and Graham was struck by the ease with which they were able to lift him. He seemed to weigh less than a firelock.

"I'll carry him myself," he said, and took the inert bundle in his arms, stumbling up the slopes, with Watson and the woman ten paces ahead. There was no path here, only a series of broad, sloping terraces where the vines grew in loose, shifting soil into which their feet sank ankle-deep, but as Graham topped the last rise the woman uttered a sharp exclamation and Watson shouted a warning, so that instinctively he flung himself down, pressing himself and the boy into the furrows as the others came slithering back to him.

"Dragoons!" the woman said briefly. "On the road the far side of the ditch!"

"Did they see you?"

"I think not, but if they did there is nothing we can do against cavalry in this place. It's a patrol, not more than a dozen or so."

They crouched together a few feet below the crest of the slope and Graham heard the measured clatter of hoofs and the soft jingle of accouterments. The sounds seemed terrifyingly close and, listening intently, he could hear the squeak of leather and the rumble of voices. Then the murmur began to recede and after a few moments died away altogether in an easterly direction. After a pause Watson crawled to the summit of the fold, returning almost at once, beaming with relief.

"They gone by up the river," he said. "If we wait on a bit we c'n get down to the ditch!"

In the brief interval of waiting Graham listened to the

wheezing breath of the drummer-boy, lying where Graham had flung him, his pallid face calm but expressionless and a wide smudge of dirt across his cheek and forehead. He looked infinitely pitiful and Graham passed his hand lightly across the boy's face, trying to remove some of the dirt. Curle opened his eyes and stared back, moving his lips as though he wished to say something, but apparently he found the effort too much for him, for he gave a long shudder and closed his eyes again.

Watson was beckoning eagerly from the top of the slope now and Graham said, "Lie still, boy, I'm carrying you to cover. We're almost there, you understand?" He gathered him up and went on over the brow of the slope, then down a steeper patch to the welcome cover of the ditch.

It was a narrow irrigation channel about five feet in depth, with a thick growth of weeds on each side. There were about three inches of stagnant water at the bottom, but they jumped into it, grateful for the shelter. Graham left Curle with Watson, to splash along to a culvert that ran out of the ditch at right angles and then under the road along which the dragoons had trotted. A mile or so to the east he could see the sun sparkling on their casques, but they were nothing to worry about now, he decided. What concerned him at the moment was Curle, who was clearly incapable of marching another step. Some kind of shelter would have to be found for him until they could set about contacting a gunboat, and he looked about him anxiously for signs of one of the grain pits which Gwyneth had mentioned earlier. Seeing none, he ducked through the culvert under the road. The swift flow of water in the ditch told him that the river must be close, for he could hear the roar of its outfall at the far end. The water reached his waist as he entered the brick tunnel at the end of the ditch, but he pushed on, feeling his way step by step. The tunnel would have been an ideal place for concealment had there been a dry spot in it, but in the dim light coming from each end he could see smooth, unbroken walls, festooned with slime and weed.

Fifty yards farther on he emerged, to find that his guess had been accurate. The outfall led directly to the shingle beach of the river and there was the broad estuary right before him, close on a mile wide at this point and empty of sail. This, he decided, would have to be their line of approach, for above ground there was no speck of cover apart from the ditch and the tunnel. He was on the point of plunging back into the latter when his attention was caught by a prolonged swishing sound that seemed to come from beyond a wide bend upstream, and as he looked in that direction he saw a shower of descending stars as from an exploding firework. Within seconds of the explosion came the steady rattle of musketry, causing him to retreat hastily into the tunnel. As he made his way back along it and into the lateral excavation where he had left the others, he was mystified by the sounds of activity along the bank, certain that they were in some way connected with the gunboat patrol but recalling no precedent for the use of rockets in a ship-to-shore attack.

The file was no longer where he had left it and for the moment he panicked, stumbling through the shallows and having to restrain himself from calling their names aloud. Then, to his relief, he saw Gwyneth waving to him from the top of the ditch and he scrambled up, a curse on his lips which she checked by an impatient gesture.

"We've found one of the grain pits," she said. "I was sure there would be one hereabouts, but you must cross the road—hurry, now!"

He leaped after her, running across the road and plunging down the farther slope, where there were the remains of a gutted cottage and near its standing chimney stack a rock, carved with a crude Maltese cross. Watson and Curle were nowhere to be seen and for a moment he wondered where they could be, but before he could ask, Gwyneth pointed to a heap of stones beside the roofless stable and suddenly Watson bobbed up from ground level and said, with a grin, "Dry as a bone down 'ere, sir, an' there's grain enough to make porridge for a regiment!"

Graham crossed the garden and looked down into the funnel-shaped aperture, to see Curle lying on a bed of maize and staring up at him with his huge, trusting eyes.

They sat slightly apart from the boy and made their plans. Rank and sex had no place in their deliberations and they might have been a trio of generals, or three sergeants neither possessing seniority over the others. They argued as delegates, as a committee of three, and their terms of reference were the boy's immobility and their own desperate situation.

Graham told them of the culvert and the tunnel and mentioned the soft explosion in the sky, a phenomenon that he could define as offensive because it had provoked return fire from the bank. Watson's face was blank, but Gwyneth said, "It must have been a Congreve rocket gun. I saw one being tested on a frigate in Portsmouth harbor before we embarked. It had just such a sound as you describe."

Graham replied, "Then there is a gunboat upstream now and I can go back through the tunnel and wait until it shows round the bend."

"In daylight? They would see you from the bank and take potshots at you," she reasoned.

Watson anticipated Graham's protest, saying, "If he waits till dark the Jacks on the gunboat won't see him, neither!"

"That is so," she said gravely, "but there are ways of reducing the risk. He must wait until it is either close to darkness or on the point of dawn and we others must remain here until he can give us some kind of signal. Only then can we carry the boy down to the beach and wait in the tunnel until the boat touches shore. When that happens we can make a run of it."

"Suppose the gunboat passes here in broad day-light?"

"Then we must wait for another one. If necessary we must wait several days. We have something to eat, have we not?" She rose, sifting the grain through her fingers. "There is one other thing. How wide is the river at this point?"

"Almost a mile," Graham told her.

"And the gunboat, how much water would it draw?"

"Not above six feet," Watson said. "I watched 'em sail close in when we was took ashore through them breakers as Lisbon. 'Andy little craft, they are, an' them Jacks can 'andle 'em smart as you'd like!"

"Well, then," she said, drawing her brows together in a way Graham had noticed when she was considering tactical problems, "they will surely haul over to the far shore the moment they stand off, so as to sail home out of range of fixed batteries. That means you will have the better part of a mile to swim, Mr. Graham."

"I could swim to the farther shore if I had to," Graham said.

"Then perhaps it is your duty to do that and we need not concern ourselves about the gunboat," she said quiet-ly. When he looked at her in astonishment she went on, "You have information of value, more value than Watson and me and that drummer-boy yonder."

Deliberate desertion of them was something that had never occurred to him, not even when he had stood on the beach measuring the strength of the current. Now that she had mentioned the alternative it seemed to him a far more monstrous solution to their problem than that of surrendering to the nearest picket post and being marched into captivity.

He said sourly, "That is not my conception of duty. Surely my first duty is to the file, Gwyneth."

Watson spoke unexpectedly, avoiding Graham's eyes and fixing his gaze on the little hillock of maize between his legs.

"Maybe she's right, sir, maybe if you got acrost you could still send a boat for us. We're snug enough down here an' we got vittles, tho' they ain't Christian vittles." And like the woman he let a handful of maize trickle through his fingers, contemplating the grains as they fell.

Graham said slowly, "If I got ashore over there it might be days before I could get inside the lines. All the regiments are this side of the Tagus and it's my guess that there won't be more than a few outposts over there. Besides, if they once got my notes how much would any of them care what became of you?"

It surprised him to hear himself saying this, to learn that the bedraggled trio with whom he had shared this odyssey now meant much more to him than the approval of the High Command, more indeed than the outcome of the war, for during the past weeks his entire conception of the enterprise in which they were all engaged had undergone so many radical changes that it was difficult to regard it as anything more than a background to the personal survival of these few human beings. It was as though every man and woman he had known in the years up to the moment the shot from the hill laid Captain Sowden dead were anonymous strangers passing the window of his consciousness and only the members of the file, both dead and living, had the substance and reality of fellow members of the human race. Their survival, and a justification of their trust in him, had become far more essential to him than the approval of beings as far removed from him as, say, Wellington, and at the same time more important than his personal survival because their needs reached out beyond his estimate of himself as a soldier and embraced everything that governed his understanding of manhood.

They watched him as these thoughts, conscious and unconscious, explored the deepest recesses of his brain. At length he was able in some measure to give expression to them. He said, "We have been through this thing together, as a file, as a unit. The fact that there are only four of us left makes no difference to what I regard as my duty. If, for some reason, I fail to stop the gunboat, then I will swim back to you and we will try some other way. Whatever we do now we will do together, the way we have come this far."

The woman flushed as he said this and the flush proclaimed her pride in him. She had found him a boy and now he was the only type of man she could understand and value. He had learned all the lessons she had read him since the night they had been deprived of the sergeant's leadership. Now he could wear the badge she had sewn for him, and the knowledge that this was so filled her with the deepest kind of satisfaction. She watched him draw off his cracked and broken boot and extract from it a hard-packed roll of paper covered with writing now blurred by water that had leaked in at the toe. He did not know if the notes he had made were still legible or could be made so and he did not attempt to unroll the papers.

"Keep it for what it is worth," he told her, "and if they are against coming ashore for you, then I shall have something to tempt them."

She took the mess of paper, slipping it into a moleskin bag that hung around her neck and tucked inside her bodice. He had never known what the bag contained and did not ask now, judging it to be some small items of personal loot that she had never disclosed. Then she rose and told them that she was going to risk a fire on the open hearth of the ruined cottage and that he and Watson must watch the road in case cavalry patrols were attracted by the smoke.

"I shall make maize porridge," she said, "for it is necessary that we have hot food in our stomachs, you most of all." She nodded and scrambled up the funnel to the open.

Watson followed at once, but Graham remained a moment to talk to the boy. All the time they had been deliberating Curle had lain quite still and Graham wondered if his silence and immobility were caused by physical exhaustion or whether in fact he was dying. His eyes showed that he was aware of what was taking place around him, but the will to contribute was gone, wasted over the long hungry marches and the spell in the wine cellar. Graham lifted the boy's hand and pressed it, feeling as he did so like a physician at the bedside of a dying child.

"We shall soon be out of this and back with the regiment, Curle," he said deliberately. "You have been as good as any grown man and I shall tell the sergeant major to give you a new side drum as soon as we get to Lisbon. Then, when spring comes round, we shall all advance and push the French back into Spain and afterward across the mountains to France. You will be marching with the regiment when they do this, Curle, and it will have been a fine thing to have chased Boney a thousand miles! You will eat the woman's porridge if I bring you some?"

The boy smiled and nodded and suddenly Graham felt his throat constrict. He rose quickly, climbing into the open and taking up his position east of the cottage where Gwyneth was already mashing maize in the battered canteen, the sole communal possession of the file. The landscape was still empty except for Watson on guard a short way down the road. A faint sound came to Graham as he stood looking toward the east. It was the irrepressible Cockney whistling a snatch from his favorite tune, "The British Grenadiers."

Gwyneth insisted on accompanying him through the tunnel, declaring that a reconnaissance was necessary on her part if they were to carry the boy to the boat when Graham alerted them by signal. He was aware, however, that this was not the real reason she followed him as far as the beach. She wanted to stand behind him up to the moment he plunged into the river and began his swim. They had been unable to decide in advance what kind of signal he would give. It would depend, she said, upon whether the skipper of the gunboat carried colored signal flares and was prepared to use them, or whether he would allow a signal to be made at all. So much, indeed, had to be left to chance and the exigencies of the moment, and now that it was within an hour of dusk and the river was quiet and empty, it was more than likely that there was no gunboat within miles. All that was settled was that Graham should maintain a shore watch from dusk to dawn and be ready to swim out if there was the slightest chance of intercepting a vessel and bringing it inshore to the north bank. It had seemed a workable enough plan when they had discussed it, but now, as they waded through the slime of the tunnel toward the pinprick of light at the far end, the entire project struck Graham as absurdly optimistic.

The beach here was no more than twenty yards wide, narrowing to a strip where the river swept around in a wide easterly curve beyond which lay the French cantonments at which the rocket gun had been firing earlier in the day.

There was a sandy hillock crowned with coarse grass near the tunnel mouth and they climbed it, taking up a position on the summit where they could look across to the southern bank and downstream for more than a mile. Their view upstream was blocked by the bluff.

The last rays of the sun lit up the sky in the direction of Lisbon. It was difficult to imagine that no more than ten miles in that direction lay Wellington's army or that upstream, and almost certainly downstream as well, were the greater part of three French army corps strung out along the bank and in occupation of every town, village and hamlet between the river and the foot of the mountains. They remained there without saying much until the light faded and a fresh breeze, rain-laden as always, blew down from the mountains, chilling them and causing them to draw together for warmth. Yet they were neither unhappy nor tense, for the sense of companionship they drew one from the other was like hot food in their bellies, spreading comfort and confidence throughout their bodies.

"The gunboat has gone," he said finally, and she replied cheerfully, "Ah so, but it will come again at first light. I shall watch with you through the night, Mr. Graham."

A shared vigil had no part in their plan, but he accepted her decision most gladly, telling himself that perhaps it was a better course for her to remain within full view of the river, where she could not fail to see any signal he was able to send from the gunboat. Watson would not fret, he was safe in the grain pit and had implicit faith in her judgment.

"Then I am still 'Mr. Graham' to you, Gwyneth," he said, smiling. "I told you my name was Keith, but you have never once used it."

"I have lost the habit of using given names," she told him, with a shrug.

"But you referred to the Highlander as Donald."

"Because his name was Donaldson. I do not remember ever calling my other husbands anything but the names by which they were known on the muster rolls."

Something in the way she said this, as though she was already anticipating a string of future file husbands, made him sharply aware that the gunboat would mean the end of their association, and the thought dismayed him utterly. He said anxiously, "If we are lucky enough to get picked up and taken to Lisbon, will we continue to meet and talk to one another again, Gwyneth?"

"Ah yes," she said lightly, "for our army is too small to get lost in and from time to time, no doubt, we shall meet on the line of march or in bivouac and perhaps, when we do, you will stop and exchange a joke or a flask of rum with me!"

"Nothing more than that? Chance meetings by the roadside?"

She turned on her elbow and regarded him intently,

and in the swiftly fading light he thought that her eyes were smiling.

"You must know that there is no provision for officers' women on the march," she said. Then, with a note of laughter in her voice, "Officers have wives who await them in the garrison towns at home, pretty, scented women, who occupy their time with embroidery until such time as their man returns to give them children to console them during campaigns overseas."

"You know well enough that I have no such wife!" he said sulkily.

"Ah so," she said, "but you will find one when you return after the war, and in the meantime there is always the bordello."

"There would be no joy for me in a bordello," he said grimly. Suddenly, seizing her by the shoulder: "You mean to take another husband if we get back to the regiment?"

She looked at him calmly. "Why, surely! What other way is it possible for a woman to follow the drum?"

There had never been a moment since the night of their first conversation after the flight from the church when he had been unaware of the impermanence of their association, yet now, as she told him unemotionally that she had every intention of forming a fourth semiofficial alliance with a ranker, he felt a sharp stab of jealousy.

"I have no intention of devoting my life to the Army," he told her savagely. "I have seen too much bloodshed and misery to encourage me to soldier until I am retired on half pay!"

She seemed astonished by this declaration. "What else can a man like you do?"

"That is something I will think about between now and the end of my present engagement," he told her, but she made a vague, chopping motion with her hand, as though impatient with his prattle.

"You talk like a fool," she said bluntly. "When this campaign ends you will be well trained as a soldier, a captain perhaps or, if you come by nothing worse than flesh wounds, a major! Why should you throw away such hard-won experience? Besides"—a note of contempt entered her voice—"you have seen nothing yet! A few skirmishes in the mountains, a few leagues marched on am empty stomach! Pah, do not let us waste our time with such idiot's talk!"

"You think there is nothing in life but marching and fighting?"

"For men such as you, Mr. Graham? No, there is nothing, not once it is well begun as you have begun it. There are men, officers and privates, who take up arms and lay them down as soon as they see blood on their blades, but you are not such a man, not now, not when you have come this far and done what you have done for men like Watson and the drummer-boy yonder!"

"What have I done?" he demanded, laying his hand on her as though striving to equalize their relationship once more. "What have I done but blunder from error to error, losing a man at every turn of the road? Tell me, then, where are these qualities of leadership you speak of? What right have I to expect men like Watson to follow me up hill and down dale in a quarrel that I no longer understand?"

She pushed him away with both hands and it seemed to him that suddenly she was angry, both resenting and rejecting physical contact with him.

"You have brought us thus far," she declared. "You have done what you set out to do, brought this file to the banks of the Tagus."

"The file," he said bitterly. "There are two left of the eight who set out under my command!"

"The two weakest!" she reminded him, and there was a ring of triumph in her voice as though she was satisfied that the strong who had fallen along the route were strays and discards outside his responsibility.

"There is glory in that," she went on passionately, "and also in the change you have wrought in yourself. When I first looked on you back where my Highlander was laid you were a frightened boy who puked at the sight of a hussar, but now you are a man fit to lead a regiment over the Sierra to Paris itself! Do you think soldiers like Crauford and Tom Picton will fail to understand this the moment they set eyes on you?"

He said nothing for a moment. Instead he lay still, looking down at the river, basking in the warmth of her declaration, for suddenly her words were like a trumpet blast summoning reserves of courage and self-confidence he would have thought were spent uselessly along the road they had traveled. And as his blood quickened to her challenge there awoke in him a terribly urgent desire to possess her again and at once. She recognized and welcomed his urgency, yet even in these surroundings she was still a slave to practical details, for she gestured to him to move down from the crest of the hillock, and when he did so she began scooping with her hands to make a little hollow in the sandy soil where they could find protection from the wind.

"It will not be light enough to watch the river for hours," she told him, "and what chance will you have if you begin your swim stiff with cold? Here, eat while I make some kind of shelter." She thrust her canvas bag into his hand and returned to her digging, undercutting the bank until she had scooped out a tiny cave where there was just enough room for them to lie under the downslope of the hillock.

He put his hand into the bag, feeling among the scavenger's harvest she had provided, but was disinclined to sample the stale scraps he found there, for he had eaten his fill of maize porridge before they set out.

"There is a flask here," he said. "Is it the vinegar wine that gave Curle the colic back at the convent?"

"No," she said without pausing in her digging, "it is a swallow or two of brandy, but you must not drink it yet. I have saved it for when you enter the water." She stood up, peering at him intently in the darkness. "Where is your cloak?" she demanded.

"I gave it to Curle," he told her, and she gave a snort of contempt.

"That was a fool's action! Curle sleeps dry tonight and has no need of his strength! Come close to me, it is as well I stayed with you!" She wriggled out of her dress and spread it like a blanket in the shallow excavation. "Lie down," she commanded him, "as far under the bank as you can get!" When he did so she crawled in beside him, taking the loose folds of the heavy material, throwing it over them and reaching across him to tuck it under his thighs and shoulders. With her right arm she pillowed his head, with the other held him closely to her breast, her hair tumbling about his face. Lying so, he was enclosed in her possessiveness, and warmth returned to him, vanquishing the damp and fatigue and suspending him between the ardors of the past and the uncertainties of the morrow. Above them the rain-laden wind came searching down from the mountains; behind, the big river warbled over a million stones on its way to the Atlantic. But he forgot mountains and river in the sanctuary of her strong, wholesome body, and this was not because of the physical protection it offered but because she was willing him warmth and comfort with the whole of her being, drawing upon the reserves of countless Celtic ancestors, each a woman whose usefulness had been measured by the solace she could offer a mate.

CHAPTER NINE

The Gunboat

~~~

THEY SAW it in the first moment of dawn, breasting up the river and looking, in the far distance, like a cloud riding the water, then as a large, leisurely swan, and finally for what it was, a forty-ton sloop with sails spread in the stiff westerly breeze and its bow wave advancing from perhaps two miles distant, a quarter mile offshore.

There was no time to deliberate, for it was approaching at a spanking pace and even as he stripped off tunic and breeches the sun caught its brass deck cannon and threw back diamond-hard rays of light, advertising the vessel's purpose there at that early hour. He said as they scrambled down the bank, "Will you wait in the tunnel?"

But she replied, "No! It's all or nothing now, Mr. Graham! I'll fetch the others as soon as I can and we must take our chance in the open. If you reach it and the captain will heave to, then our chances are good, for there is nothing here to fire at them. Go now and God give you strength, boy!" She seized his hand and kissed it, then ran swiftly toward the culvert, her dress bundled under her arm.

The first plunge snatched at his breath so that he rose gasping and spluttering, the slow current lifting him and, to his relief, slanting him upstream more or less in the path of the oncoming sloop. He realized this at once and fought to use it to his advantage, swimming overarm at an angle of forty-five degrees to the bank in the hope that their paths through the water would converge at a point his side of the wide bend. He knew that if he misjudged the distance, or failed for one instant to maintain his pace, he was lost, for despite his boast he now realized that he would never have the strength to swim back to the shore but would be swept by the slow current clear around the bend and into the presence of the enemy shore pickets. He thought as he struggled, We've been so lucky up to now, lucky to get this far and luckier still to find this blind spot in their patrols. It is for me to use that luck and reach the middle of the river before the sloop passes within view of the French. And he gritted his teeth and struck out with all his power, using the crawl kick that his father's gamekeeper, Rowley, had taught him in the river reaches as a child, keeping his head down but raising himself every dozen strokes in order to keep the prow of the gunboat in view.

He had forgotten the cold now, for he was fighting a different enemy, a dizziness that sought to confuse sky and water and gave him the feeling of struggling in a world without substance or gravity. The weak sunlight blinded him at a moment when he needed his judgment more desperately than he had ever needed it in the past. The water was choppy out here, and twice he swallowed great draughts, the second dragging him below the surface, but when he rose again there she was within yards of him, looking as huge as a man-o'-war, with snouted cannon peeping from the bows and the jib sail rushing down on him like a huge white bird. He threw himself over on his back and raised one arm, reaching up out of the water and shouting with the full power of his half-drowned lungs. Then the bow veered sharply away from him and as the bow wave struck him something smacked into the water within a yard of him. Without in the least realizing what it was he shot out both hands and took hold of a bulky cork float to which a rope was attached, and he knew, as his nails dug into the yielding substance, that he had succeeded, that the vessel was indeed veering to starboard and dragging him through the water at what seemed to him a prodigious rate. Then he heard voices,

British voices, very close at hand, and there was another hard splash, this time almost on top of him, and somebody shouted, "Haul away, haul away, damme!" and the feeling of disembodiment engulfed him altogether, the sky and water meeting in tumbling confusion and the sun twinkling on a million points so that he could see nothing but the cordage binding the cork float clasped to his chest.

He came to himself when they were holding a bottle to his mouth. He could hear his teeth clattering against the neck and instantly recalled his purpose, thrusting the bottle aside so that rum gushed onto the deck as he pointed frantically toward the shore. Two sailors were on their knees beside him, slapping and rubbing him with hard, crusted palms, and an officer in dazzling white breeches and stockings was looking down at him with an expression of angry concentration. The rum they had forced down his throat brought a glow to his belly, and as he struggled to his knees, pushing aside the hands of the sailors, he managed to gasp, "British stragglers on shore—through the lines—vital information—Lisbon!" before rum met the water he had swallowed and seemed to boil inside him, causing him to fall forward on hands and knees and retch over the officer's buckled shoes.

Despite his stern expression the man did not appear to resent this indignity but bent down and raised Graham to his feet, waving the grinning sailors on one side and fixing Graham with a pair of piercing blue eyes.

"Stragglers, you say? How many? Where did you come from?" Without waiting for a reply, he stood smartly aside, grabbed the rum bottle from one of the men and thrust it into Graham's hand, saying, "Get some more of that into you!" and, turning, "Hard to starboard! Ease her off there!" as the boat shuddered around and the jibs cracked like a salvo of cannon shots above their heads.

Graham steadied himself, deliberately swallowing two mouthfuls of rum. When he lowered the bottle he noticed the envious expression of one of the sailors, whose tongue shot out around his lips as he dropped his gaze to the pool of spirit on the white deck. Then the officer was back with them and addressing Graham in a rasping voice.

"Who the devil are you? Where do you come from? How do you come to be drowning in the middle of the river?"

The second draught of rum must have had a powerful restorative effect, for almost at once Graham's head and vision cleared, sufficiently so for him to note that the sloop was now on an almost reverse course, tacking aslant the breeze with mainsail flapping and bulwarks rising and falling sharply on the tide.

"Ensign Graham, Fifty-first Regiment of Foot," he gasped. "We came over the mountains from the Mondego. The others are in a culvert on the beach and you must send a longboat at once before the dragoons pick them off!"

He did not address the lieutenant as "sir," did not in fact so much as notice his rank, but his urgency melted some of the frostiness in the man's voice and eyes and for a moment the lieutenant seemed bewildered.

"God gut me!" he suddenly snapped. "You want me to send a boat ashore? Here and now?"

"There are no French close enough to take you if you went in and out at once," Graham said, holding his breath as the lieutenant gauged the distance to the shore and then looked at the ship's boat towing astern. As the man still hesitated he said deliberately, "We crossed the French line of march and I made a tally of their strength. Everything is there, written down for General Crauford, but the woman has it!"

"There is a woman with you?"

"A camp follower from the Forty-third Highlanders and two of my men, one of them unable to walk. We have been hiding in a grain pit and the woman is fetching them now!"

As he said this a squat bowlegged seaman approached and saluted with the careless lift of the hand that passes for an acknowledgment of rank among seamen. "She's losing way in the scour, sir! Should we drop anchor? There's four fathoms hereabouts!"

"No, damn you!" roared the lieutenant. "Heave to and take four men ashore for stragglers. And be sharp about it! If they run out one of their field batteries I shall scud away and leave you to it! Gantry!" he bawled at a knot of pigtailed seamen standing between twin cannon in the stern. "Keep your guns trained on that hillock yonder, but if you fire without orders I'll flay the four of you! Ensign," he flung back at Graham, "in the name of God get below and find some clothes."

Suddenly, as the vessel swung in a slow, graceful circle toward its former course, the deck erupted with running figures and Graham was hustled below and pushed into a tiny cabin amidships, where someone flung him a jersey and a pair of canvas trousers. They offered him food, but he refused it, hurrying on deck and taking his stand near the wheel. Here he hardly noticed the mad bustle around him but fixed his attention on the strip of beach immediately adjoining the hillock, gazing across the gray stretch of water in an effort to pinpoint the half-submerged tunnel mouth through which he had waded the previous day. He could not see it and for a moment his belly contracted with fear lest the tide should have carried the vessel upstream out of reach of the spot where he had commenced his swim. Then he recognized a hump in the shingle where the culvert ended and he knew they were no more than two hundred yards upstream of the outfall. He watched the longboat pull around in a close circle before shooting inshore, the harsh rattle of its keel carrying across the river. His mind was now frantic with calculations of time and distance, how long it would have taken Gwyneth to wade back through the tunnel, climb the culvert bank, summon Watson and Curle from the grain pit and return the way she had come.

The lieutenant had said he could not wait, that if fired upon from the shore batteries he would abandon boat and crew to their fate and stand off out of range, and Graham found himself praying for the trio battling their way through the waist-high sludge of the tunnel. He heard himself muttering over and over again, "God make them hurry, God give them strength!" Suddenly somebody jogged his elbow and, turning, he saw the lieutenant, his glowering expression softened somewhat by a quirk at the corners of his mouth.

"Take the glass! There are cavalry coming down the road, but I doubt if they're mad enough to ride in under our guns! If they do I shall liven them up with grape." And the lieutenant strolled aft, calmer now, to address a group of gunners standing between the two brass stern-chasers with linstocks and slow matches in their hands.

Graham's hands trembled so violently as he lifted the brass telescope that at first he could see nothing but the empty stretch of shingle between hillock and culvert. Then the boat and its crew leaped into focus, and as it did so two of the sailors began to run up the beach toward the culvert. Leaping ahead of them, Graham's glass picked up three bunched figures coming out of the dip. It was the woman and Watson, carrying the boy between them, and Curle seemed to be held semi-rigid on what looked like a length of pole. In spite of their burden the two seemed to cross the shingle with great speed, and Graham, in his eagerness to keep them in focus, overreached the group and swung to the left. Then, before he could pick them out again, he saw a little cloud of horsemen jostling down the gully higher up the beach and he swung the telescope down like a flail, screaming the news to the group beside the cannons. But the gunners had already seen them and Graham's warning shout was lost in the roar of the guns, and when he raised his glass again the gully was empty and the little group of figures were already swarming around the boat.

A single discharge at French cavalry appeared to have mellowed the lieutenant, for when he returned to Graham he was grinning like a schoolboy. "The cavalry never learn," he said casually, "perhaps because they once captured the Dutch fleet with a squadron of hussars! That was in the Texel years ago and anyway the ships were icebound. Yesterday I dropped a shrapnel shell into the middle of a bunch of cuirassiers. It was like cracking lobsters with a belaying pin!"

Watson had seen the cavalry a few moments before the woman came storming up the bank and across the road to the grain pit. He had climbed into the open to get Curle some water and because the canteen was half full of maize porridge he used his battered shako, dipping it in the running water at the bottom of the culvert. On his way back across the road he saw a stout oak beanpole and it occurred to him that if Curle had to be carried through the tunnel to the beach this might prove useful, so he tucked it under his arm and was on the point of jumping down into the garden when he saw the group of horsemen approaching from the west.

They were still more than a mile distant and he was certain they could not have seen him, but he was alarmed for the woman, who at any moment might emerge from the tunnel, climb the bank and cross the road in full view of them. At that moment, as he crouched under the wall, he saw a pair of herons soar up from the point where the culvert entered the tunnel and he knew instinctively that they had been disturbed by her approach. For a few seconds he dithered, wondering whether to leap into the grain pit or run across the road and warn her, and then he realized that if he did the patrol would be sure to see him on the way back, for the distance between them and where he stood was narrowing and they seemed to be advancing at a fast trot. The early-morning sun flashed on their casques and breastplates and at once he identified them as cuirassiers, who did not move at the speed of the light cavalry, and the memory of this decided him. He left Gwyneth to take care of herself and leaped into the pit, dragging Curle to his feet and shouting, "We gotter run for it, son, we gotter get out o' here!" When the boy sagged Watson gasped with dismay, realizing that Curle did not possess the strength to climb out of the pit.

In that moment he thought with rage of Strawbridge's slow, ponderous strength and how his file mate would have lifted Curle like a small portmanteau and hoisted himself into the open, across the road and into the safety of the tunnel. He reckoned that he had perhaps two minutes before the cuirassiers came within pistol range and in that period he had somehow to get Curle out of the pit and across the road, drop into the culvert and seek help from the woman. He was a very small man, not much taller or broader than the boy, but the urgency of the situation gave him a measure of ingenuity as well as an access of physical strength. He jerked Curle to his feet, scrambled out of the pit without releasing his hold on the boy's collar, shifted his grip to the armpits and dragged the drummer into the open like a man extracting a tent peg from a bed of clay. As soon as Curle was clear he snatched his crossbelts and began lacing the boy's wrists and ankles to the bean post, and as he worked at feverish speed he cocked an ear for the rattle of hoofs on the road. What he heard first, however, was Gwyneth's shout as she rushed across the road and appeared on the wall of the cottage. When he glanced over his shoulder and saw her standing there in mud-spattered corset and drawers, the incongruity of her sudden appearance made him pause in his work and gape with astonishment, for she did not look like a woman at all but like a bedraggled fury, her matted hair half obscuring her face, and her mouth wide open in a shout of warning. Then she was down beside him and he did not have to explain to her why Curle was lying at their feet like a trussed fowl, for at once she grabbed the end of the pole nearest the boy's feet as he seized the other end, and between them they set off at a stumbling run, mounting the broken wall and scrambling down onto the road in a matter of seconds.

They were only just in time. The leading file of cuirassiers was about a hundred meters down the road, and the moment they appeared, dashing across the road and up the bank that enclosed the culvert, the leading horsemen bellowed a view-halloo and urged their horses into a canter. Their outcry was taken up by the files in their rear and the column bunched a moment before rushing down on the cottage in a body.

Watson got no more than a fleeting glimpse of the charge before he was down the bank and into the culvert, and after that he had no inclination to look over his shoulder at the men who came pouring over the bank in pursuit, yelling like excited huntsmen within a few strides of the death.

What saved the quarry was not speed and agility on the part of Watson and the woman but the collapse of the bank under the weight of the horses. The second of them became involved in a miniature landslide of mud and stones, and for a few vital moments the narrow stream bed was blocked by a confused mass of slithering horses and cursing men, all getting in one another's way as the troopers struck at the horses with their long, straight swords. In the brief interval that it took the leaders to fight clear of the melee Watson and Gwyneth reached the tunnel, where the water rose to their waists and no horse could follow them. The leading cuirassier, who had not been involved in the struggle, thundered along the culvert, swung himself out of the saddle and entered the tunnel, but he was hopelessly handicapped by his heavy topboots and spurs and after a few strides turned and groped his way back to the culvert to assist his comrades in getting their excited horses back onto firmer ground.

The tunnel seemed endless. With the pole resting across their shoulders they just managed to keep the boy clear of the water, but it was as much as they could do to maintain a footing on the slime-covered floor. Neither of them spoke as they struggled toward the exit, but when at last they struggled out onto the beach Gwyneth gasped,

"If the cavalry find a way down to the beach we're done for, Watson! Stay here with the boy and I'll show myself. We've nothing to lose now. It rests on how quick they are with the boat."

"We should ha' kept 'id an' let the bleeders go past," he grunted, but she was already running along the shingle to the knoll, where she could keep road and river under observation. The sloop was there, broadside on to the tide. As she watched the longboat cast off, its crew pulling aslant the current and heading directly for the tunnel mouth. A moment later she saw the cuirassiers, cavorting about on the marshy strip bordering the road but unable, it seemed, to approach the river directly because of the waterlogged ground. She thought for a moment of the soggy roll of papers in her moleskin bag and wondered whether to throw them away, for she was under no illusion as to what would happen to her if she was caught and searched, but a glance at the river showed her that the boat was now more than halfway to the shore and she ran down from the hillock shouting and waving and along the beach to where Watson waited with the boy.

"Come," she said, seizing her end of the pole, "we must chance their fire. We are lucky they are cuirassiers, they have no carbines, just pistols." And together they lifted the drummer and set off to the water's edge as the boat swung around and shot inshore.

They heard the roar of the guns, and to Gwyneth, slithering across the last few yards of beach toward the knot of sailors, the sound came as the final salute of the campaign. A moment later the seamen had them and Curle had been dragged into the boat, and as the sailors thrust off with their long sweeps she caught a fleeting glimpse of horsemen scattering beyond the rim of the dunes and busied herself unbuckling Curle from the pole, chafing his wrists where the leather had bitten into the flesh.

Watson, watching her with a small, crooked smile, said, "Well, we done it!"

But the boatswain, looking reproachfully in the direction of the sloop, said, "Aaron Gantry has been at the rum again. That grape was ten yards short of the nearest of 'em!"

The lieutenant addressed Graham as he went aft when the shot had scattered the cavalry, but Graham did not hear what he said. He was too intent on the boat as it shot into the current, then spun in a slow circle as the crew bent to their oars, heading for midstream a quarter mile below the sloop. The vessel was pitching violently now and it was impossible to focus the glass on the group huddled in the stern, in addition to which, renewed bustle was taking place about him. A sense of loneliness invaded him, as though, from the deck of an alien vessel, he were watching his homeland recede and rain fall on the last of his kin in the boat astern. For a few moments his sense of time was suspended, past and present merging one with the other as in a dream. He stood quite still, gripping the rail, looking beyond the boat to the flat, featureless shore and the outline of mountains beyond, and as he stood thus the file marched across his memory like a procession of proud beggars who wore their rags like ermine and bore their arms like kings. Morgan and Fox were there, climbing the slopes of the first ravines, and Lickspittle, with his sullen mouth, and Strawbridge with his foolish countryman's grin. Then Croyde, poised on the rock and looking fearfully at the rope bridge, and last of all Lockhart, with his firelock crooked in his elbow as he marched on ahead, searching out the path they would follow.

The boat was making fast now and sailors were crowding the bulwarks, shouting down the inevitable jokes that had passed between tars and infantrymen over centuries of warfare, but as Graham moved to get a better view of the figures in the stern his feet tangled with a coil of rope and he stumbled, falling forward on hands and knees, his forehead striking a projecting stay. It was no more than a touch and he hardly noticed the shock, but when he tried to stand upright his knees buckled and his hands slid across the deck as the confusion of sky and sea that he had experienced in the water settled on his brain with the density of mountain fog, and the slap of bare feet on scrubbed planks sounded in his ears like the drumbeats of an advancing army. The glass slipped from his hand and rolled into the scuppers as more men came scrambling on deck and the sloop bore around into the full drag of the tide.

They had carried Curle below before anyone noticed Graham stretched unconscious on the deck, but they raised him gently enough and carried him after the boy. The lieutenant watched them go and after them Watson, still able to twist his mouth into a wry grin that was part triumph and part anticipation of a double noggin of Navy rum. Last of all came the woman, treading the decks as one well accustomed to shipboard, and holding the sordid remnants of her incongruous green gown. With more than half his attention on the ship's way, the lieutenant noticed these things, the helplessness of the ensign and the drummer-boy, the jauntiness of the guttersnipe Watson, but more striking than either of these was the bearing of the half-naked camp drab, and although he had been at sea since he was a child of twelve and was well accustomed to these things the lieutenant knew pity and was ready to recognize and salute the undefeated. As the woman passed down the companionway after the others he said, half to himself and half to Gantry the gunner, "All the way from the Mondego on their flat feet!" He turned to the quartermaster at his elbow, adding, "Feed 'em with the best you have aboard, Marriott, and don't spare the rum!"

Then he moved aft, lifting his glass and searching for signs of enemy movement among the bluffs beyond the bend.

CHAPTER TEN

Vale

❧

GRAHAM WAS discharged from the officers' sick quarters in the Convent da Estrela on the fifth day of December, four weeks to the day after the sloop *Prometheus* had disembarked the survivors of the file at a ration wharf in Lisbon. They had not waited until he was fit or clearheaded before they set to work to wrest from him a detailed account of the march south and southeast from Coimbra, but had pestered him quite mercilessly with relays of officers, British and Portuguese, who probed his memory, double-checking the almost illegible notes that had been copied out under the supervision of Crauford himself. Presently Crauford called, not to praise or congratulate but to query Graham's figures regarding the number of mule teams in the transport train of the Second Corps. Only when the somber master of the Light Brigade was on the point of taking his leave did Graham summon enough courage to make two personal pleas, one in respect of the boy Curle, the other concerning Watson, who was back in the bosom of his regiment. It was in pursuance of these two applications that Graham went out into the windswept streets on the fifth day of December and picked his way across the crowded city to the quarters of the Fifty-first, behind the public abattoir, where the men lived in shanties during the rest periods when they were not on duty in the hill forts and outposts of Torres Vedras.

Almost the first man he encountered on entering the stockade was Watson, crouched over a miserable fire, engrossed in the obviously agreeable task of frying salt beef and mashed vegetables in a long-handled pan. The mess in the canteen sizzled and spat. Motioning the Cockney to continue the preparation of his meal Graham sat down on a tub and offered Watson a Brazilian cheroot, one of a box sent out for invalid officers by the ladies of the Peninsular League at home.

Watson seemed fit and cheerful, in no way the worse for an experience that made Graham thankful for the upturned tub after his unsteady walk through the city, and as he watched Watson savor the cigar he reflected that perhaps Gwyneth had been wrong to class the little man as one of the two weakest of the file. Watson looked as if he had already forgotten stumbling marches through the woods and defiles and nights in the open when they had shared a single rabbit snared by Lockhart. His narrow face was still grimed with dirt, through which his brown eyes twinkled with pleasure on noting a lieutenant's chevrons on Graham's tunic. He said, with the faintest touch of embarrassment, "Can't get enough o' this chow inside me, sir. Been on double rations for the best part of a month, I 'ave! Right careless wi' their vittles is this lot. Leaves 'em lyin' around for anyone, they do!" Sniffing appreciatively, he jabbed the pan with the ramrod that he was using as a stir-pot.

Graham said quietly, "As a lieutenant I can have a permanent soldier servant. I came down here to tell you that you can be my servant if you wish. You would have better quarters than this and as much food as you can eat, so long as we are in garrison. I would pay you myself, so there would be no waiting about for arrears as you do now. Does the notion appeal to you, or would you rather remain with your friends?"

Watson licked his lips, forgetting the pan for a moment as he glanced across at the huddle of shanties surrounding the fire. Smoke rose from a hundred fires, and half-dressed men came and went about their routine tasks.

"Friends, you said? I got no friends among this lot, sir.

Old Turnip'ead Strawbridge was my real mate and I'm gonner get quits wi' them murderin' Portuguese one o' these days! Turnip'ead, an' arter him Jimmy Lockhart as we left behind in the clink. As fer this lot"—he jerked his head contemptuously toward the camp—"they're noo to it, most of 'em, and if they'd 'ave been cut off like we was they would 'ave given up the first day, I reckon. Takes luck to find sodjers like Turnip'ead an' Jim Lockhart, it do!"

"Then you'll come?"

"I'd be right glad to, sir, 'specially when we git movin' again. Yes, sir, I'd be glad to and I'd do me best for you, you c'n lay to that. I'd keep yer clothes smart-like an' I c'n cook better'n most of 'em. We won't go short o' nothin', not if it's left lyin' around, sir!" And he saluted without moving from his seat.

Graham smiled, finding that the sweep's lively acceptance of the post renewed his faith in the future, inasmuch as it offered some kind of continuity. "Where will I find Curle?" he asked, and noticed that Watson's face clouded.

"Curle? He'll never campaign no more, will the boy, sir!" he said resentfully. "He's still in sick quarters over beyond the slaughterhouse. Seen 'im every so often, I 'ave, an' took 'im food more'n once, but somehow he don't put on flesh, not like he should. Mebbe it's the consumption?"

"Perhaps," Graham said soberly. "They told me he was ill and I've got his discharge papers here. He's going home soon."

Watson looked startled. " 'Ome? Curle fer 'ome, sir? Wot 'ome's he got, barrin' the regiment?"

"My home," said Graham. Then, because it embarrassed him to pose as a benefactor before this grimy little sparrow, he rose abruptly, adding, "I have quarters close to the Convent da Estrela in the city. Most of the officers of the Fifty-first are thereabouts, so pack your kit and

report there tomorrow after reveille. Meantime, take me
to Curle."

They found Curle in a large stable behind the slaughterhouse where the stench reminded Graham of wounds,
grease and unburied offal. The stable had been set aside
for disabled men who were more or less able to take care
of themselves, and noisome as it was it was sanitary
compared to the hospital wards in the main building.
Here the sick lay in close-packed rows on truckle beds,
cared for by three or four elderly nuns, fugitives from a
convent in the north, and it seemed to Graham, as he
traversed the long building, that most of the patients were
beyond hope of recovery.

They found Curle sitting on his palliasse carving a
piece of wood, and when he saw Graham and Watson his
hollow cheeks flushed with pleasure and he made a show
of rising and saluting. Graham was shocked at the boy's
condition. He was even thinner than he had looked during
the march and his huge, melancholy eyes stared back at
them with the mute appeal of a sick calf. Two or three
crippled men lay close by, engaged in a desultory game of
cards, but they were too far gone in boredom to take
more than cursory interest in the visitors. Anger rose in
Graham, but he checked it, reminding himself that his
resources were limited and that he was not here to
crusade for a reorganization of the army hospital service.

He said, with a forced smile, "I would have come
before, Curle, but I have been in hospital myself until
today. I am getting you out of here very soon!"

The boy's eyes tormented him and he was grateful to
Watson, who sidled forward and said with a swift grin,
"Mr. Graham's got yer discharge, son! Think o' that, nah!
You're fer the boat!" But the boy looked stunned, laying
aside his wood carving and placing his hands protectively
on the knapsack that served him as a pillow.

The instinctive action was not lost upon Graham, who
said, "I told General Crauford about you, Curle, and he

asked for a report on you from the regimental surgeon. After the General told me of this I wrote a letter to my father and asked him to find a place for you at my home. You will live with Rowley, the keeper, and he will teach you to trap like Lockhart. To fish too, perhaps, in the river where Rowley taught me to swim."

Still the boy did not seem reassured, and Graham realized that he must be more explicit. He sat down on a hogshead beside the pallet, with his back to the men playing cards. "You are not strong enough to follow the regiment when we move out in the spring," he went on. "You would fall out on the second day's march, but if you go home to Kent and get strong you can take the shilling again when you are a year or so older. As you are already a veteran, they will surely start you as a sergeant."

The boy spoke suddenly and Graham saw that his lip trembled so that he looked more childlike than ever, a mere infant faced with a decision that he was unequipped to make. "You will be going, too, sir?"

"Not until after the war, until we have chased the French over the mountains. Then I shall certainly go home on furlough, and when I do I can teach you to ride. We have some good horses at Addington Court!"

Watson intervened, pitying the strange helplessness of the gently bred when called upon to state the simple truth.

"Fact is you'll croak if you're left here, son," he said brutally. "Now get aboard one of them transports, eat some o' their vittles and breave fresh air, an' you'll perk up! Besides, suppose you do foller the drum when we get moving, ain't a dry bed an' reg'lar vittles a bleedin' sight better'n bivvyin' down in pourin' rain an' makin' do on 'arf-cooked 'orsemeat when we're on the march? *Ain't* it, now? Besides, you got no choice, 'ave you? You bin discharged, son, just like Mr. Graham says!"

Graham picked up the boy's knapsack and, making sure that no one but Watson observed him, he slipped two gold pieces under the flap. He knew that Curle was too

professional to let the knapsack out of his sight, even
when he visited the latrines.

"Watson's quite right," he said. "You will be taken
aboard a transport in a day or so and until then he will
stay and look after you and see you fed." And he nodded
to the boy and hurried out into the comparatively sweet
air of the yard. He knew that his request to Crauford for
the boy's discharge could save Curle's life and that the
drummer would never bear arms again. He was aware,
however, that Curle could not be expected to regard this
as a service, for it was as Watson had said: in Curle's
vocabulary the word "home" was the same as the word
"regiment."

Watson fell into step behind him and they returned
through the maze of shanties to the stockade. As by
unspoken agreement neither of them mentioned Curle or
his chance of survival, for both identified the boy's condition with the deadly attrition of the file as a unit. Then, as
they reached the gate, Graham saw the woman.

His excursion to the camping ground of the Fifty-first
had been a tying of loose ends in respect of Watson and
Curle. What he had done for each of them represented
the closing of the book on their odyssey, and he had not
anticipated finding Gwyneth here—in a different but
scarcely less tattered gown, with an old chip bonnet
clamped on her unruly hair. The shyness he had experienced on meeting Watson and Curle returned to him as
he advanced to where she stood, her arms folded across
her breast, her weight resting against the square bulk of
the gatepost. Many times during his convalescence he had
rehearsed words he would say to her when they met
again, but now he was as tongue-tied as a youth at his
first tryst and their differences in age and experience
seemed greater than ever. Watson drifted back to his fire
as Graham advanced uncertainly, his face stiff with a
forced grin.

"I did not know you were in camp, Gwyneth. Watson
said nothing . . ."

She at once assumed command in the way she had made decisions during the march, taking him by the hand and leading him through the gate to a steep cobbled street that sloped down to the waterfront. As he glanced at her he was struck once again by her essential freshness and bloom, suggesting a background infinitely remote from that of a squalid camp teeming with unwashed men and rank with the stink of wood smoke and cooking fat.

They exchanged no word until they had left the hutments behind and emerged onto the quay, where the bay lay open before them. Across the ship-studded water lay the white terraces of Almada. The only movement out there was the beetlelike progress of lighters and wherries plying to and fro from the anchored transports and men-o'-war. She pointed to one of the dram shops fronting the quay, most of them empty at this hour of the day, and they passed under the awning and sat down at a table. A pair of excessively fat friars were conversing in low tones in the farthest corner, but they were too engrossed to pay any attention to them. An olive-skinned slattern came forward to serve them with thimble-sized cups of coffee.

When the woman had withdrawn Graham said, "Crauford came to the hospital and I arranged for Watson to become my servant and also for Curle to be discharged. I am sending the boy to my home in Kent." Then, truculently, "You have found another man, Gwyneth?"

"No," she said, with a half-smile, "but I am considering offers!"

He had the impression that she was mocking his youth and inexperience, perhaps even his clumsiness as a lover, and at once his temper flared. He was no longer the leader and officer, concerned in maintaining his dignity and social ascendancy, but a young man whose blood was quickened by the presence of a woman he had twice held in his arms and who yearned to do so again and again, but on his own terms, not hers. So urgent was this demand that he reached forward, his fingers enclosing her bare arm, his eyes glancing furtively at the muttering friars in the corner of the room. The laughter went out of her eyes as he declared passionately, "Everything I did out there I did on your account, Gwyneth! What purpose was it all if we are never to see one another again?"

"What purpose?" She stared back at him without withdrawing her arm from his grasp. "We got through, the four of us! Besides, out there you needed me!"

"I need you now and always, Gwyneth!"

But she shook her head. "No! You understand nothing of women, not even women of your own kind, but because of me you will learn when you go among them again. Do you think that a word from you could change me into the kind of wife you will need when you rise in rank or live among civilized people once more? What would I do in a great house such as yours, with servants to scold and linen to count? And if, so be it, I found myself in such a place, do you think for one instant I would be content to stay there whilst you were away somewhere campaigning? No, Mr. Graham, you cannot play the rich young suitor with me, and you cannot pack me off home like the sick drummer-boy yonder! This is my place and in your heart you know it to be so. All else is no more than a boy's fancy!"

"Do you believe in God, Gwyneth?" he asked suddenly. "In the God who brought us together out there in the mountains?"

She seemed to give his question consideration. "I believe in a God of battles, the God who stood with us when we escaped from the partisans' camp, who put the file into Lockhart's hand and then gave you the strength to swim the Tagus when you were numbed and starving."

"No God of love, Gwyneth?"

"Love!" She spat the word, her full red lips curling. "What have the likes of me to do with love that poets talk of? I use my body to give strength and comfort to those whose trade is my trade! Love is for the women at home, to go along with their frills and petticoats and lavender-scented closets! You make me blush for you to make such claim on me!"

She stood up as though half in mind to turn her back on him, but he seized her hand, suddenly contrite.

"You want nothing more than to go on forever like this, until you are old and worn out and have too much damp in your bones to follow the drum wherever it leads?"

"Why should I want anything different? All the men who have used me have been good soldiers and I would never permit anyone but a fighting man to spill himself into my body! That I invited you to do so was because you had become one of the brotherhood and had acquitted yourself like a man when you were alone and desperate! This is my purpose here and without it I am nothing."

For the first time since he had seen her kneeling beside her dead Highlander he came close to understanding her true nature. There was, he reflected, no profit in confusing her with women who bore children and taught them their manners and their catechism. She was at once more than a woman and less than one, a creature whose body was a refuge for the only male creatures she accepted as men, warriors unsentimentally dedicated to the arms they carried and the exercise of their own prowess and valor, savages who exulted in their strength and their ability to overcome all obstacles interposing between them and survival. She was something out of the long-distant past, when tribes lived out their short, dangerous lives in forests where death lay in wait for the unwary and the weak, where a cleft in the rocks was hearth and home, and a man's family was fed in relation to his prowess with bow and spear. He saw this as something revealed by a flash of light on a dark night and ceased, in that instant, to quarrel with its finality. Yet a current of warmth and comradeship for her gushed through him, flushing away the cloying sweetness of the yearning he had felt for her a moment since. He understood, too, that her rejection of him was temporary, that if, in the months ahead, he had need of her, then she would make herself available, perhaps on the eve of some desperate venture, and because of his access to her ripe, vigorous body he would go into battle like a lion.

He said, smiling, "Very well, Gwyneth, when we move out in the spring I will send word to you by Watson, and the man you take is more fortunate, I think, than if you brought him a dower chest filled with all the loot in Lisbon!" He bent swiftly, kissing her brow, and walked out of the shop into the hard afternoon sunlight playing across the ruffled bay.

She let him go, a quiet smile playing about the corners of her mouth, not wishing to speak to him of his child which she knew lay in her womb, for this was something she would keep always for herself, nursing the knowledge as a statesman harbors his solution to a vexed and complicated state secret.

It would be a child conceived in war at the very moment of its father's transition from boyhood to manhood, from dependence to independence, from uncertainty to proud and fearless conviction, and thus, in a sense, it was a beginning for child and man in the same moment of time. Contemplation of this pleased her, prolonging the smile until he had reached the corner of the steep street and lifted his hand in farewell.

She sat on for a time, sipping her thimble of coffee and letting her mind explore the significance of the conception, of the place where it happened, under the mountain among the wrecked wagons and the crucified Frenchman, of his clumsy eagerness once the encounter was started so that, as in everything else, it was she who had led and directed. She mused also on the sense of fulfillment it had brought to her, something that had been absent from her submission to other men. She did not understand why this should be but only that it was, and that in bringing solace to him she had succeeded in demonstrating her usefulness to the whole profession of arms, and that now, between them, they had done a little to bridge the gap between the two worlds fighting a common battle among the mountains and torrents of Portugal. The fancy intrigued her so that she wondered briefly what status his child would have as the issue of a raw young officer of the line and a Welsh camp follower in search of a fourth husband. For a moment only she was half resolved to tell him when the child was born, and then she knew that she would not, for the confession might prompt him to begin again his tiresome talk of love and urge upon her an impossible alliance.

Yet she knew that if the child was male she would tell him about Graham, for it would help to mold his pride and initiate him into the greater fellowship of fighting men everywhere, bringing closer the day when the barriers of class crumbled and all men who went to war fought under the banner of comradeship in the field. For this surely was the banner they had woven together in the mountains and had carried in triumph from the Mondego to the banks of the Tagus.